Enemy

Kimberly Amato

Little Crown Media, LLC

For my family members who fought for change against immeasurable odds.

Contents

Chapter One

I'm going to kill President Laskin.

    Agent Ellie Goldman scratches the words onto a worn, wrinkly piece of paper, the edges long tattered and color yellowed. She pays no mind to the nub of a pencil between her fingers and thumb as she traces over the same letters again and again as if putting them to permanent memory.

The radio in front of her, old and beaten like everything else in the subterranean living space, crackles a bit as it comes to life. The makeshift antenna of copper wires attaches to a rusty pipe overhead that drips into a cup on the edge of her desk. She barely registers the cloudy look of the contaminated water, but drinks it all the same.

"On this, a beautiful Sunday, the first day of January 2045, we celebrate the wonders the world has provided us all. We also take heed of humanity's past indiscretions and focus on change to facilitate a better tomorrow." The voice distorts as it filters through the speaker and into the ether around Ellie's head. The words on her page continue to darken with every pass of the pencil.

Her notebook, open on the metal desk covered in dirt and detritus, is full of ramblings of a mind that's lost its way. The words, written in all directions, offer nothing coherent to another person. Her shoulder-length salt-and-pepper hair hide her face from the rest of the world. Her nails are chewed to the meat, some missing altogether, covered in the muck and mire of her space.

"We owe it to the future generations to educate them on the realities of the global world," the garbled voice continued. "This year, the twentieth anniversary of the Final War, we must come together more than ever. There are enablers who prefer the underbelly of darkness rather than the light of life. For those who have never seen the horrors, we must remember the pain and suffering of years long gone."

The static cackles as shuffling sounds echo out of the radio. Ellie drops the pencil, her attention focused on the change in the background. Her pain-filled blue eyes stare as though looking through the speaker to the other side. Low voices hit her ears, some mumbling, others begging, a few praying.

"We start this New Year with a lesson and a gift. Criminals infiltrated Buckingham Palace to assassinate the prime minister. Their desire to reform the royal family of the United Kingdom failed. They undermine everything that we stand for. They come out of the underground, reeking of wrath, jealousy, and fear. These rapists, murderers, and drug addicts will stop at nothing to take your children and convert them to the ways of an impure world."

The sound of guns being loaded are crystal clear through the device. Ellie leans back, her chair fighting her movement as her dead eyes remain focused. She's keenly aware of what this means. She's seen it in person before, lived it in real time, and fulfilled her orders. They were just faces then. Nothing more than a picture on a page with a detailed file and a criminal record. The goal of every operative was to protect the greater good.

"By order of King Valkov, the one true ruler, we send these sinners to the depths of hell for their crimes. We pray Satan will have mercy on their souls."

The radio continues to break up as gunshots ring out. Ellie's eyes close as she hears the low thudding sounds of bodies hitting the floor. She tries to count them on one hand, but the connection isn't clear enough.

"If you see or hear of these individuals in your city, notify the authorities immediately. The safety of our children is at stake. Happy New Year."

The broadcast cuts out. Ellie switches the radio off and turns her attention back to her page, her haven of reminders. She feels Anton's presence behind her before he speaks. The chipped lead paint cracking underfoot gave him away. So did his breathing, deep and slow like hers.

"Anton." Her voice is low, but sharp.

"London's fallen," Anton says from the doorway, his hands clasped in front of his muscular frame.

"I heard," she responds. Ellie walks across the room to the water-stained cement wall to where an old global map hangs from a metal ceiling beam. The frame bangs against the broken cement wall, shaking dust to the floor as a subway train rattles above. Using the pencil, she marks a large *X* over London, adding to the many fallen cells. Cities once thought to be strong holds are now long gone. Paris, Florence, Cairo, Johannesburg, Cartagena, Buenos Aires, and Los Angeles to name a few. "Anyone else?"

"No word from Beijing, Tokyo, Toronto, or Sedona," he answers quickly.

"Give them time, could be a technical issue," Ellie says, looking over the map where the few penciled loops cover major cities and some outliers. Her expression remains the same as her eyes dart from town to town. The coalition against the tyranny of the king was dwindling faster than anyone expected. The only unique marking on the map is of a red circle covering a small area named Churchill in Canada.

"Agent Goldman, it's been three weeks," he begins, trying to grab her attention. "We're getting encoded messages of raids throughout the resistance strongholds. We're running out of time. I think we might want to consider leaving the city."

She ignores him and places the small pencil behind her ear. The once flourishing lands of the world now stare back at her as a decrepit tic-tac-toe board.

"Do you think we had any to begin with?" The coldness of her tone lowers the temperature in the room. "This has always been endgame. From the moment United States citizens voted for emotions over rationale, social media over actuality, the ticking of the doomsday clock began. As they and other countries allowed rights to be swept away by the waves of perceived fears, humanity's death march began."

"I don't believe that, Agent Goldman. No one chooses this life." His naivete oozes out with the deepening of his tone.

"Did you ever have a choice? This began decades before either of us existed, when corporations and profits were more important than balance. They put compassion into terms of entitlements. The top tiers took more while paying less. History books long since burned in the cleansing spoke the truth we rarely hear." Ellie stands in front of her second-in-command, his height towering over her. "We've been fighting this cancerous disease for decades. We're outgunned, outmanned, and have a pittance of their funds. We've been fighting our extinction since this began. I appreciate your idealism, but let's not lose focus on our reality. People like us, the ones who stand up, we're going to die out soon enough."

Irritation gets the better of him, and Anton walks around his commanding officer. He looks around the room—the sparse furniture, the blank walls—for any sort of connection. Finding none, his eyes land on the pages on Ellie's desk. His left hand traces the scribbled words.

"The resistance is more than you or me. Freedom isn't just some fantasy. Democracy can—"

"What do you know of it?" Ellie's scream bounces off the walls and echoes down the tunnel leading to her room. "You're a child. Twenty-two years old with dreams of green pastures and happy times. You don't understand how hard it is to maintain those freedoms. How difficult it can be to allow someone with different beliefs to scream in your face, wanting your death all because of who you are, who you might love."

The words fall on deaf ears. Anton might have been born during the time of some equality, but by the time he could walk, it didn't exist. He and his sister, Nadja, spent their days surviving tests and intense training, each activity ending in a numerical value that found its way into their dossiers. All for the pleasure of an existence doled out by the regime.

To refuse this choice, thinking outside the box or speaking up, led to immediate termination. Anton could vividly recall those on the playground challenging a teacher. The small voices demanding more time on the slide or refusing to go inside for their next training session. The sound was jarring at first, but he acclimated. They all had to.

"I've seen enough." His voice was level and firm. "I know this world can be better. There are people within it that can make it happen. This is bigger than your personal vendetta, Agent Goldman." He walks over to her map and takes in all the large *X*'s and the one circle within Canada. "So many have died for our right to fight. As a kid, I wanted to see the polar bears. Imagine being a child and reading about Churchill and the poisoned ice. Learning how it was a biochemical weapon testing site to see how flesh would respond. All on those innocent creatures. They deemed it so horrific that they refused to use it again and shut down the entire area like it was Chernobyl."

"They were smart. Nothing would survive in those conditions," Ellie adds.

Silence engulfs the room, leaving Ellie and Anton in a staring contest of sorts. The wills of two individuals struggling to find their place within the world they currently know. The one where sun is a rare pleasure, fresh water and air a commodity, and life a secondary thought.

"The directors will be in the conference room for our meeting." Ellie breaks the tension. "I understand your sentiment, Anton, I do. The last president we had told us that, globally, we were a cornucopia of diversity. One that would foster change and bring about the peace for a global society. In her last address, before the traitor took over, she said that we were all small ripples in the ocean of life. Alone, we're small and easily broken. But if that ripple gets attention, more ripples might join it to create a tsunami. It would be one so powerful it could eradicate the greatest of evils."

Ellie grabs her worn, green army cap and places it on her head with a deep exhale. "His death might only be a small ripple, but maybe it is the beacon others need to see to start the wave of change we so desperately need."

Ellie walks out of the room, slowly taking in the state of life for her people. The dank, rat- and roach-infested living quarters were becoming too crowded. She'd accepted the smell of rotting flesh and sewage long ago. The rest of her team seemed to struggle with it. Their desire to go topside and the want to give up was always strong around this time of year.

The sound of their boots is the only noise the two hear as they walk through the abandoned subway tunnels of the city. The sounds of traffic above and nearby subway cars rattle the walls. Plumes of lead-laden dust fill the room as Ellie continues to breathe normally. Anton coughs slightly, but easily regains his breath. This is their life, their normalcy.

"Agent Goldman?" A frantic voice echoes down the hallway.

Ellie turns, hands up in a defensive posture as she pushes her second to safety behind her. A woman, half carrying, half dragging a child with her, scurries down the tunnel like a rodent. In the limited light, Ellie can see that the dirt covers her skin like a wetsuit, her hair full of knots and ill-kempt, while her teeth shine yellow with tinges of blackness at the root. It's easy to see they're malnourished and, from her tone, terrified.

Ellie watches as two of her security guards knock the woman down to her knees. They hold their guns raised and press the muzzles to the back of her head as a precaution. Ellie understands it's necessary since the price on her head is higher than the majority on the Most Wanted List. A former Multinational Security Council Operative, her training is beyond that of any military outfit and her access to classified information is—or rather was—extensive. None of her past makes the vision in front of her easy to process. She's numb to the death, but not to the children being subjected to it.

"Agent Goldman, please . . ." she pleads, pulling the child close to her chest.

"Shut up!" the security officer yells over her.

"Agent Wei Ni sent us!" the woman screams in desperation.

The name stops Ellie cold. She ignores Anton's pleas behind her and walks up to the pair. She kneels down as her military cargo pants soak up the rancid water below. Ellie raises her right hand to the woman's face—who flinches. Gently, Ellie runs her thumb against the cheekbone of her intruder. The simple act of a kind touch forces the woman to tear up as her shoulders shake.

"It would behoove everyone to remember where we are. The tunnels aren't as secure as our private rooms. They're conduits for sound, and we don't need topsiders coming down to investigate this racket, now do we?" The guards nod and the hallway returns to the low murmuring of conversations. "Now, what's your name?" Ellie's soft voice surprises everyone. It was a side of her that was rarely, if ever, seen among the men during their tenure in the resistance.

"I'm Iris and this is Toby." Her body remains protective of the young child in her arms.

"Hello, Iris. My name is Agent Ellie Goldman. We have some protocols you have to follow first, but then you can have a nice shower and a meal. Sound good?"

"What kind of protocols?" Iris's voice cracks slightly. "We both know they're not meant to help people like us. Please . . ."

"A simple scan for implants, history of your whereabouts. Nothing like topside." Ellie helps Iris stand and looks directly at her officers. "One of my officers will take you to security first; after that, a shower and some food."

Her attention turns to the smaller of the two guards.

"You will escort them to security before meeting back at your post. I assume you left it unmanned?"

Their lack of an answer confirms her fear.

"While finishing your shift, get your stories straight before explaining to Anton how an elderly woman with a child in her arms made it into the deeper tunnels of our camp. Now go!"

The taller soldier spins around and rushes down the tunnels. The other leads Iris and Toby away from Ellie. Unmoving, she stands there, watching them go, steadfast even after they are out of sight.

"She took an enormous risk coming down here. Security should have shot them the minute they ran. I'll fix it. Maybe stagger the schedules and mix up the teams. Might help fix the issue," Anton says.

"She had no choice." Ellie's voice remains soft, almost weak.

"We need to verify no one followed her down here." Anton continues his train of thought, hands moving about.

"They're black," Ellie whispers.

The words sharply shut down anything her second was planning to say. His hands slowly lower; realization takes over his expression as he turns to the empty path.

"Oh god."

"They are under my protection. No questions."

Ellie's voice rises back to the firm, powerful tones which end all discussion. Shifting in the sloshing water, she steps further down into the dimly lit depths.

"If she's a plant? Someone meant to infiltrate our ranks? It wouldn't be the first time they've done that. You've heard the reports of torture on Riker's Island. They manipulate and brainwash prisoners for nefarious purposes all the time. We need to be cautious," Anton continues as the two walk through the maze of twists and turns.

"It would be easier to fill these tunnels with gasoline and light them on fire. More satisfying for their sadistic desires," Ellie tosses out.

"Also, costly. I have to question your judgment on this one, Agent Goldman. Maybe you're . . ." They stop moving abruptly.

"Be careful of your next words, Mr. Blanca," Ellie says as her body remains facing the darkness of the tunnel before her.

Anton turns to his commander. "They might be alive. Have faith."

"Faith? When I came home, they were all gone. Their door wide open, alarm disengaged, graffiti on the walls inside. Flies swarming around the spoiled food on the counters and in the fridge. Their clothing hanging in the closets upstairs. My niece and nephew's half-finished puzzle forgotten on the playroom floor. Every piece of furniture with a thin layer of dust, letting me know so much time . . ." Ellie's voice cracks. "The upstairs bathroom . . . the grout was red with blood. I know what I saw. Those willing to talk spoke of soldiers going door to door. Removing anyone on their lists."

"I didn't know," Anton whispers.

"Why would you? Faith and hope . . . they're worse than death. They serve no purpose but to distract me from the tasks at hand. Down here, we have living people in need of leadership. My family is dead."

"But what if they aren't?"

"My imagination creates horrific scenarios of what happened in that house. If I could have stopped it, could I have protected them from whatever happened? It's a constant reminder that soldiers threw my brother-in-law, sister, and two young children into a truck like garbage. I pray it was swift, because the alternative of Riker's Island is beyond my capacity to process."

Ellie continues walking, ending the conversation. Citizens of the rebellion move around her, nodding or saluting. It's something she's well aware of, but she gives it no credence or power. Coming to a heavy steel door, Anton steps in front of her and bangs three times. It rattles as the locking mechanism disengages. Anton and a man behind the door struggle to open it, allowing Ellie to walk inside. Using their combined strength, the two men push the door shut once more.

The room, shaped like all the rest, houses a beaten, square wooden table in the middle. White men line the walls, their clothing in various states of disrepair, all attempting to look like the military in history books. Ellie sits at the head in one of the mismatched chairs around the table. Anton takes a seat to her right. Four other men sit at the other end, waiting.

"London's fallen." Ellie's words disrupt the silence in the room. "Anton informs me we've been out of contact with several other resistance cells for several weeks. Sam, what can we do to reestablish connections or gain confirmation of their destruction?"

Sam Flynt sits upright, toned arms on the table, hazel eyes looking at his dirty hands.

"I can try to access our dark web portals. If the king and his hackers shut it down . . . well, we won't be able to get much," he relays.

"Why not just hack the president's files for information?" Anton pipes up.

"I doubt he's looped in on other countries' dealings or situations. They might consider Jerrik Laskin next in line for the throne, but that doesn't mean he has all the information out there. I could try to get into some of the Pentagon's files, but they've increased their security since we got in last time."

"Do whatever you can within reason. We can't risk exposure at this point." Ellie turns her attention to the only man at the table with a real military uniform jacket. "Major Trent, has recon turned up anything?"

"We've intercepted information regarding construction for Forty-Second and Seventh Avenue. They're expanding Political Plaza to include several more streets before and after 1515 Broadway," Trent states. "They're building housing and various other complexes to protect those involved in the government, higher-ranking officials, and more."

"Any confirmation about the rumored bunker?" Ellie asks directly.

"Not yet, but the new plans show all aspects of DC will be in an official capacity in New York City," he answers.

"During this construction period, the area will be vulnerable. We should consider—" Anton begins.

"No one has the arsenal or the manpower to even get out of the subway, let alone to Laskin's penthouse." Ellie cuts off her second-in-command. "Something feels wrong about this move. Why bring everything onto an island? One that cuts you off from the outside world and isolates you. It doesn't seem like a good strategic move," she finishes.

"Why would they worry when their citizens live under an iron fist? No one risks going against them," Anton answers.

The lights above flash as the ceiling rattles from a nearby working subway train speeding by. As the dust falls from the surrounding walls, no one moves. After the room stops shaking, Ellie takes her hat off and smacks it a bit before placing it back on her head.

"How are our supplies?" she continues.

"I wish I had better news. We need to make a run, but we're running out of options. I think it's time to go outside of the city limits to scavenge," Milo Jones answers.

"That would require some soldier support we can't afford right now," Trent cuts in quickly.

"We're all dead if we don't eat, Trent. Seriously, it's common sense, asshole," Jones, the only one of them with a job topside, argues with the major. "We need to feed these people. We also have to secure more water rations as well. We can't survive down here much longer without both. Military support or not, this is something we have to do."

"We can drink the sludge off the floor for all I care! We cannot afford to waste bullets or human resources for some extraneous people!" Trent stands to continue his argument.

"Sit down, old man." Ellie raises her voice slightly.

"You can't seriously be entertaining—"

"I said sit your ass down, now!" Her voice shakes the confidence of the major, and he slowly lowers himself into his chair. "Jones, you were discussing water rations?"

"The filtration system needs to be worked on. Jason informed me we're down to our last set of filters. We'll need to stock up again as well as repair some pipes. While we might have the tools and duct tape to accomplish the tasks, we need more people willing to assist him. I know it's not a job the laypeople want, but it has to be done."

"Jason?" Ellie asks the tanned-skin man sitting quietly at the table, who is in charge of repairs.

"I've put them off for as long as I could, but we've reached the critical point. If I have six people willing to get their hands dirtier than normal, repairs might take a week or two. If everything goes well, the pipes will hold until we figure out a better solution. If Sam can find the specs for topside's filters, maybe one of our engineers can create something similar from the junk we have. The water won't be as clean, but it'll keep us going," Jason whispers.

"We need to focus on our military and making a significant strike to the bastards up there. We can easily tap into the power lines that run below the city. Filtration and water would no longer be an issue. We should make better use of our resources. Have the engineers focus on tapping into the main water supply lines that run through nearby tunnels. Then, we can continue to train the men and women for a strike on Riker's Island and free our people. We came here to make a stand, not play house and barely survive at all," Trent continues to argue. "You need to stop thinking like an emotional woman and be the soldier you once were!"

The elder gentleman's words force the entire room into silence. Trent's face, full of wrinkles from years of fighting the world above and beyond, stares defiantly at Ellie. His eyes and words betray his true belief system. To him, Ellie is merely a woman, an inferior fighter to the power a man can wield. The rules of the topsiders allowed for this old archaic ideology to flourish among them.

State by state, the freedoms women held dear fell back into the distant past. First, it was their own medical care and choice. Unwitting female participants defending these laws and restrictions as ways to save lives. It began the slow roll to their jobs, property rights, bank accounts, and more. The state-run media spun the moves as eradications of unemployment and murder of the innocent. Women lost everything to men like the major.

Trent, with his white hair perfectly cut into a military style, his fists balled together, waits. Ellie watches him, her face passive. The other members of the room dart their eyes to one another, gauging the need for intervention.

"You seem to forget I was never just a soldier." Ellie's voice is low, laced with threatening undertones. "I rarely had any backup, machinery, or technology to protect me. I was unseen, unheard, and unknown. I was a ghost, meant to be forgotten if things went south."

"You fought back, you killed when needed, and you didn't sit on your ass begging for volunteers!" Trent stands again, his fists firmly planted on the table. Ellie remains calm as the others move to subdue the major. With a simple wave of her hand, they retreat to their former positions.

"You want to tap into the city's water supply, but how would we explain the increased usage in our vicinity? They calculate and ration every gallon of water used by individuals throughout the city. Rations, I might add, set by the president and the council to ensure his climate initiative continues to succeed. If you push those numbers up even a half a gallon or less, we will put innocent citizens in jeopardy. Worse yet, if they track the increase closer to our location, we risk exposing ourselves. For what? So you can hold your dick high in the air to prove it's bigger than mine?" The darkness oozes out of every word Ellie utters.

"If those individuals cared about the world around them, they would fight alongside us and not support the enemy!" Trent continues his diatribe, regardless of the feeling in the room.

"Your words condemn us all," Ellie finishes calmly. "Jason, find volunteers and keep us informed of your progress."

"Why do I bother coming here if you consistently ignore my suggestions of an attack to prove our seriousness?" Trent says, pleading with the surrounding men to support him.

"I take everything you say into consideration. I agree we need to make a strike to show our strength to the locals. Work with Milo and find a food source that will target the powerful, but not the poor. Bring me the plan, and if I approve it, you will have your military action," Ellie concedes.

"And Riker's Island?" Trent asks as he lowers himself back into his chair.

"As I've told Anton, we cannot just go off half-cocked. The attack on Riker's Island would be the largest mission we've ever attempted. We're also discussing the assault on Political Plaza. Both will be complex and likely cost lives and significant resources. We need to be precise in our movements. That means having all the intel, from blueprints to insider information. If Macalov grabs even one of our men, we will follow London to the pits of hell. There's no room for error here," Ellie says to the room.

"Maybe I can help with that," Sam says from his small corner of the table.

He leans forward and his jumpsuit zipper slides down, showing his clean, aboveground clothing.

"Have they assigned you to either location?" Ellie asks curiously.

"Not at the moment. My physical attributes make me a candidate for security detail, but according to my practice tests, I'm the poster child for the intelligence community. If I get that position, they will station me within the plaza and give me entry level access to the global network of systems. It might assist us," he finishes excitedly.

"Yes, well, appearance is everything. Having a good-looking male with higher grade levels is one step toward retiring the imperfections of those currently staffing the agency. If they choose your physical prowess, however, you'd get keys to the jail, weapons to your heart's content, and permission to defile all the women in captivity. Either way, you're a perfect specimen to them. A poster boy of the new world they wish to protect. A success story, beauty and brawn." Ellie's harsh sarcasm slices through the room.

"My brother Tim has keys and access. He drinks himself to sleep at night, so I know the job weighs on him. He's a good man. Maybe he can help us, indirectly of course," Sam finishes quietly.

"Sam, you've been a part of the resistance since we arrived from Georgia. We were badly beaten and had lost so many during our travels. You were here, setting up our communications system. Not once did we see him by your side or offering help," Anton says.

"Because of our mom. His job gave him access to the vaccine registry. Fourteen months ago, she began her Alzheimer's treatments. If he gets caught, we lose those weekly installment shots. Docs say she might remember me in a year as the medicine builds up in her system. She'll never get the cure, that's not available to people like us. So, no. He can't risk openly helping."

"Yet you offer information that could compromise her healthcare daily. If you're caught, the same rules apply. Hell, what's stopping him from turning you in to get the full cure?" Anton questions.

"I would risk the world for my mother to have access to the one-shot cure. Denying her the right because she was born across the river is . . . just wrong. He has downtime. Depending on where he keeps his security cards, maybe I can duplicate them. If he turns me in, well . . . my implant is up to code." Sam's back is straight, his chest puffed out a bit more.

"Your mother would die if this goes wrong," Ellie adds.

"If she's a pawn to keep my brother in servitude, she might be better off."

"If anything comes to your attention that requires immediate action, you know how to get in contact," Ellie tells him. "If there's nothing else, this meeting is over."

Trent mumbles some attack ideas to the men who follow him out of the room. Anton waits for Ellie, but she waves him off. Soon, the only sound is the dripping of water in the corner and Ellie's breathing. Reaching into her left cargo pocket, the only one still attached to her pants, she pulls out a small, square, folded piece of old paper.

Carefully, Ellie pulls the edges apart as to not rip it along the creases. The faded photo shows a much younger Ellie, with dark brown hair, bright eyes, and a vibrant smile, holding two children. Their light brown curls bounce off their shoulders, and they wear ear-to-ear smiles as their arms wrap around her neck. They have hazel eyes, and their skin a beautiful two or three shades darker than hers. Ellie runs her fingers along their faces as the dripping in the room becomes louder.

The little boy in the photo, Ellie realizes, looks just like Toby.

Chapter Two

*A*bandon all hope, ye who enter here. The phrase is from the warden's favorite book, *Dante's Inferno.* On his command, they erected the words on an archway across the small two-lane roadway where directional signs used to be. The metal plaque held up by two rusted poles attached to the Riker's Island Bridge over the East River greets old school buses carrying the people deemed unworthy of outside life. Like the decrepit transportation bringing them to the area, the rest of their existence will be in servitude.

A small parking lot of cars rests on the right, filled with various luxury vehicles that seem to be clones of one another, distinguished only by the different logos on their fronts. Their owners work across the water at one of the nine buildings on the 413-acre island. A blue bus carrying employees pulls away from a small trailer and onto the road toward the jail complex.

All the buildings look identical from the outside with cinder block construction, black roofs lined with solar panels, and bars across all the blacked-out windows. The crisp, white numbers ranging from one to nine, the only differentiating characteristic between the units. Soldiers pull inmates out of vans and buses, shackled at the waist, wrists, and ankles, their heads covered with cloth hoods, their bare feet leaving a small trail of blood behind each one.

Colonel General Gregor Macalov stands by his window, drinking a large cup of imported Italian espresso as the screams of victims roll past his window. The letters on his door read *Warden Colonel General Gregor Macalov.* The silk oriental rug covers the cold cement floor. His snakeskin shoes reflect the light as he walks across it to rest on his soft black leather couch. The walls hold accolades and awards for the warden's work. A purely narcissistic and ego driven room with cold and inhuman undertones except for one photo on his desk: the picture of a white woman and her son . . . the spitting image of Macalov himself.

The warden opens the morning paper, a staple of the new world holding onto old traditions. The headlines in Russian speak of the end of climate change and how the planet has shown significant signs of healing. Another smaller title speaks of "Chernobyl's Cleanup," developers plan for new lower-level housing to free up land for the oligarchs in the vicinity.

Flipping the pages, he sips his coffee and folds the paper in half. The article reads: *King Valkov deems South America to be Exile Continent. "The treacherous land, resurgence of the deadly local wildlife, and the lack of interest from political leaders makes it the perfect location for those poisoned individuals to live out the rest of their days."* Macalov chuckles at the king's quote.

A knock hits the doorframe before it swings open, revealing a male reporter in a perfect suit, his pale, white face cleanly shaven, teeth gleaming, and hair styled to perfection. Macalov looks unimpressed.

"General Macalov, my name is Hugh Winters from the *Times*. We were hoping to talk with you about the advancements that keep coming out of Riker's Island."

Macalov folds the paper closed and looks at the soldier behind the reporter. The young man appears terrified, his hands shaking at his sides and his eyes focused out the window.

"I am not sure where you were born, Mr. Winters, but we have procedures here. Knocking and being received are two of the most important. One cannot simply knock and casually walk into any room they desire on this campus. Had I been on a call with the king . . . Well, it wouldn't be wise to continue this practice."

"I apologize profusely, General."

"Colonel General," Macalov says, sipping his coffee and glaring at the reporter. Hugh squirms a bit, his discomfort clear.

"Colonel General Macalov, we have a scheduled interview. Would it be to your liking if we begin?"

Macalov places the paper on the small, antique coffee table and carries his coffee to the desk. The reporter waits until Macalov sits before following suit on the other side.

"Would you like something to drink? Coffee? Tea perhaps?" the warden offers with an uncomfortable softness to his tone. The reporter hesitates, unsure if he should accept or decline. "Give the man some water, soldier. He looks scared of my options."

"I'm okay, thank you," Mr. Winters squeaks out.

The soldier hits his heels together before leaving the room and closing the door behind him. The reporter, attempting to appear confident, looks more afraid as his right leg bounces uncontrollably. His eyes dart around, the true isolation of his surroundings sinking in.

"Shall we begin?" Macalov asks.

Winters places his cell phone on the desktop. "With your permission, I would like to record this to ensure accuracy."

"Considering the security of this location, the same rules apply before publication."

"Of course. My editor has assured me you will receive a copy to approve before it goes live."

"Good," Macalov begins, his accent thicker on the harsher sounds. "Go ahead."

"Riker's Island was closed in 2020 when it was still the United States of America. Scrolling through the archives, it was due to, what the people called"—he flips through the pages in his pad—"'cruel and unusual' living conditions, along with egregious expense. Considering their reasoning, opening this facility could be considered controversial. Would you share why the jail was reopened?"

"It depends. Would you rather have the ill living next door to you? We give them a place to heal, die in peace, and help humanity. You believe in the greater good of humanity, yes?" Macalov counters.

"Of course. It's a privilege to be where I am," Winders replies robotically.

"But it isn't a right. That's where the worlds of the past were wrong. Assuming equality, giving it freely on a whim is not good for mankind. We must earn what we have. That's why we have the laws on the books protecting men from the tendrils of the black widows."

"You mean women of lower standing going after men of higher positions. Are you aware of men that do that as well?" Winters asks.

"Yes, but those men are working it to their advantage. It makes them look more powerful among their peers to have brought a woman down with him."

"Have you witnessed such cases?" the reporter presses.

"A few. One sticks out in my mind, though. Maria was from a noble family and betrothed to a man in the political circles, older but well established. Six months after the wedding, citizens saw her in the pits with a man several status levels beneath her."

"What was her punishment?" Winters asks, staring down at his notes.

"Now, Mr. Winters, we do not refer to the execution of our most basic laws as punishment. It's just and true." Macalov pauses. "The law stripped her of all power her original status provided her. Her family and friends parted ways with her rather than following her down the wrong path. The governing body swiftly provided an annulment of marriage to her spouse. She married the harvester, bore his children, and lives in a small shack on the outskirts of her original husband's property. They dispersed her wealth and privilege among her former family members. She lives in the mud, muck, and mire like the rest of the filth."

"May I ask what her defense was? I assume there was a tribunal?"

"Yes, a very short one. The magistrate was unconvinced of her innocence. Man may be many things, but magicians we are not. Women have a choice in this world: live within your position or not. There was no brainwashing, as she claimed. There are millions of individuals respecting the rule of law. They work hard to ensure our society is safe and free." Macalov stands and walks to the window. He waves the reporter closer, and Winters dutifully follows with his cell phone in hand.

"This is the essence of controlling an out-of-control populace. We cannot have the genetic pool muddied by women defiling the sanctity of our establishment. Any male found guilty of the same crime pays significant fines. Beyond that, they face repercussions connected to their actions until the rumors subside. If they do at all. Either way, it could prohibit their family's growth. The world is clear: a man brings more to the global economy than a female. Without the power and wealth we possess, the world would flutter and die."

"And those below?"

"Those people stay there and work for the privilege of breathing the same crisp, clean air we get to enjoy. It might seem—how did the archives say it?—'cruel and unusual', but we follow Darwin's Theory of Natural Selection. The more genetically advanced procreate to contribute to innovation, creation, and the future of this world. The rest of the masses are the foundation upon which we build. Without their brute strength, we wouldn't have the utopia we live in today. Is that so cruel? Some must suffer for many to live."

"So, was that the reason behind the reopening of Riker's Island? To protect the public and to innovate or create change?" Winters questions.

"Yes. There will always be detractors to our way of life. Some remain from the old world, still holding on to an ideal burned long ago with their flags."

"And you are uniquely qualified for this position because of your military birthright?" Winters asks as he continues to jot notes down. Macalov smiles proudly. His eyes glance down at the medals on his chest.

"It is my duty to protect our society. The global constitution and ramifications detailed within bind every citizen to a rule of laws. The magistrates dole out the sentences. I ensure the worst of those individuals never stand before the courts again. Here, there is no recidivism. There's no opportunity for our guests to re-offend."

Macalov fixes his jacket, puffing out his chest.

"Life is precious, and you have a choice. Live in the beauty that is our way or not. Those who resist, as they so eloquently say, are a brand of vitriol that this world needs to eradicate. Our police and military forces will do the same. We will hunt them like the infection they are and remove them one at a time if we must. It's a long, drawn out game of chess, but it is one I am honored to partake in. We will protect all of our people, the entire global federation."

"How do you keep the recidivism to a nonexistent level?" the reporter asks innocently.

"The moment transportation crosses the bridge, the rights of the outside world cease to exist. In simple terms, Mr. Winters, you are no longer entitled to them. We develop useful members of society within these walls. The hallowed tenet of treatment: come in a malcontent, leave as obedient property for those donating to our research. Those individuals shine as beautiful products of the future. They also serve as deterrents for those willing to break the law."

"And the scientific advancements, how are they achieved here?"

"Well, not every program works perfectly. We have guests incapable of adaptation. Those individuals spend the rest of their days serving our science department. Their bodies become vessels for change. They show us how future outbreaks, vaccines, and more would or could ravage our bodies. Their sacrifices pay for their crimes. Their dossiers clear and their family is properly compensated upon their demise. It is the godly thing to do to honor their courage."

A knock on the door breaks the conversation. Winters stops the recording under Macalov's watchful eye. "Come," he bellows with authority.

A tall man with jet-black hair cut to military code, piercing hazel eyes, and a built physique stands in the doorway, his uniform clean and fitted, his firearm strapped to his leg with the leather lock in place. He's the perfect physical representation of the new regime. The patches and pins on his uniform show his rank and loyalty to the regime.

"Nature has a hierarchy. Our biggest weakness is believing human beings all deserve equality in life. Once we break that train of thought, we can fully remove those with genetic abnormalities from the planet. When our cloning program is ready, this man will be on the forefront. Full of modern vaccines, these chosen few perfect physical specimens will revolutionize the future. The genetic revolution is fully within our reach. Diseases a thing of the past. Death avoidable," Macalov says in a hushed tone to Winters. "Make sure you print that."

"Warden?"

"Yes, officer . . ."

"Officer Tim Flynt, sir. You requested the updates of the day."

Macalov waves Tim in, but his gaze remains on the reporter. Flynt takes two steps inside the room, his black military uniform highlighted by wisps of red, white, and blue along the pockets, his name patch held by Velcro over his left breast. The United States flag, with its newly amended look, rests on his left and right arms, the stars representing the states long since replaced with a white hammer and sickle.

The men remain silent as the reporter's focus darts between the two men. Macalov stands at attention, waiting for Winters to get the hint. His forehead creases with every passing second, his mind a flurry of activity, but his expression remains hard and cold.

The reporter visibly gulps as he takes in the full expression of the Colonel General. Without saying a word, he expeditiously packs up his gear. Macalov follows his every movement until the man dashes out of the door, leaving it swinging open.

"Speak." Macalov turns his attention back to the movement outside the window. His lip quirks up as guards force Winters into a bus for transport back across the water.

"Admin finished processing the transfers from the western systems. They're currently on medical hold for decontamination. Then they'll be ready for gen pop. Two inmates were members of the Toronto Resistance Fighters. They are uncooperative at this point, and it is unclear if that will change."

"Unless they can share information about other cells, it would be useless. These resistance fighters aren't stupid. Those with any actual knowledge are dead or in hiding." Macalov waves away the concern hanging in the air.

"They may shed light on the eastern sects that we have yet to identify," Flynt interjects.

Macalov pauses and spins around on his heels, his arms still locked behind him.

"Did you know that history books tell of the West being won by settlers, pioneers, and the original railroad?" the warden states flatly.

"No, sir. Our history began when the new order fell in line with the king," Flynt responds mechanically.

"Ah yes, you're too young to know all the old-world legends. In that case, you're blessed. Too many remember the old ways and wish for them to be returned. They cannot understand it was a speck of time with unique circumstances. Yet, here we stand, watching the rats gorge themselves on the promise of returning a democratic republic to the world. Their historians were wrong then, and they're wrong now."

"I don't follow."

"The railroad only gave people the ability to travel. They conquered the land with guns, violence, theft, and destruction. Like everything else in this world, the powerful culls the weak. Only then can society innovate, create, and move on. No one is safe as long as someone else is waiting in the wings to remove them. Do you understand?"

"Yes, sir, but I am unclear of the intent."

Macalov turns from the window and rushes up to Flynt's face. He takes in every aspect of his clothing, stance, and demeanor.

"You are one of my best, yet you stay within your station instead of ascending the ranks. If you believe these resisters could hold information, I expect you to take initiative and extract it from them. If nothing else, it will further your training."

"Yes, sir."

Macalov takes another step into Flynt's personal space and lowers his voice considerably. "You will report directly, and only, to me. Follow my orders explicitly and you will rise like a phoenix, or stay and be an expendable worker ant."

"Understood," Tim answers.

A different voice cuts through the room. "If you wanted to kiss, just do it already. If you're trying to get info out of the man, just kill him for sport."

An overly muscled man, clad in a camouflage military uniform with dark sunglasses, leans on the doorway. The top buttons of his shirt hang open, showing small skull tattoos covering every inch of his neck. His hands show more of the same.

"Mr. Flannery," Macalov greets with distaste in his mouth. "Officer Flynt, please head back to your ward and report back at the end of your shift."

Flynt hits his heels together, keeping his arms locked as he turns perfectly in position. He closes the door gently behind him. Flannery watches him go before removing his sunglasses and hooking them in his shirt. A scabbed wound rests over his left bloodshot eye. He drops into a chair in front of Macalov's desk, propping his dusty boots on the pristine wood.

"Jesus, Flannery, what the hell happened to your face?"

"A woman with too much energy and a flair for dramatics. She surprised me with a hidden blade and a wild swing." His southern drawl adds to the dripping disdain in his voice.

"Is that why you're here? Bringing me more clientele?" Macalov asks, pulling out a bottle of Russian vodka and two glasses from his desk. He fills them both halfway before Flannery raises his eyebrow. In response, Macalov fills the glass to the brim.

"No need to waste taxpayer's dollars." A sinister smile washes over his face as he drops his boots to the floor and retrieves his drink. "She cut me, so I destroyed her in so many unique positions."

"And the remains?" Macalov sits back down, keeping the desk between the two men.

"Someone's got to feed the bottom dwellers some fresh meat." Flannery leans back again, gulping his liquor and placing his boots back on the desk.

"Of course, you butchered her. Your reputation is spreading throughout the nation." Macalov leans back in his chair, taking a sip from his glass.

"Thank you. That makes me proud."

"While I appreciate your methods, it's your appetite for women that needs to be discussed. You can explore those predilections within these walls. Outside of them, you must be more discrete."

"You're just jealous, old friend. The great Colonel General Macalov, tied down to this place while I get to roam free. I know it's tough, but in here you get so many pleasures too. Admit it, you couldn't handle doing what I do."

"Pleasures some, not all," Macalov finishes before taking another sip as Flannery takes another full gulp. "Our visitor hasn't spoken recently. She seems rather tight-lipped."

"Then cut them off." Flannery's laughter bounces off the cinderblock walls. Macalov's lack of response confuses the American soldier. "Her lips, man. Slice them off if she—"

"I understood you the first time, Flannery. She might be of some further use to me. One doesn't pour sauces onto the food before you've taken a bite."

"One doesn't waste time with bullshit when one can make them scream. I can pontificate with the best of them." Flannery laughs into his glass. "Hell, rip her teeth out one at a time to raise the level of excitement."

"What are you really doing here, Flannery?"

"Volkov called me. Apparently, there's an uptick in unrest in the area. He wanted me to check it out personally." Flannery finishes his drink, places the glass on the table, and pulls out a bowie knife. He cleans his dirty fingernails, flicking the detritus onto the floor.

"The king called you directly," Macalov scoffs. "We both know he only speaks to President Laskin or myself in this vicinity."

"Maybe he did, maybe he didn't. Point is, word has come 'round of the last resistance fighters showing up in New York City." Flannery smiles.

"I'm sure the president would appreciate hearing about this."

"You speak like he isn't fully in the know. He's aware you have a beautiful little princess in here that's rumored to be connected to the Multinational Security Commission. If that's true, then she knows more than she's letting on."

"They disbanded the MSC during the first wave of purges. The king's own intelligence guards have confirmed such information. Therefore, logic, something you continue to lack, dictates that she is nothing more than a rebel trying to prevent the inevitable," Macalov counters.

"Maybe, but where I come from, they base rumors on a grain of truth."

"Shall we not discuss where you originated from? I doubt one can hang their hat on the Deep South. Your kind of blind followers throwing their neighbors to the pyres because they were different. When the rest couldn't pass our tests for placement . . . Well, they burned as well. But you, you were a special case because of your unique abilities. Allow that to include following actual certainties and not unfounded information. If there is a pocket here, we will find them and handle it ourselves."

"I'm not here for your job, old man. I'm here to keep the money flowing and put those that stop the way things are . . . Well, I put 'em in the ground. That's all," Flannery says, stabbing the knife into Macalov's desk. He sits upright and cracks his neck, the lighthearted feeling of his movements long forgotten.

"Excuse me?"

"Rumors are deadly things. They plant these seeds of hate, ya see. And rumor is you're not the same hard ass you used to be. The king wants to keep the high society happy. That requires someone willing to get dirty. You don't have to like my methods. I don't give a shit if you do, really. All I care about is making those ingrates in custody give us all the information we need. Then I just report it back. Simple."

"I don't see . . ."

"Yes, you do. I have my orders to look into it. Before you get your panties in a twist, I'm not science and shit. I don't give a fuck if you attach a man's hand to his penis as punishment for spilling his own seed too often. I really don't give a rat's ass what you do behind those doors."

"Then why are you inspecting that sector?"

"To make sure it stays on course. If you need new patients, money, whatever, that's what I'm here for."

"The armory is already being refurbished; everything else is moving along smoothly." Macalov answers quickly.

"See, that's the kinda thing I have to tell them. We need that working sooner. That means money and workforce. I need to see everything with my own eyes too. It's part of the deal. You don't give me what I need to report back, then I have the green light to remind you who you work for."

"Hollow threats from a pathetic man." Macalov stands with his hands planted firmly on his desk, the veins pushing out from his skin. "You shouldn't pick a battle you are incapable of winning."

"I don't threaten." Flannery stands and places his hands near his knife. "I know you've got that small pistol under your desk. If you think you have time to grab it and shoot me first, you're more of an idiot than I thought. I'd slice your throat before you could aim it." He motions to the knife standing upright on the desk. "Your body would spasm, firing the damn thing in a random direction as you desperately try to stop bleeding. Your boys would rush in, and I'd have to shoot more people, and I hate the paperwork. So, let's not waste our energy with the eventual outcome and just play our parts. We work together, no one gets hurt. We fight, you either die or end up in Siberia for the rest of your life."

"They would never send me there. They'd kill me first."

"We both know they'd keep you alive until you wished you were dead. Then they'd deny ya," Flannery says with a straight face. "Agreed?"

"We are on the same page, yes."

"Good, then show me around this lovely place. Maybe I can taste the exotic fruits while I'm here. I did travel a long way."

Flannery pulls the knife out of the desk and slides it back in the small scabbard along his belt. He cracks his neck one more time before holding his hand out for Macalov to take. The two men shake hands in agreement, but their eyes remain firm, neither one fully trusting the other, but both understanding the larger chess board.

Chapter Three

"We must indeed hang together, or, most assuredly, we shall all hang separately." The words of Benjamin Franklin rest on a worn-out piece of paper taped to the wall of Anton's room. The young soldier is barely aware of who Mr. Franklin was, let alone the true meaning of his words. Yet, he holds onto his personal interpretation.

His sparsely furnished place, with chipped walls, rusty desk, old wooden chair, and a full bed built out of spare parts, is his home. Nothing new or shiny, everything reclaimed from a forgotten time. His room has one thing above the others: no leaking pipes.

Anton rests at his desk, moving pieces of a chessboard around by himself. He makes a move, spins the board around, and then studies it before making the other side's move. Each time, he mouths the position silently. To his right are an old map of the area and some worn down pencil nubs.

"Who's winning?" a voice half buried under the patchwork blankets mumbles. Two arms stretch out toward the ceiling before black hair pokes out. A woman, thin but extremely toned, sits up in bed. Her heavy-lidded dark brown eyes blink several times, adjusting to the harsh lighting. Her pin-straight black hair cascades down her shoulders to her hips. She runs her hand through her hair, taming the few wild pieces back in line.

"Me, or well, maybe me. I'm not sure," Anton says, staring at the board with a smile on his face.

"There's a ton to unpack there, and I haven't had enough coffee so it's going to have to wait." She stands, slips on Anton's boots, and wraps her arms around his neck. "You didn't sleep well, did you?"

Anton turns in the embrace, pulls her to straddle his lap, and kisses her hard, his hands playing in her soft hair. "I thought you were going to get it cut," he whispers when their lips break apart.

"You try finding someone topside willing to cut my hair," she says softly, kissing the side of his neck.

"I'm sure the barber down here . . ."

"That hack with the tools screaming for a tetanus shot? No, thank you. I'll see if a topsider will do it for triple pay next week."

"Osaka, you can't spend your money like that," Anton says, rubbing his eyes. "They have to help you."

"Anton, I'm an Asian woman. My father might have been a white, high-ranking official, but my mother was a Japanese immigrant. If not for my pale skin and my father's name, I'd be in the brothels or dead. You know all this. No one will touch depraved hair without inflating the cost three to tenfold."

"No, you'd—"

"I'm lucky to be where I am, but I don't hide the fact that my father is the reason I'm in the position I'm in."

"You're my girlfriend, and I think you're stunning exactly as you are," Anton says with a seductive undertone.

"You also live underground with a bunch of sweaty old men who think they know better than the woman who coordinated secret military operations." She moves to stand, but Anton pulls her back down. "Anton, I love you, but let go." He releases his grip and allows her to get up.

"It's a never-ending game, back and forth. Eventually someone has to win," Anton says, spinning the board again. "She's afraid of making the big moves. Ones that could advance our cause."

"She's also kept everyone alive, no matter how many times she's forced you to migrate. I know being in the city is hard, especially how we have to live—"

"You don't have to live here. I do," Anton spits out.

"I choose to live here, with you. I put my life at risk every moment of every day . . . more than it already is, for you." Osaka's voice rises ever so slightly. "If I ever get pregnant . . . If they ever raid this area . . ."

"They would sell you and our child after its birth. Name or no name," Anton answers solemnly.

"I take these risks to fight for the greater good, but selfishly, I fight . . . for us. So, stop with the bullshit of where I could live, how to spend my money, or whatever. Stop mansplaining the world to me. I see it every goddamn day when I read about my people. I know my father bought and paid for my mother. I also know he sold her to a hard labor camp when she was no longer useful."

"I understand, love."

"Do you? Because at any moment my skin tone will mean nothing, and I can't hide my facial structure." Osaka squats down in front of Anton, her hands holding his. "You've been here a year, and you've lived more in the shadows than I have in the light. Please, just be patient with her. Let the plan roll out as it's meant to."

"She wants a raid on neighboring towns for supplies."

"Sounds reasonable. Long Island is all but abandoned to the undesirables. Our armed people could use the old Long Island Rail Road tunnels for access. They'd be on foot for some time, but theoretically they could overpower anyone in the vicinity."

"And they'd have to pass inspection stations en route."

"Those guards are of inferior quality. A five-year-old could make a passport that could easily get you through. The testing level for that post is almost basic level, the bottom rung of the middle-class tier."

"Can you get a copy of the tunnel maps so we can mark out the checkpoints?"

"I can do my best. I don't believe they've switched positions for some time, but I will find out," Osaka answers. "We'll get Nadja back. Ellie promised we'd fight to free her."

Anton stares at the chessboard again, his mind wild in thought. "When? There's been no word from our people on the inside. We've all heard the stories of what goes on in that place. They could subject my sister to anything while we're out here playing house!" Anton swipes at the board, scattering the pieces onto the cement floor.

Osaka picks up the queen and places her on the proper square to start. "Then we pick up the pieces and keep moving on. Ellie has never broken her word to our people. That's why she chooses them carefully. Trust her. You used to. What's changed?"

"The men don't. There's a push to unseat her," he answers, bowing his head.

"A mutiny in the ranks does nothing to benefit anyone. They have to see the bigger picture. It's our job to support her and make them understand what she's doing. Ellie chose you, Anton. Not because of the notoriety of the resistance cells you were a part of. She didn't pick you because you and Nadja came back home with her to fight. No, Ellie chose you because you're a good man who understands the long game."

The young woman stands up and kisses the top of Anton's head. "I have to get ready for work. I'll see what I can do with getting those plans." Osaka opens the door just as Major Trent raises his hand to knock.

"Sir," Osaka says as she passes him out of the room.

"You ought to be careful with that one. She'll bring an unwanted light on you, boy." The major walks into the room and closes the door. "Use her to keep your bed warm, but don't let her into your heart. Her kind aren't good for such things. Understand?"

"Who I spend my time with is none of your concern, or would you like me to bring up the gentleman that leaves your residence frequently?" Anton quips back defensively.

"And what?" Trent laughs. "I know not to fight my nature, and I'm too old to care about the regime or following their archaic ideals. What I don't do is give in to the youth thinking they know more than the older generation. Experience is true power. There are only a few of us decorated officers left alive, and you all act like we're ignorant children running around this place. I won't tolerate that," Trent counters, pushing out his chest to show medals from a bygone era.

"Good, because I'm sick of people from years gone by telling me how to run my life. Your way of life died decades ago. Get over it." Anton stands and lifts a purple heart medal in his hand, rubbing the dirt off with his thumb. "These mean nothing now. We've all got experience, Major. It's called life after the invasion. One that your proudly decorated people didn't protect us from. What was the oath of your people? To protect against enemies foreign and domestic? Didn't see you all running in the streets while they burned people alive."

The major slaps Anton's hands away. His breathing increases with each step as he paces back and forth in the room, mumbling the entire way. Anton lets the man be and picks up the chess pieces, placing them back on the board. Anton sits and stares at it, spinning it around before moving an off-white pawn to e4. He spins the board, but a hand plunges into his view, effectively stopping Anton's movements.

"We need to remove her for the safety of our remaining people," Trent mutters as he moves the chipped black pawn to e5 to match the second-in-command's move. "Maybe I don't want to make the same mistake twice. This is where I defend my people against the domestic terrorist."

"That's a big word, but it doesn't matter. We don't have enough clout nor physical strength to make a go of it," Anton says, attention firmly on the pieces in front of him. He grabs the off-white bishop and moves it to Bc4.

"What if I could find the missing pieces of the puzzle?" Trent moves his knight to Nc6.

"I'd say you'd sell out our entire community to do that." Anton quickly grabs his knight and moves it to Nf3.

"I'd say that's a chance we should be willing to take to preserve what brief life we have left." The major moves his knight to Nd4.

"And what would we do if we remove her from power?" Anton looks over the board before moving his knight to Nxe5, capturing his enemy's pawn.

"We would plan a full-scale attack on the president's motorcade, or maybe take back Riker's Island. Blow the bridge and use the guards as markers, like the Romans used to." Trent takes his queen and moves it to Qg5.

Anton rushes to move his knight to Nxf7, capturing another black pawn. "Like the Russians do in Siberia. We don't crucify people here, Major. Those days are long, long gone."

Trent says nothing as he moves his queen to Qxg2, claiming an off-white pawn. Anton grabs his castle and moves it next to his king, Rf1. He sits back, smiling at the game in front of him.

"Those days might be long gone, but the moves are still the same." Trent moves his queen to Qxe4+. "Checkmate is still checkmate, and that my boy, is where we are. If Agent Goldman isn't prepared to move forward, we need someone who will."

Trent finishes before leaving the room as he entered, unwanted.

"Who says you're not the true enemy, Trent?" Anton says to the empty room. He turns his attention back to the board, spinning it to try and figure out the moves that left him in a no-win situation.

Osaka walks up the steps from the subway at Fiftieth Street in Manhattan. Her spring dress flows elegantly down to her ankles, the light colors complementing her skin tone and makeup. Men turn their heads and stare at her physique until they see her face. In disgust, they turn and focus on the people in front of them. Women walk around her as if she is an infectious creature housing the vilest of diseases. In a sea of white Anglo-Saxon people, Osaka is an anomaly.

She walks freely among the highborn, the ones chosen by tests and genealogy, as if she was one of them. Her father broke the law ensuring she got an education. She knew the action wasn't for her benefit. He used her as a ploy to further his image and power. She performed like a trained seal at parties, playing piano for his guests. They lauded him for giving someone so depraved a chance at life. As if he did her a favor by bringing her into this world.

The only thing she would never stop thanking him for was the access to books. Memories of hiding under her bed to read great tales of faraway lands and heroines make her smile through her discomfort.

She should be used to it after all the years she's been walking this path, but time hasn't eased the discomfort. She hums a song her mother sang to her as a child. She has no knowledge of its heritage, but the connection to the unconditional love of a parent grounds her.

Armed guards wait by the cornered-off construction zone from Forty-Eighth down to Thirty-Ninth streets. The tip of his AK-47 runs up the side of her left breast as she waits patiently to pass. The guard pushes her hair away from her neck with his chafed free hand and he presses himself into her back.

"You carrying?" His smoke-filled breath hits her nose.

"No, sir. Reporting to work," she says, slowing her breathing to a calm level.

"What floor? What politician wants to sink himself into you?" His hand slides down her side, grabbing her dress and hitching it up in plain view of the surrounding crowd.

Osaka stills. Any movement might lead to accusations of treason. There are no laws on the books protecting her from violence. If the guard wanted to harm her, she'd have to accept it and move on. The desire to grab his already hardening cock and dig her nails in until it bled makes her heart pound violently.

"Get your hands off her right now!" A booming voice forces Osaka to open her eyes and look for where it originated. The guard, however, ignores the order. "I said you are to remove your hands from my employee or face the consequences," the voice reiterates.

"And who are you?" The guard spins around and comes face to face with Jerrik Laskin.

"The President of the United States of the Russian Federation. Who might you be?" The lanky man with floppy brown hair and matching eyes stares down the guard. Two men in black suits flank him, and a limo idles directly behind them.

"Officer Nelson, sir." The guard stands at full attention, arm bent and fingers barely grazing his right cheekbone.

"This is my personal assistant and secretary, Officer Nelson. You've assaulted her."

"Sir, with all due respect, she's not one of us . . . sir."

"Her father is. Her skin is as pale as mine, Officer."

"But her face, she ain't like us, sir. They belong downtown, unless she's . . . well . . ."

"What, Officer?"

"Your property, sir."

"She is no more my property than you are, Officer. Now, you will never lay a hand on Ms. Yen ever again. There will also be a formal report on your assault given to one of my employees. For each second your hand was on her person, I'll dock five thousand dollars from your salary this year. We will use the CCTV to verify the time allotted. Is that clear?"

"Sir, that's . . . I wouldn't be able," the officer pleads as the president, his team, and Osaka walk beyond the gate. "I have a family to support."

"A different punishment then." The president stops, pulls out a small caliber gun, and fires. Officer Nelson falls to the floor, a bullet lodged in his brain. "You." Laskin points at one man in black. "Take care of this and ensure they dispatch loyal guards to this entrance. No one in or out until then." He places his weapon back in his holster before turning back to the rest of his entourage. "Ms.

Yen, would you mind ensuring his family gets the proper severance package? I understand if you don't wish to handle this specific case at all."

"It's no problem, Mr. President. May I speak freely, sir?"

"Of course."

"Thank you for intervening," Osaka says honestly as she stares at the body of her attacker. Laskin places his hands on her arms and smiles as a father would at a child.

"Your father was a great man with a long legacy. There is so much of him in you, and I'm proud to have you working on my team. Men like Nelson are a dime a dozen. Women like you are a rarity." He kisses her forehead. "I wish you would reconsider the facial reconstructive surgery. I would pay for everything, and it would remove these inconveniences."

"When the side effects and rejection rates have gone well below the accepted medical standard, I will take you up on that offer," she says, trying to stop her body from shaking.

"Come, let's go inside and get you a warm cup of tea."

The entourage walks through the construction site and into 1515 Broadway. The building, a landmark due to its classic design of the old world, showcases the metal spines that remind Osaka of the jail she lives in. The lobby, newly renovated with the security cameras, scanners, and guards, greets them. Everyone salutes as they walk by, no one giving Osaka a turn of their head or a negative glance. No one would dare with the president around.

A soldier holds the elevator open for the group. Once inside, the soldier steps in and waits. Laskin places his hand on a screen. It scans before turning green and the number fifty-four illuminates automatically.

Laskin breaks the silence in the elevator. "There's much to discuss today. Maxim is at the office. Maria dropped him off before heading to some first lady meetings. I would appreciate it if you could help him with some of that blasted homework of his. Ask me about our history or the law and I have it covered. This science and math side continues to overwhelm me."

"Don't worry, sir. I would love to help him. If you have time to sit in with us, maybe I can make it be easier for you to understand as well."

"I don't know if I'd like that." Laskin chuckles to himself as the doors open on the top floor.

The three exit the elevator car, but the soldier remains. He hits a button and allows the doors to close. The remaining man in black stands with his back to the wall while Osaka and Laskin walk into the open penthouse floor.

"No matter how many times I look out the window, the view still takes my breath away. Excellent decision making this my home and office. Plenty of space, wall to ceiling windows, and Maxim always has some gadget at the ready if I need him to be quiet." Laskin smiles, his arms outstretched as if absorbing the light from the sun. "I feel invincible today."

"Osi, is that you?" A young boy with bright blonde hair and sky-blue eyes rushes around the leather couches of the living room and into Osaka's open arms.

"Hello, my prince. What are you doing home today? No school?"

"No, Mommy said I didn't have to go today. I had a tummy ache when I woke up."

"Max, why don't you get your homework, and Ms. Yen can work with you on a few things."

"But I wanted to p-p-play." Maxim's nerves cause his voice to stutter. Jerrik's face hardens as his son continues to struggle. "I'm s-s-s-sorry, Father."

"Max, I want you to look at me, okay?" Maxim turns to face Osaka, who remains kneeling. "Remember what we talked about. When you feel the nerves jumble up inside, you . . ."

"Take a breath and think about my words before saying them."

"That's right. So, let's try it."

The two take a deep breath in, both puffing their cheeks out like chipmunks. After ten full seconds, they exhale slowly. Osaka waits for Maxim to meet her eyes before nodding to his father.

"I'm sorry, Father. Can we play after we do my homework?" he says, speaking slowly and clearly.

"Yes, you can. But if I need Ms. Yen for other work, there will be no complaints." The boy runs off without saying another word. "If he doesn't break that damn impurity."

"He will. You've been working with him. He knows not to speak outside these walls if he feels unsure of himself. No one will ever know or report it."

Laskin walks into his office with Osaka right behind him. He removes his blazer and hangs it on the back of a leather high-back chair. His desk, made of thick antique oak wood, holds pictures of his family and a laptop. The blue carpet under their feet showcases a large white hammer and sickle.

Osaka moves to her desk in the corner. The much smaller one with little space to house anything other than a phone is more than she ever expected to use. The comfortable, yet not as elegant chair is perfect for her working needs. She picks up the 1950s replica phone with rotary dial and calls a number she knows by heart.

A deep, authoritative voice answers. "Yes, Ms. Yen?"

"President Laskin has removed Officer Nelson from his duties. He requests his family receive a severance package."

"The usual severance, burial fees, medical for a year . . . I know the drill. You mind telling me what happened?"

"I'm not at liberty to discuss that, Mr. Jones."

"I can't keep paying out these people, Ms. Yen. Tell the president to control the temper of his personal guards or we'll have to investigate this further." The voice coughs at the end of the forced diatribe.

"I will pass that along."

"See that you do!" The phone disconnects. Osaka places the handset gently back down.

"I take it human resources wasn't pleased," Laskin says, not looking up from the document on his desk.

"They are threatening an investigation if we do not control the tempers of the team, sir."

Laskin leans back. The springs of his chair creak with age. His hands fold together as his brow knits tightly in thought. "Please call them back again. Get the same individual on the line."

Osaka looks over to a locked file cabinet behind the president's desk. If there were blueprints of the building, they'd be in there. If she were lucky, there would be a treasure trove of information for Anton and the resistance. Laskin always opens it when he arrives in the morning, but rarely leaves his office during the day. Osaka would have to create a much more detailed plan to get him to leave long enough for her to search. She breaks out of her reverie and does as she's told.

"Yes, Ms. Yen, what happened now?" The same gruff voice radiates in her ear. Laskin walks around his desk and casually holds his hand out to her. Taking the receiver, the president smiles at Osaka before looking back out over the skyline.

"Yes, this is the president."

"Yes, sir. What can I do for you, sir?"

"You can pack your things and get off the premises within the hour, or I will send my temper laden men after you. You will immediately report to the military officer and your rank will never rise above private. Wonderful doing business with you." Laskin hangs up the phone without a second thought. He walks back to his desk and resumes reading.

"Osi, can you help me now?" Maxim stands in the doorway, backpack hanging over his shoulder.

"Sir, may I?" Osaka asks politely.

Laskin drops a pile of folders on her desk. "Of course, but I need you to process and remove these criminals from the database."

Osaka looks down at the large stack and takes a shuddering breath. These were the names of those put to death for varying reasons. Many were from Riker's Island, others chased like prey in the charity hunting tournament. Either way, she had a great dislike for this side of the president. He might have accepted her, but his disdain for lives other than his own family made her feel ill. The man's agenda was clear. Remove anyone in the way of his reign, which he only gained by marrying King Volkov's daughter, Maria. He was an opportunistic man who bled green like his money and thought in terms of his own pockets.

One day, Laskin might want to collect on all the protection he'd provided for Osaka over the years. A chill runs up her spine at the thought of his demands. She'd seen what he was capable of with a weapon or just his hands. She knows her training would be useless, but she'd fight back. Either that, or she'd throw herself out the only window that opened. Whichever was easiest.

"Ms. Yen?"

"Apologies, sir. I will handle these once I return."

Her eyes once again fall onto the pile of file folders and the air in her lungs rushes out with force. The top reads Nadja Blanca. Her boyfriend's sister is dead. The young boy grabs her hand and pulls her out of the office, her mind running a mile a minute on how she was going to break the news to Anton.

Chapter Four

T im Flynt pushes the scrambled eggs around the frying pan as they cook. His uniform pants, held up by a black belt with the double-headed eagle logo, hold a black muscle tank top in place. He flips off the stove and splits the eggs among three plates, filling the space next to gray-colored pseudo-meat and white rice. He squats down and carefully balances them in his overly chiseled arms.

Entering the dining room, Tim places one plate in front of his brother Sam, who is busy trying, and failing, to do a proper Windsor Knot with his tie. The other plate he puts down in front of a woman. Her eyes stare straight ahead, unfocused. Her hands twitch slightly as a bit of drool hangs from her mouth. The rest of her body remains eerily still. He kisses her forehead before sitting down himself.

"Stop messing with it, Sam. I'll show you how to do it after we eat lunch," Tim says, shoveling a spoonful of eggs into his mouth.

"What's this?" Sam asks, pushing his fork through the gray meat.

"Protein replacement. It's all I could afford," Tim answers with his mouth full. He puts a bit of food on his fork and raises it up to the woman's mouth. She mechanically opens it before slowly chewing. "That's good, Ma." Her mouth falls open again, showing the food resting on her tongue. "Ma, you gotta swallow before I give you more, okay?"

"I miss bacon," Sam mumbles, pushing the food around his plate.

"You can't miss what you never had. You know I can't afford stuff like that. We're not on that level. I'm doing the best I can, buddy."

"I know, just . . . why the hell do they get everything? Better food, cleaner water, and medicine?" Sam starts, his voice slowly rising.

"Sam, stop. You sound like one of . . . those people." Tim continues to feed his mother between bites for himself.

"Like what? Someone who resists the bullshit? If we had access to the cure, Mom wouldn't be suffering right now! One shot and she'd be talking to us, cooking breakfast, and fucking teaching me how to tie this thing!" Sam throws his tie onto the floor. "But no, we get the gradual care. She gets an injection every two months and we pray that she's cured in a year or two. Do they realize the delay between shots prevents any positive change? The one dose works. This plan, no fucking clue, but hey—if you want any hope at all—follow the rules or you're shit out of luck!" Sam continues to yell.

"Enough!" Tim's voice booms as he slams his fists onto the table. His glass of water sloshes back and forth, his chest heaving as he attempts to catch his breath. A small bit of water spills on the table and rolls onto his mother's lap. She remains unmoving as her mouth hangs open once more. "I know you don't think it's fair, but this is our life. We're fucking blessed to be where we are, you hear me? Mom's disease could have knocked us back into the underground dwellings."

"And you think that makes it better? We're not in the sewers, so it's okay? You think them having money justifies how they treat people?" Sam counters harshly.

"What I think and feel is irrelevant. I have to take care of Mom and you. I've done it for the last six years, and I'll continue to do it until you're placed in a work position. Then you can help me out. After that, we'll see."

"I don't want to work with you at Riker's."

"You won't," Tim says flatly, going back to feeding his mother.

"You can't guarantee that."

"You're too smart. Depending on your scores, you might be a jumper. Then you can have all the bacon you want."

"Then Mom and you will come with me. She'll get the shot, she'll be cured, and everything will go back to the way it was," Sam says, his tone lighter than before.

"Baby brother . . ." Tim takes a large gulp of his slightly yellow water. "It doesn't work that way. If you jump, we stay here. At most, you'd get to send us an allowance. That's it."

Sam looks at his brother and his mom before placing his fork back on the plate. "Then I won't—"

"Don't be stupid, Sam. You're going to take the test. You're going to go where they send you, and you're going to stay alive. You don't have a choice. It's the test or imprisonment."

"Then lock me up," Sam says flatly.

"Dammit, Sam! Think about Mom." Tim sips his water, giving himself time to calm down. "How's your tech club after school going?" he says, trying to change the subject and get through the meal in peace.

"It's fine. I've got it every day this week, so . . ." Sam looks everywhere but at his brother, his body betraying the fact that every day after school he runs to the resistance outpost underground. "If I don't take this te—"

"You will, and that's final," Tim answers firmly, his eyes darker, as if he's holding his full rage at bay. "Please, baby brother, just do what I ask of you? Please."

Tim's cell phone rings in the kitchen, and he leaves the table to answer it. Sam moves quickly and pulls a small box out of his back pocket. Flipping a switch on the side, a row of five red lights flash continuously as he sits in his brother's chair. Sam grabs Tim's work identification card and slides it into the small opening. The lights blink a few more times before one switches to green, then another, and another.

"Sam, keep feeding Mom. I don't want her food to get cold." Tim's voice rings out from the kitchen.

"Come on, you stupid thing," he says to the box. Four lights are green, but the last keeps flashing red. He grabs a forkful of food and lifts it up for her to eat. Her eyes are on him as if she understands her youngest is betraying his brother. Sam's eyes dart down, away from her gaze as they've done so many times before. It might be the leering motherly look he thinks he sees or the embarrassment of the shell she has become. Either way, he can never look at her for too long.

Her youngest son glances down at the box in his lap, willing the lights to turn green faster. Spoonful after spoonful, Sam's mother obediently swallows before opening her mouth again. He dutifully wipes her mouth after every four servings, catching the saliva-soaked food before it ends up in her lap. Her shaky hand falls onto Sam's lap, hitting the box as the last light changes color.

"I know you think I'm going to get Tim in trouble. I'm not, I promise. I'm doing this for all of us. You don't deserve to live this way, Mama," he whispers. "I'm just trying to do what's right, make it better for you and people like us. It's for the greater good. Just like you taught me."

The last light turns a solid green, and Sam places the card back in its protective sleeve. He shoves the box into his pocket before feeding his mother some more. Tim walks back in and pulls the shirt off the chair.

"I have to go in early. I'm sorry, Ma, but there's something I've got to take care of. Sam will take good care of you before he heads to his test. The nurse will be here when he leaves." Tim kisses her on the head again as he buttons up his shirt. "You better be at the school today or else."

"I will."

"I'm serious, Sam. You can't mess this up. There's no plan B here," Tim finishes before walking out the dining room.

Sam continues to feed his mother in between feeding himself. "I know this isn't what you wanted for your two boys. I don't blame you, Mom. I hope you know that." Silent tears roll down her face. "I know Tim's trying to take care of us the best he can. He didn't ask to be put in that position, but it's time he sees the bigger picture. He's twenty-three now, has a job that keeps us in the lower middle class, but it's not enough. I don't care how, but if I get placed above our station, you two are coming with me. I'll figure it out. I won't leave you behind. If everything goes well, maybe there will be a more stable setup soon. Wouldn't that be great, Mom? If everyone had access to the same things? Equality across the board?"

Mrs. Flynt finishes her meal and flops her head away from Sam. Her moans of displeasure fill his ears as her body twitches. Her answer is clear. Whatever her son was doing, she was not happy with it.

Sam clears the table and hides his card reader in the bottom of the cookie jar. He pours the oatmeal raisin cookies back over it. "Thankfully, Tim hates raisins," he mutters to himself before heading into the dining room with several bottles of medication. "Mom, time for your medication."

"Mr. Flynt?" a voice echoes from the front entryway.

"In the dining room," Sam calls behind him as he lines up the rainbow-colored pills.

Nurse Capellini enters the dining room and smiles at the two of them. It's obvious she's lived a hard life by the tiredness in her eyes and the deep-set crow's feet that encase them. Her short and plump stature and well-groomed salt-and-pepper hair indicate a woman having access to things well above her means. She's one of the best nurses around, but still in a job that holds no power in the world as it is. She is a slave to her clients as much as they are to her.

"Nurse Capellini, how are you today?" Sam asks. His eyes look over bottles and pills to verify he has all of them set up in the proper order.

"How many times do I have to tell you it's Nurse Anna, sweetie? Calling me by my last name makes me feel old." She places her small medical bag on a chair and looks over at the horrible attempt Sam is making. "You leave that medication to me, young man. It looks like you threw confetti on the table for fun."

"Tim said they added new ones, and I don't know what's what yet. Might take me a day or two, but I'll have it."

Sam's hands shake a bit as he opens bottle after bottle, putting the pills back so he can start all over again. Slightly wrinkled hands cover his own, stopping his motions.

"You just stop all of this nonsense. I'm here now. Let me handle it." Anna leans down and picks up the one runaway pink-colored pill. She grabs the proper bottle and drops it back inside. "Tim says you have your levelling exam today."

"Yes, ma'am." She gives him a stern look. "Nurse Anna, I just don't know what to expect."

Anna walks over to the long-forgotten tie tossed away in anger. She picks it up and walks back over to Sam, her eyes never leaving the woven fabric of the simple design. "I remember those days." She holds the tie in the air, one eye closed as if measuring the length needed to wear it properly. "My husband wore his father's tie. Of course, we have three beautiful girls, so they had no need to wear one. They each got to wear the lucky necklace my mother gave me, but they carried that darn tie in their pockets." She reaches around his neck and lifts his shirt collar. "This your daddy's?" she asks, sliding the tie around his neck.

"No, his job didn't require one. Tim gave me one of his."

"If your daddy could see you now . . ." Anna angles the tie correctly. "It was such a loss for our community."

"Well, he died protecting our city from murderers. A good detective, who somehow got out of wearing one of these damn things."

"He was a great man, but not just because of his job, Sam. He was a good man in spite of it. He had power over people and never once took it to heart. He put the people in his district and his family above himself. I remember him driving me home when it wasn't safe. I miss his smile as he would say I should call him when I need a ride. I miss his laugh when I'd give him homemade cookies as a thank-you. I miss that kind of integrity and humanity, Sam."

"He was a great dad, Nurse Anna. He also did things . . . things I can't quite forgive him for." Sam watches as she swings the tie around itself and loops it through.

"We all do things we're not proud of, sweetie. It's called life. Sometimes it's just about survival." Sam watches, amazed, as Anna continues to swing the fabric around with practiced ease.

"Anna, I know everyone is so quiet about this thing, but do you know what's on the test?"

Her hands halt and her face falls.

"Nurse Anna?" His voice is soft and filled with concern.

She shakes her head to remove the fog, finishes his tie, and lowers his collar. Her hands brush his shirt, removing any unwanted dust or wrinkles before taking a step back and smiling brightly. "You look so handsome. Just wait until you're matched with a lovely woman worthy of you, Sam. You'll be the talk of the town." She moves around the table to Mrs. Flynt and starts lining up the bottles properly. Sam watches, his face etched with confusion as his question goes unanswered. "You better get going, young man. Subway's already full with kids heading to the site. Better make haste."

"Yes, Nurse Anna." He hugs the older woman and kisses her on the cheek as her face erupts into a full smile. "Thank you for all you do."

Sam rushes to the front, but turns back to look at his mother and Anna. His mother's eyes stare through him and into the beyond as Nurse Anna pulls one pill at a time out of the bottles. His brain rattles dramatic scenarios as he wonders if this will be the last time his eyes see the two women in this setting. If he scores high enough, would they whisk him away immediately? If he fails, would he be terminated on site? The horrors of his imagination flare behind his eyes as he closes the door behind him.

The red brick building and tall blue pillars with the name West End High School in large, silver block letters look imposing from a distance. The generic title rests over the ghostly image of the previous name, the laws having stripped all honorary monikers from buildings nationwide. The new plaques marking scholastic buildings remind those who enter of the privilege to be educated, the gift bestowed upon them by the king himself.

This was also Sam's home for the last four years. Athlete, straight-A student, leader of the robotics club, and so many other accomplishments litter his high school resume. None of them matter very much in the grand scheme of things. Whatever this test is, Sam knows his future is riding on it. He can handle anything thrown at him as long as he has the time to process the question.

Sam takes a few steadying breaths before looking at his watch: one twenty-nine.

"Real—" he sputters. "Reality is what I make of it. I'm in charge of my destiny." The entrance opens automatically, beckoning him inside with a swooshing sound. He walks in, hearing the inaudible murmurs of all the other attendees waiting for their turn.

The door slides shut behind him silently. The watch on his arm vibrates. It reads one thirty; he barely made it. Loud banging sounds pull the entire crowd's attention to the doors. One by one, they rattle as the locks engage. A large gate creeps down from the ceiling until it hits the floor. Clamps extend out from the wall and grip it tightly. The message is clear: no one is leaving, and those late arrivals have already failed.

A man in full military uniform, complete with an AR-15 hanging across his chest, splits the crowd and stands in front of the blocked exit. Tinted lenses block the soldier's eyes as his hands hold the weapon close to his chest, his finger ready to pull the trigger. Tim's warning rings through Sam's mind. The punishment for those banging on the doors for entry seemed obvious. He was more concerned about how each participant would leave after. It might be to a new job or in a body bag.

One by one, they announce names on the speaker system. Each time, an arm pierces the crowd and rises toward the ceiling and a new soldier, sporting their tinted lenses, stands beside the student. Silence hovers over them all until the soldier hooks his free arm under the student's and drags them away. It's always the same, somewhat aggressive, interaction. Sam wonders if it is to instil fear in the candidates so they won't lie on their exams. Maybe it was a way to get the blood flowing for when they thrust the actual pencil and paper into their hands. No society could survive with a top-heavy upper class. They need most of those tested to bomb out and be the foundation so the ones above could continue to thrive.

With every passing moment, Sam's anxiety rises, the fear of being dragged into the unknown weighing heavily on him. If it was an interview test, one that required interaction with a trained mediator, he would fail. He would shovel shit on a farm with no future. His last name begins with an F, placing him in the middle of all the alphabetical assignments.

But this was different. Names were being called in no particular order. His watch reads two thirty. One hour in and the crowd is a third of what it had been. A soldier appears, dragging one of the first kids called. The student, eyes glassy with an awkward smile, as if he were in a hallucination, holds a piece of paper in his free hand. Another soldier, one with a large scar along the side of his face, grabs the document and smirks. He waves over two additional men, and they carry the student away through another door.

The anxiety rushes through him like a shot of heroin. Would that be his result? Carried away to an unknown fate without ever telling his family goodbye? The lobby is almost empty at two fifty, with the last four of them standing so far apart as if the other is diseased. One young woman, visibly shaking as she shifts back and forth on her feet, digs her nails into her elbows as her lips move. Sam wonders what she's trying to do to calm down. He was counting to ten with every inhale and exhale, trying to gain control.

"Flynt." The name hits Sam's ears with a start. He raises his hand, although it seems unnecessary with so few of them there. A soldier marches over to him, grabs his arm, and drags him away. The only thought in his mind is *At least I wasn't last.*

They stop in front of a solid wood door with no number on it. Sam had walked these halls for four years, but couldn't remember anything about the layout at the moment. If this room had been there the whole time, he couldn't tell you anything about it. The soldier slides a keycard into the entry panel, and the door unlocks. He pushes it open for Sam to enter, and reluctantly, he does.

A white metal table rests in the middle, a small U-shaped section to support your head and neck at the top. Sam is three steps into the room before the door shuts behind him and the telltale sound of an electronic lock clicks into place.

"Mr. Flynt, please undress and put on the provided clothing," the speaker above Sam's head tells him. A drawer on the right wall opens up and slowly rolls out. A pair of pristine white boxer shorts are inside. Nothing more. Sam looks around the room for privacy, but finding none, he changes. "Place your current clothing inside the drawer."

Sam folds his dress outfit neatly, like Tim taught him when he was younger. His skin erupts with goosebumps, but he's not sure if it's from the temperature of the room or the fear coursing through his veins.

"Lie down on the table and relax."

Sam climbs onto the table, finding it warm from what he assumes are heaters underneath the surface. His head rests comfortably on the soft contraption, and his emotions settle slightly. Robotic arms drop from the ceiling, along with an enormous dome-shaped helmet. Most of the arms move around him, placing electrodes in strategic places, while two meticulously place smaller ones around his forehead and scalp. Once done, all arms retract back into the ceiling, leaving the dome behind.

"Lowering the holo. Please, do not move your head."

The helmet covers Sam's entire face and locks onto the table below him. His nerves spike, and sweat beads form on his chest. Within seconds, metal clamps grasp his wrists and ankles, preventing all movement. Claustrophobia creeps down his neck and through his entire body. He struggles to get free, but everything tightens as he does. If he continues, he'll choke himself to death. His hands shake, muscles tensed, as he focuses on his breathing.

The screen inside the lens displays an open sky, giving the illusion of space. It helps a bit with the trapped feeling, but his mind isn't so easily tricked. The video blocks his eyes from seeing his surroundings. Metal arms lower once again, this time fitted with needles housing a dark red substance. They hover above his legs, arms, and chest, waiting to deploy.

"The test shall now begin."

Put the numbers in order. Varying digits flash across the lens quickly, and Sam's eyes dart over to the next one in the sequence. He's gotten some wrong, but once it hits one hundred, the screen stops.

Pick the criminal. Images of white men and women fill the screen. In the photos, they all seem to be happy, with a proper life, but then there is one of a shooting. A poor man holding a makeshift rifle stands over the bodies of his victims. His face is etched in anger, and blood covers his white shirt. The shock of the image pulls Sam's eyes to it. His head tries to rationalize what he knows is a fabricated item, but he can't in an association game.

After several more questions, Sam has calmed down and chosen properly throughout. He sees the patterns and smirks a bit at how quickly he has finished things. Anyone with an above average intelligence could hack this test as quickly and easily as he did.

"Starting the last test."

The needles slam into Sam's body, and he screams at the top of his lungs. The fluid pushes into his bloodstream as red lines move around his skin, each one alive and independent of the others. His body shakes violently as they travel around, into his organs, muscles, heart, and finally his brain. Blood trickles out from the needle marks onto the white table.

The last thing Sam remembers is the pain and his voice leaving him.

Tim stares at his watch; it's a little after three, and Sam hasn't called with his results. He rests his hand on his utility belt, and he begins the long walk down the hallway of cages inhabited by criminals in the eyes of the law. One victim is clinically insane, strapped to his bed as he screams obscenities in a language no one has ever heard before.

"That's a new one, ain't it?" Arnold George, a blonde-haired, blue-eyed, almost perfect Aryan prototype says, walking up behind Tim. "One day I might listen to the fucker and try to decipher it."

"Arnie, you ain't doing shit. You couldn't even learn Russian in school, and that's our second language here." Tim laughs at the guard as they walk down the hall together.

"I know enough to get by."

"Curse words don't count," Tim answers quickly as he glances at his watch again.

"Sam call?"

"Nah, and it's got me worried. If he's a jumper, I'll be happy for him. I just want to know he's okay."

"Man, you know how those tests go. It could be a while."

"I was thinking about it, but I don't even remember my test. I remember getting to the school and my results, but that's it. You think they . . ."

"It doesn't matter, man. Let it go." Arnie continues walking away from Tim. "The future is more important than the past," he yells over his shoulder.

"Where are you going?"

"I have a lovely inmate to visit," he says, turning and making a crass sexual gesture.

"Punk ass fool," Tim says mostly to himself as he continues his walk through the cells, inmates trying to get his attention through the bars as he goes by.

Using his key, he opens a gate into the forty-seven hundred section and locks it behind him. The walls are solid concrete, and the doors have only a sliver of plexiglass for light and a slot for a food tray. This is where the alleged traitors to the crown remain. The lights inside the cells flicker as regularly as the dripping from the sinks. Everything in this section is colder and more calculated than the rest. It's meant to drive the convict to confess in exchange for a better location and thirty minutes on the quad. It's also designed to drive the will out of those who resist.

Tim once watched a man die from a seizure induced by the flickering LEDs above his cell. The man screamed for days, begging the guards to fix it. He even kept his face in his pillow for hours on end. But he never gave Macalov what he wanted, so Macalov removed the pillows, sheets, and mattress. With no place to hide, the man had a small seizure within a week of the new arrangement. Then the doctors came in to study the cause and effect. They toyed with the settings, making them flicker faster or slower. He had several smaller seizures until they perfected the frequency. The massive one forced the inmate to bite through his tongue and aspirate on his own vomit as they all watched and took notes.

Tim was on duty that night, and he struggled with the outcome. In the end, he did as he was told and kept his head down. It's what he's good at. At least that's what his test said. He scored exceptionally well in sections of the exam involving physicality, loyalty, and ability to follow instructions. If he was being honest with himself, Tim continued to question what his other results were, if any. They assigned him to the correctional detail and he hasn't looked back once. Good pay, good benefits, and good retirement options. That's all he ever wanted for his family. Like his father before him, Tim understands the duty to his job and his family might conflict. Unlike his father, his job doesn't require protecting anyone outside of his house. He simply prevents those within the cement walls from escaping.

He places the key in cell 4711 and turns it. He slides the door open and steps inside. He pulls the door closed slightly behind him, but not enough to block out the world. A woman stands in the center of the small cell, her eyes closed and her arms swaying in calculated motions with her legs. There is a fluid peacefulness in her expression that Tim envies. She continues, even as her eyes open and take in the intrusion.

Her long, black hair, matted and dirty from her incarceration, hangs over her shoulders, hiding the slight protrusion of bone. Her thin frame is skinnier than normal because of sustenance being withheld as punishment. She pauses, brings her hands to center, and bows in front of Tim. They stand, staring at one another warmly, her smile genuine, and his nervous.

"You need to tell me what you know," Tim speaks softly.

"The rabbit never gives the tiger a way into the burrow," she says, sitting down on the bed and folding her feet under the opposite knees.

"Wei Ni, this isn't a riddle. This is real life. They're going to torture you. Violate you in ways you never knew possible. Fuck, there's a testing site . . ."

"I know what they're capable of. I've seen it first-hand, Officer Flynt. Please don't protect me. I am more than capable of dying with dignity."

Tim slides the door shut and moves to stand in front of her. He stops, fully aware of the cameras in the ceiling watching his every move. "They will kill you . . . I'll have to kill you."

"Then I die with honor." Wei Ni smiles. "But I appreciate all your concern and . . . assistance. But I am not like you. I have no place outside these walls. So, whatever shall happen, may my ancestors guide me home," she finishes firmly.

"You don't understand what you're saying . . . what you're asking of me." Tim runs his hands through his hair. "I'm in charge of you now. Your number, your body, your . . . everything belongs to me."

Wei Ni stands upright and looks Tim in the eye. Her hand grazes across his cheek as he struggles for composure. "You feel pity but not remorse over things you have yet to do. I hold nothing against you, Officer Flynt. In war, we are all merely pawns."

"I have a family I need to provide for. I need to know—"

"I cannot tell you."

"My brother sneaks away from school, bullshits me with after-school pro-grams I know he's not a part of. I followed him into the subways. Is he part of this?"

"There are many destinations throughout the city that those trains travel by. Beyond that, I've told you—"

Tim grabs Wei Ni by the wrist and spins her around, her face hitting the concrete and cracking her front tooth. His body presses up against hers, his mouth right near her ear, sweat and saliva mixing as it rolls down his face.

"I don't want to hear it. I want the truth. If Sam is with them, then he's a dead man and so is my family," he spits.

"Asking me if I know everyone is like saying every Asian person knows one another. We do not. We are but blades of grass within a bigger field. I know this angers you, but you must look within yourself to understand why you are truly full of rage."

"You're playing games and fucking riddles with me. My mother is dying. My brother's a fucking traitor, and I can't do anything to stop him," he fumes. "Trust me, I understand my anger."

"Yet, you choose not to turn him in," she whispers.

Tim's body recoils at her statement, at her words tumbling out like a bucket of cold water. He's known of Sam's assistance to the resistance for some time. He's followed his brother, seen him with people of interest, but never once felt the need to turn him in. The ramifications of such betrayal of the government would mean no medication for his mother or worse. His face hardens, and his hands mindlessly remove his belt and baton. Tim drops the belt on the bed and snaps the weapon to its full length.

"If you won't talk, then you'll scream."

"As you wish." Her words of defiance echo in the small cell. Her body recoils each time the baton hits her flesh. But she never gives him the satisfaction of hearing her screams. Even as he ravages her body inside and out, Wei Ni remains silent, turning inward for peace.

Chapter Five

T oby sits on the makeshift bed, touching the mattress with childlike curiosity. The two metal frames, held together by rope and old rusty wires, creak with each little movement. His clean hand-me-down pajamas are expertly cuffed at his ankles and wrists to shorten their length. His tan skin is glowing in the underground light, and his smile and the lively look in his eyes bring a vibrance to the world that Ellie has lost sight of during her tenure on it.

Iris watches him, ever vigilant, her hand on a bag housing what little possessions they have. Their old clothes are hanging in the corner, dripping dry. Two small plates rest on the empty table behind her, crumbs highlighting the meal they've already consumed. A pitcher of water and two cups remain as well, barely touched. She looks tired, her eyelids closing before her head pops back up at attention.

The small room might be a chance for a new life or another prison. Ellie knows this all too well as she hovers in the doorway. She takes in the image of one innocent to the world around him and the other fully aware of the atrocities they've escaped. Most children are raised to understand the differences in society from a young age. Ellie made sure all the children raised below the surface were allowed a childhood, but since they would be at the mercy of the police force above if any of them snuck out of the tunnels, each child was given an implant from the age of five on and knows how to defend themselves. It is the sad reality of their current lives.

Ellie watches as Toby takes in the new world around him. Iris acts as if the next shoe will drop, forcing her hand. It's a hard one to decipher. The child has to know something, anything about the world he exists in. She had to teach him to steal food or how to survive, right? If not, what was she teaching him this entire time? How did she explain his parents being gone? That's a conversation for another day. For now, she's more concerned about who they are and why they knew Wei Ni's name.

"Did you have enough to eat?" Ellie asks softly.

Iris jumps at the sound of Ellie's question, her body already holding the bag and one arm around Toby, as if ready to flee.

"I'm sorry! I didn't mean to startle you." Ellie holds her hands up in submission. "You're safe, I promise. I should have knocked. It won't happen again."

Iris places the bag at her feet, but her arm remains protectively around Toby, her body language that of a woman ready to fight to survive. The glimmer of scars on her arms are a testament to the physical and mental costs of the constant battle for survival she had waged. Ellie wonders how she overcame the torment of deep physical wounds and mental anguish enough to escape with her life.

"May I sit?" Ellie questions, motioning to the old table against the wall.

Iris says nothing, watching as the agent walks across the room, her body shifting to stay in front of the young boy who remains oblivious to the standoff. The chair scratches the floor, filling the emptiness of the room as Ellie sits down.

"I'm sorry we don't have more hot water to offer for your showers."

"We appreciate a shower, regardless of the temperature. It beats cleaning up in a puddle or whatever else we come across."

"I'm glad. I know it's difficult out there," Ellie begins. "Did you get enough to eat? The two of you look hungry. I'll get you some more." She quickly picks up the plates and tries to make an escape.

"We're fine." Iris pauses and takes in Ellie's appearance. "Are you?"

Ellie places the plates back down, ignoring the motherly stare Iris gives her. It's the same one she'd gotten when she was younger when her mother caught her eating a cookie before dinner or beating up a bully.

"You look haunted, Agent Goldman. I've seen that look on many people in my lifetime," Iris says, forcing the agent to stop all movement. "Only difference between you and them . . . you never raised your hand to me and hid behind the law. You didn't look at us with disgust. You saw people you knew, didn't you?"

"And if I did?" Ellie asks, her back remaining to the room.

"I'd say you were human. More human than those on the concrete above us."

Ellie leans against the back of her chair. Her eyes scan the ceiling of the room, trying to home in on any aspect of the goodness inside of her.

"I don't know how much humanity is still within me, Iris. Each day it bleeds out a little more." Ellie's voice seems more like a whisper as the bodies of those she's killed flood her mind.

"Maybe so, but you allowed us a place to clean, eat, and spend the night. I am grateful for that kindness."

"You are welcome to stay as long as you like. The only requirement is to carry your own weight. Because of your age, we could find something suitable—"

"I am no frail old woman, Agent Goldman."

"Ellie . . . please, just Ellie."

"Toby might not be able to do much around here, but he can put a smile on anyone's face. Me, I can cook, clean, fix an engine, and I used to be a teacher. I am not a woman unable to hold her own."

"I apologize again. I shouldn't assume . . ."

"Color doesn't mean ignorant or weak."

"No, it does not. I based my words on your age, nothing more." Ellie reaches into her left cargo pocket. Her hand trembles ever so slightly as she does. Pulling out the worn photo, she looks at it before handing it to Iris. "They were my world. Each time I would go away for work, I would send them a picture of where I was. Their father, a black man, would show them, and they'd play a game to figure it out. Once they did, they'd stick a pin on the map. Then I'd get a photo of the pin and their smiles. If they got it right, they got a rock from the location."

"Their mother must have loved that." Iris looks over the photo, and for the first time, smiles. "Though I think the rocks would have ended up in my garden."

"I thought so too, but Leandra, my sister . . ." Ellie pauses and tries to find her words. "After the purge, I found a case in the basement. She was always a builder, and she made this beautiful trunk. Each drawer held a small container with the rock, where it came from, and the date. Some even had the two pictures. That's where I got that one from. I never knew she did that."

Ellie falters for the first time since sitting down. Her eyes become glassy with unshed tears as she looks at Toby.

"He reminds you of your nephew," Iris says, looking down at the picture again.

"Yes," Ellie says without emotion.

"He's not that child. I don't want you to assume . . ."

"No, ma'am. I would never. But everything in me is screaming at me to protect this boy like I couldn't protect my own. I can't promise you that we won't have to run, but I can give you right now. We take it one day at a time down here." Ellie fights to regain her composure.

Toby moves around the bed and slides to the floor. Kneeling, he rummages through the bag and pulls out a ratty old toy: a stuffed bunny, once white, now gray with one ear and eye missing. He pulls it to his body, looks up at Iris, and smiles before walking right up to Ellie. He looks up at her, eyes wide and curious. She says nothing, but allows the child to play with her cargo pocket and poke her pale skin. His other hand never relinquishes the stuffed animal during his movements.

"Toby, be careful," Iris says in a soft, motherly voice when he tries to pinch her.

"He's adorable."

"He is such a beautiful soul in all this . . . mess."

"How old is he?" Ellie asks as Toby pulls a nub of a pencil out of her right cargo pocket, his wide smile revealing how many teeth he is missing.

"Seven, but I swear sometimes he is much older."

"Did you find Toby out there alone?"

"No." Iris looks Ellie over, her hand still on the bag by her feet. The pattern of running away from people with Ellie's complexion is strong, but the need to rest is more powerful. "He's my grandson."

"Your family?"

"In the camps, dead or enslaved." She releases the bag for the first time since Ellie arrived.

Ellie pours the woman a full cup of water, Toby watching her every move with curiosity. Iris takes it and swallows about half of the liquid before stopping. "We started out in Alabama. Beautiful little town that you'd see on television. My daughter and her husband owned the local general store, and I taught at the middle school. Kids just playing everywhere, laughter fillin' the void. I wish you could have seen it."

Iris stops for a second and looks at the picture in her other hand—the smiling faces of two little children lost to the war that raged outside their walls. "But then again, I'm sure you had something similar." She holds out the photo, and Ellie looks it over, her thumb grazing the edges.

"They keep me alive to this day. I can still hear their voices, but it fades bit by bit, year by year."

"The purge started because our governor changed all the voting laws and districts. They corralled people of color into smaller land masses, and then we were just illegal altogether. The powers that be systematically took property away from everyone. Before they hit our town, my daughter and our husbands planned an escape. We had heard about resisters up north who started the underground railroad again. Those kids were so young, but at that point, Toby and I had no family left to run with. That was 2019."

"Where did you go?"

"Kentucky, Tennessee, Nebraska . . . We traveled all over the country. We'd stay in the shadows, working odd jobs for those who gave us shelter. Fed off whatever we could afford or scraps smuggled our way. Never stayed too long in one place, but we managed."

"Twenty-six years is a long time to be on the run." Ellie looks over at Toby, who is happily drawing on the concrete wall with his little pencil.

"We were safe in Canada for a long time. It was pure bliss. Even though the war was coming our way, we felt separated from it. Felt safe. Then the country fell, and we went underground with the resistance."

"Toby?"

"Was born in Toronto under a beautiful blue night sky. His mama knew it would be difficult to raise a child in this world, but with no access to birth control . . . well they were consenting adults, after all."

"Clinics were available . . ."

"I believe in those choices, Agent . . . Ellie. They just weren't for our family. We're godly folk." She finishes her drink and holds the cup with both hands.

"Would you like more water?"

"Got anything stronger around here?"

"It's not topside liquor, but I can get you a glass of the tunnel's finest moonshine. I can't guarantee the flavor, but I promise after one cup your chest will burn but nothing else will. Side effects include dry mouth, desire to walk around and fight everyone, plus a significant hangover in the morning."

Iris smiles as she hands her cup back over. "I think I will stick to water until this little one is asleep. Maybe we can talk more about what we can do around here to chip in." Ellie refills the cup to the brim.

"I know this is tough, but no one really knows we moved to this location. Your scan came up clear, so how did you find us?"

"My daughter had a hard labor. Toby was a quiet baby, but without the medical care accessible to her . . . well, she got an infection. When the raids started again—"

"Toronto fell?" Ellie asks. "We've been trying to reach out to them for months, but no one replied."

"Not at first. The first raid forced us into a different section of the city. My daughter was getting worse with each day that passed. During the second raid, she couldn't move. She begged me to take Toby and go. So, I did. We were the only ones of my family left at that point, so we stayed with the Toronto group. We'd move every few months with no worries. They had someone in the local police department that would tip us off each time. Worked until Toby was six."

Toby looks over at the women, waving his free arm. The two women look over to glance at his stick figure artwork on the wall. He bounces up and down before turning back to the drawing, making another circle much smaller than the surrounding people.

"He doesn't talk much." Ellie watches as Toby continues creating what looks like a bunny on the wall. "Can he? I know it must be difficult teaching him anything right now."

"Yes, he does. He can also read and write, though his chicken scratches give my eyes a run for their money." She rubs her eyes before taking another drink of her water. "I'd read the signs to him. Teach him what words were bad or good. He'd barely leave my side, so he learned from all the refugees. It takes a village to raise a child, but I had a small group who willingly helped. It really was a nice found family feel . . . for that time, anyway."

"You were saying it changed when he was six?"

"Yes, they burst through every possible entryway. The men in power directed women and children toward the back exit. It was a small grate that we could move and travel into the sewers to get out. Those soldiers are merciless, but not if it means smelling like feces when they go home. Not much power in smelling like a cow's bum."

Toby giggles at his grandmother and points to the concrete. The contorted image of a bunny with the telltale one ear and eye smiles back at him. Two tall people stand guard, and one smaller figure holds the bunny's hand. With no prompting, he's drawn his environment in his childlike framing. Innocent and unique to his vision.

"We got out to higher ground, but the dogs barking was a bad sign. We moved along the border as fast as we could. Didn't sleep until I couldn't hear the noises anymore. By then, I'd lost the rest of the people I was with. It was just the two of us until we made it down through the thicket and into Buffalo. Slept in the woods by day and migrated by night. Safer that way."

"That's smart, but it still doesn't explain how you found us," Ellie says, growing more serious as the conversation went on. She felt an affinity toward the two of them, but the lives of the entire camp were her responsibility. If Anton was right, they could be wasting valuable time while the military got its forces ready. "I'm not trying to be rude. I just need to know more than you're sharing. I hope you understand."

"The woman who helped us said you would be compassionate but firm." Iris takes a sip of her water. Ellie watches in rapt attention, waiting for the rest of her story to unfold. "She met up with us after I crossed into Buffalo. We were starving, scrounging around for anything to eat. We were waiting in the shadows like always for a restaurant throwing out the scraps before closing. Before we could get in the dumpster to collect anything, a woman in all black came out of hiding. She grabbed all the food she could, packed it in small bags, and shoved it into a backpack. Toby made a noise. Maybe out of pure hunger, I'm not sure. She noticed us right away, but wasn't afraid."

"She helped you." Ellie exhales, fighting her emotions.

"Yes, she traveled with us the entire way to Manhattan. Kept us fed, fixed Toby's bunny when its ear tore off. That boy kept staring at her eyes. Never saw an Asian woman before. She put up with all his questions while we walked. She was on her way here. We're just blessed she let us tag along. In case of separation, we were to come straight here and fight our way through to you. Wei Ni saved our lives."

The name grips Ellie's heart like a vice. Wei Ni was the MSC operative she always worked with in her former life; the reason she traveled so many times, fixing things in other countries by the light of the moon. The blood on Ellie's hands from the years gone by was haunting, but nothing like now. Knowing her former colleague, Wei Ni would never casually give up her name or location. Their training meant understanding that capture equaled death.

"She isn't here with you?" Iris inquires.

Ellie replies with a quick shake of her head. "Where did you split?"

"We were running through the park, trying to get to the old subway entrances, when a patrol spotted us. She closed the entry behind us before giving me the quick rundown. Then she fled. I assume she gave herself up to the authorities to keep us safe, but I hoped she was here."

"I had been broadcasting our MSC codes to other resistance holdouts in hopes of more highly trained operatives coming to fight. She must have heard it." Ellie rubs the back of her neck and takes in what it all means. Those in the Multinational Security Council received her message. That no one had physically made it to them was disheartening.

When the conflicts of hacked elections and false information began spilling out globally, the MSC was on the forefront of stopping it. Operatives took several trips to the town of Veles, in the Balkan nation of Macedonia, trying to uncover the truth and stop the wave of lies. They made threats against anyone who stepped on freedom of speech, even if it did not guarantee those rights in other countries. But it all ran deeper than anyone could know.

They set traps. One by one, operatives kept going off the grid. Wei Ni and Ellie were two of the few who remained to the very end. Eventually, those running these misinformation factories exposed the MSC in a negative light, and those who ran it became traitors to their home countries. Their deaths aired on global streaming stations, if possible. Whether hung or stoned, the crowds watched and blamed the victims as villains. In America, members received untold amounts of torture in Guantanamo Bay until they exposed others.

Ellie and Wei Ni made it to Central America on a cargo ship after a massive amount of money went into the captain's hands. They worked their way through Mexico and followed the old drug tunnels back into the United States. That was 2021 or 2022, Ellie couldn't remember. Time lost all meaning over the years.

The two women agreed to fight against all enemies of freedom, regardless of their affiliation. Their oath to protect humanity from the demagogues who threatened to rule it running through Ellie's mind with her memories. War brought them together, and war tore them apart.

"I'm sorry, we couldn't help her." Iris whispers after some silence.

"She wouldn't have let you stay. She sent you to me for protection. It was her . . . our bond, our commitment to one another. You have my word; no harm will come to you while you are here." Ellie stands, her muscles tense, back rigid. "Thank you for your time. I'll have someone come talk to you about helping around this place."

"She might still be alive. If you love her, find her."

"How'd you—"

"A woman always knows."

Ellie stands stoically, her eyes focused on a far-off point in front of her somewhere. "I'm sure she is, but our relationship . . . it was free until it wasn't. We've both lost so much, we're not the same. Iris, sometimes death is a gift over the imprisonment this country would give her if they truly knew who she was . . . who we were together."

"I always believed love was a gift, no matter what the form. I've also heard the rumors of Riker's Island. They wouldn't do that to her, would they?"

"Rumors are like old wives' tales. They might've spun out of control over time, but they started in truth."

Toby rushes to stand before Ellie, blocking her exit. His hand shakes as he holds up the pencil for her to take. Ellie smiles, kneels down, and takes in the boy's features, reminding her so much of the life she left behind, the life she begs for in her sleep. She covers his hand with her own and steadies her breath.

"You keep it, Toby. I'll try to get you some paper and maybe a newer one when I can."

Toby holds out his bunny. Ellie's eyes glaze over as she pulls the toy in for a hug, her head tucked into it as if hugging a small child. She opens her arms to hand the stuffed animal back, but Toby rushes forward and wraps his arms around her neck.

In one swift motion, Ellie's defenses crumble and tears march down her cheeks, the weight of the world rolling down along the once perfect toy between them. Both people, broken, missing pieces of themselves, finding comfort in a simple hug. Iris sits on the bed, drinking her water and taking in the scene. She knows the future is dark and most likely impossible, but as they all stay in the room, one thing remains true in the silence. As long as there is breath, there is hope.

Chapter Six

The small, golf-cart-like vehicle bounces on the uneven pavement of the Riker's Island complex. Macalov sits up front, his hand firmly gripping the safety handle as the officer takes another corner faster than he should. In the back, Flannery sits with one leg up on the bench as if the jerky movements don't bother him. He nibbles on his left index finger's cuticle and swallows the piece of flesh he bites off.

A large white building at the edge of the complex comes into view. Cement barricades emblazoned with NYPD in blue spray paint prevent the cart from getting any closer than the main road. The police, now a division of the military, man the barricades in numbers that would give anyone pause. These men have been given mandates to shoot first, then ask questions, but they are there to absorb the damage if an attack comes. If an attack wipes them out, replacements will arrive before cleanup is completed. Like clones, they are the front-line fodder.

The words *MEDICAL WING*, carved into the brick above them, show where they are. When the more powerful investors visit, they see a complex offering assistance to those who need it—a beacon of hope on an island of despair. That's why the fundraising checks never stop coming in. Giving money to those in need always soothes the guilty conscience of the one percent. It also helps that disease vaccines bear their name. They never inquire beyond the promotional schedule for their appearances.

The cart stops with a shriek of its wheels against the tar-covered ground. Macalov glares at the driver before getting out and fixing his appearance. Flannery walks by the driver, pats him on the shoulder, and laughs. The officer drives away as fast as he arrived, the squealing as he turns heard from the other side of the complex. The two men walk past the cement blocks and up to the two large, black metal doors.

Two soldiers, holding their modified AR-15s across their chests and wearing holsters with a 9mm on each leg and a full Kevlar uniform with matching black helmet and black visor, stand guard. As Macalov approaches, the guards move in synchronicity, opening the doors for the two men to enter. They step inside and the doors close behind them, clicking in place with an automated lock, enveloping them in darkness.

Flannery flips open his lighter and lets the flame burn the edge of a hand-rolled cigarette. Several small red dots appear on both of their chests, the unmistakable laser sights on the security protocols. The smoke Flannery exhales highlights the beams from the source.

"Bit overkill, don't you think?" he says between inhaling the carcinogen.

"Prevents any unauthorized individuals or those attempting to escape," Macalov says as he presses his left hand to the wall. The scan blinks green and the laser sights disappear. The lights turn on, revealing an entire metal room. The backs of the doors, walls, and ceilings are a sterile aluminum, while the floor has pockmark holes throughout it. It's the only surface that isn't completely pristine; small orange spots litter it. "They're dead before they get out of here."

The doors ahead of them unlock and another soldier stands there, waiting. His uniform is more in line with Flynt's black one with the flag patch on his arm.

"Apologies, sir. We weren't aware you would come by this afternoon," the guard says before saluting Macalov.

"This is my guest, Michael Flannery. He and I are touring the facility today. Keep the knowledge of our presence to a minimum. We don't need to disturb anyone from their daily tasks."

The guard nods, salutes, and walks away from the two men. The doors close and another automatic lock sets in place.

"Where'd you want to start?" The southern drawl of Flannery's accent comes out as his excitement grows. "Let's start this way." He turns left and heads down the long, white hallway. A camera hangs from the ceiling at each intersection. "You overdoing the security a little, doncha think?"

"One would assume that, but if individuals knew the true essence of this area, it wouldn't bode well for the facility," Macalov answers blandly.

"Could use some color, though. Like a delicate blue; they say it's calming. Might stop the screams as you rip an eye out. I mean all this white paint screams white nationalism. Can't have them thinking that, can we?"

"Flannery, we keep things clean and simple on this island."

"Too bad, missing the chance to expand your horizons here." Flannery walks past a nurse in a short skirt, and he spins around, watching her walk away.

"Doctor Soleil, do you have a moment?" Macalov says, catching the doctor coming out of the lounge.

"Of course, sir," the older man with salt-and-pepper hair replies. His average height and build fill out his black suit perfectly. The white coat hangs off his broad shoulders and falls to just above his knees. "How can I help you?"

"Michael Flannery." The other man holds his hand out without waiting for an introduction.

"Doctor Soleil, pleasure to meet you." The doctor refuses to take Flannery's hand in his. "You'll forgive me, but we deal with varying infectious diseases here . . ."

"And your hands look like a petri dish of bacterial infections," Macalov finishes for the doctor.

"He has a good physical structure, muscular, and excellent features. Has he been considered for donation?" the doctor continues.

"That would be up to Mr. Flannery. If he wishes to go through the testing, then you have my permission to add him. The more submissions we have, the better off the results will be."

"Donations? You talking about cutting me up, doc?" Flannery jokes.

"Of course not, unless you donate your corpse, of course. We're discussing a perfect future."

"We can discuss this at a later time. Would you mind giving me an update on our testing? As long as we aren't interrupting anything."

"Of course not, sir. I was planning on doing my rounds to check on the status of a few items." The doctor turns and bounces with the exaggerated steps he takes. Flannery walks double-time to keep up with the other two men, passing one bright orange door after another.

The doctor stops, placing his hand on a gel keypad. After it turns green, he stands in front of it, holding his right eye wide open.

"Bet that don't work with glasses or contacts," Flannery says with a laugh.

"That would be true, but considering a simple surgical procedure perfects vision, it isn't an issue."

"Not everyone—"

"They wouldn't be chosen to work here, Mr. Flannery," Doctor Soleil says quickly before the door opens, allowing them all to enter. Flannery walks in first as Doctor Soleil looks him over. "Your colleague's physical features are lovely, but the brain leaves something to be desired."

"It can be corrected," Macalov says as the two men enter the room.

A woman lies lifelessly on a bed in front of the three men. Tubes run down her throat, into her arms, and out of her sides. Machines beep, showing the vital statistics of her body. A nurse enters from another door across the room. She takes the woman's limp right arm and moves it through some exercises. Then she takes two pumps of a lotion and rubs it in. A pregnant belly protrudes from the frail frame.

"They sent Miss Mildred to us from the Northern Territory. No family, no cognitive ability because of an accident on school grounds. Her genetic markers were exceptional, so we matched them with a male from the higher level," Doctor Soleil says, looking over the numbers on the machines. He pushes a few buttons and scans the new numbers that flash across in succession.

"How far along is she?" Macalov asks.

"Who knocked her up?" Flannery adds crassly.

"Approximately seven months. Sonograms are normal, bloodwork is exceptional. If this pregnancy succeeds, she will be ready to carry another shortly thereafter." The doctor turns his attention to Flannery. "And the donation was mine."

"Should I even ask how you delivered it?" Flannery says with a widening smile.

"Considering a man of your standing might not be aware of our procedures here, let me enlighten you. Freezing or altering any of the genetic markers of those who are donating is strictly prohibited. That's why there is extensive blood work, DNA testing, and a litany of other tests before any individual may become one of us. If they pass, donations or deposits are delivered the natural way. We've found that has brought about the highest success rate," Doctor Soleil says in a tone reserved for parents and science teachers.

"And if they fight back?" Flannery pushes.

"They are restrained, Mr. Flannery. If they resist, we have medication deemed safe in order to calm them down. If the patient is already unconscious, we leave them that way. If they are awake, we prefer they be aware of what is going on around them. Acceptance ensures a safe delivery and successful connection. We work diligently to ensure the fetus never experiences undue stress."

"I'm all for fun, but if you restrain them, that's gonna stress the patient out."

"And that is why some perfect patients receive continual deposits until one takes or they accept the inevitable." Doctor Soleil defends his position firmly.

"So, you rape 'em until they just take it like a good girl?" Flannery says with a sick smirk on his face. "You know, for science."

"This coming from the man who brutally assaulted a woman because she cut his face," Macalov interjects.

"There's a difference between revenge, extracting information, and destroying them in the name of science. I might be a piece of shit, but even I have my limits. If they don't accept it, knock 'em out permanently. No kid needs to be fucked up in the belly before hitting the ground running, that's all," Flannery says, his voice rife with anger.

"Not all women respond well to the approved drugs. That being said, if the warden approves it, we will look into at least calming them down for the process."

"After we're done here, Mr. Flannery will come to visit you and your lab techs to not only see if he is a viable subject, but also to assist with all of your birther projects. Mr. Flannery will report directly back to me and then the president to ensure everything is going smoothly." The words falling out of Macalov's mouth ring hollow.

"Of course. If you'll follow me, I will show you our newest project that you green-lit a few months ago." Doctor Soleil walks back out the orange door with the two men on his heels.

A nurse opens a door to their left and walks into the hallway. Macalov pushes it open and looks inside. Several beds on both sides of the rectangular room house women in various stages of pregnancy. A generation of perfect children. Eradicating the imperfections of old was a pipe dream of the past. Now, however, with the ever purifying of a populace, the future is brighter and safer than before. In less than two months, the first child will be born to the breeders. The father will then take responsibility for the infant and raise it as a perfect being. A lifetime of doctor's visits, blood tests, and psychological exams will make or break the program. Above all, the test on their eighteenth birthday will either be the nail in the coffin of the birther trials or its award-winning achievement.

"How many are there?" Flannery asks as the other man stands next to Macalov, marveling at the sheer number of women in the room.

"Currently, fifteen women are in the program. We have more shipped to us daily, but it takes time to figure out their scientific standing. This program has been our priority, but if they aren't a suitable candidate, we place them elsewhere," Doctor Soleil states as he turns and continues to walk down the hallway. The two men follow closely behind, watching the doors move by one by one.

"One of the projects?" Flannery asks as the men turn left down another hallway. "How many you got here, doc?"

"This is the medical wing. Sometimes, we treat minor injuries or illnesses that occur on the island. It's a rare occurrence and only happens if individual wards are ill-equipped to handle the situation."

"Good afternoon, Doctor Soleil." Another doctor walks past the three men and into a room to their right.

"That was Doctor Grant. He works on the diseases that emerged when the ice melted during our climate change period in addition to the standard cancers, AIDS, and heart disease. He uses that knowledge to protect our society, but also engineers them for biochemical warfare."

"So, you save people just to kill them?" Flannery asks. "Sounds counterproductive."

"Yes and no. Smaller things like heart disease or certain cancers can be cured, but genetics come into play. We can fix those, of course, but that is up to the obstetrician. Other diseases—smallpox, anthrax, the plague, and these prehistoric bacteria— can prevent an uprising and wipe out a resistance quickly. In order to do that, we have to test all these concoctions so we understand how the human body will respond to it. Therefore, we have several quarantined areas where subjects are exposed to anything from toxic gas, radioactive materials, and airborne viruses to many other things," Macalov adds, showing his knowledge and complete control over the full complex.

"The colonel general is correct. Everything we do here is to further the best of mankind and limit the influence of negative traits." Doctor Soleil stops and turns to his left. The bright orange door is unmarked, with the same scanner as the previous rooms. Two armed men stand at attention on either side, staring forward, undeterred by the doctor and his guests. After a keycard swipe and scans of the doctor's hand and retina, the door unlatches. "Now, before we head inside, I need to warn you that what you see within this section cannot be shared outside of these walls. I've been funding this project out of my pocket . . ."

"Unsanctioned? We've spoken about this, Doctor Soleil. I've turned a blind eye the first few times because of your notoriety within the community, but you signed—" Macalov begins.

"Yes, and if you wish to reprimand me, I will readily accept it. I'm asking that you be patient and judge only after you see what we're doing."

"Be patient? I've shown this in the past, but using my facility costs me money. You don't pay for the mundane things keeping this island afloat. We have a business to run, and the bottom line doesn't have a kind heart. It is a simple case of profit margins."

"I assure you this could increase our profits while lowering the overall expenses to the government," Doctor Soleil finishes as he walks inside.

The black-painted front and back walls suck out the light from the LEDs overhead. The right and left walls are half one-way glass and the rest a panel with monitors, switches, and buttons. An assistant in an off-white coat rests at the controls on the left. Doctor Soleil walks to the panel on the right and flips a switch at the top of it.

The lights on the other side illuminate a sparsely decorated room and a soldier standing facing the glass. His eyes pop open, black as night over the ocean. A green light hits the soldier's face and his arm stretches mechanically to its full extension, saluting his superiors in the other room. His small, wiry frame looks harmless and useless to the cause. The black cargo pants hang on his hips, and the black tank top shows his clavicle and lack of muscle definition.

"You brought us in here to see a fucking twig that's useless on the battlefield, let alone in any physically demanding job?" Flannery pipes up from the back.

"Sit down at your console, Zero." The doctor speaks through a small microphone attached to the console. The soldier walks to his small desk and flips the top open. A holographic screen flickers to life and scrolls through various layers of code. Zero's eyes follow each line. "Activate One," Doctor Soleil says to the assistant.

Another flip of a switch and an identical room fills with false lighting. Another soldier, just as meek looking, with a large scar from the top of his head to the base of his neck, stands at full attention. "Time to play, One," the assistant says. One walks over to his desk, sits, and opens his computer. It loads, but his eyes are slower and slightly sluggish.

"Two useless human subjects for the price of one? Just what kind of facility are you running here, Doc?" Flannery taunts.

"While my colleague might be off in his terminology, his concerns are valid." Macalov's accent showcases his distaste for the situation.

"I know this doesn't look like much, gentleman, but believe me, this is only round one of a much more ambitious plan. Zero has had extensive intercranial surgeries. Everything that made him human has been overridden and replaced by a complex system of computer coding."

"So, you're telling me that both their brains read in zeroes and ones? And you actually named them Zero and One? Doc, we need to work on your creativity here."

"I assure you, Mr. Flannery, I reserve those attributes for my studies. You can name our next subjects."

"If we allow this to continue, of course," Macalov cuts in, running short on patience.

"Zero?" The doctor speaks into the small microphone again. "I want you to fight and win a ground war against One. Do you understand?" The soldier nods. "Failure is not an option. Are we clear?" The soldier once again moves his head affirmatively. "Activate the program."

The assistant begins the trial, and both panels light up in varying sequences of color. Both soldiers frantically touch the holo-screens in order to get the upper hand. Neither one breaks a sweat, but Zero's eyes are faster, his movement a hair quicker.

"How are they waging war against one another?" Macalov asks, watching Zero's hands move faster than his best men.

"A simulation of historical battles from the archives."

"Those are forbidden."

"I understand that, sir, but that makes them perfect fodder for these tests. They have no prior knowledge or experience with them; therefore, we can twist and manipulate everything. It's the best environment for these trials. We've also updated things to include cyberwarfare similar to those attempted by the resistance."

Monitors on both panels scroll through the biomedical readouts of each patient. Other screens showcase complex coding moving so fast it's difficult to catch a line, let alone a word or two.

"You have kids playing video games. Good job, doc." Flannery laughs.

"No, Mr. Flannery, they are not playing video games. They are fighting each other to the death. Whoever loses faces severe punishment dictated by the guard on duty. They feel pain, I assure you."

"But they're not showing any emotion."

"No, sir. They can't. After a myriad of tests, I've found the way to genetically shut down all aspects of their brain that correspond with remorse, fear, or the more human traits. Pure primal biology is all that rules these two men. They eat, sleep, pass waste, and seek pleasure. Beyond that, they go through daily testing scenarios."

"They're beaten if they fail, but if they win?"

"As I've said, these men only feel pain and pleasure. Therefore, they're rewarded with whatever satisfies their urges. Zero has only lost twice. When he wins, he prefers women. He's killed a few with his exuberance. One, on the other hand, prefers food, chocolate mostly. They have been completely deprogrammed, yet they are as individual as you or I."

"While this is a rather intriguing premise and could be valuable in shutting down insurgents, I fail to see how this could be lucrative. Historically speaking, the militaries of the past rarely needed the grunts due to technology. Drones have created the disassociation needed to grow a ruthless killer. What makes this more valuable to the patriarchy?" Macalov asks seriously.

"If nothing else, it would be great to fuck with people, right? Like have Zero there do party tricks or kill someone for entertainment," Flannery says, moving closer to the glass. Zero seems to move even faster than before as One appears to slow down.

"While I disagree with Mr. Flannery's crude example, he is correct. If this works consistently, think of the applications. We can train individuals to spy on those the crown deems suspicious. They could do the jobs we use the lower tiers for. They could fill out a workforce we deem expendable. The savings to the medical system alone would outweigh the costs to start the program en masse. We can expand it to create subservient women for those with the money to buy them. In the end, a fully functional human, without the cost or upkeep of a independent one," Doctor Soleil says with a smile on his face. His hands move about wildly with excitement over his new ideas. "The applications are endless."

A red light flashes on the left panel. One hangs his head, closes the desk, and stands at attention in front of the glass. The assistant mumbles something into the microphone and three fully armed soldiers enter One's room. They beat him with batons. His slight frame hits the ground, but he makes no noise. Blood hits the white floors, and his body twitches, but his eyes continue to look at the glass.

The three men turn to look at Zero, who simply stands with his hand raised at attention. Doctor Soleil mumbles into his microphone before standing and fixing his lab coat. The door to Zero's cell opens and two guards drag a naked woman into his cell. They drop her to the floor and exit just as quickly. Zero wastes no time with pleasantries as he drags her to his bed. The doctor flips the switch, and the room descends into darkness. The screams of the woman being brutalized and the batons smacking One's skin fill the room.

"Can he impregnate them?" Macalov asks seriously.

"We've sterilized our test subjects and, before you ask, the women we provide have outlived their usefulness to our other tests. They're here strictly for the pleasure of Zero and those on my staff who wish to indulge," the doctor answers coldly.

"You've proven the trial's worth, but why only two subjects?"

"These are the first two to survive the surgeries, let alone be successful. We lost seven men on the table," Soleil answers.

"I'm sure we can find you more suitable candidates. Would you consider expanding it with women?" Macalov inquires.

"I believe we are ready to expand the program. If you fund it and send me more . . . appealing candidates, I don't see why we couldn't."

"Excellent. Have all the papers drawn up and sent over to my office. I want everything, doctor, from the moment you began. If Mr. Flannery is to report to the president, he will have to showcase its value." Macalov pushes Flannery outside of the room and blocks the doctor from following. "That being said, you went behind my back again and made me look out of control in front of our guest. That's not something I can just ignore, doctor. You will give up your entire month's salary to this complex. You will spend the entire month in the dorm building working on all the nonviolent patients. You will assist the nurses in maintaining their care. You will not partake in any pleasure, enjoyment, or depositing your DNA in another breeder. You may be a genius, but if you break the rules again, I will remove your dick and feed it to the inmates. Are we clear?" Macalov finishes, his tone hard and pointed.

"Yes, sir," Doctor Soleil almost whispers, with his hands protectively over his genitalia.

Flannery stands in the hallway, his head tilted slightly, appreciating the female nurse as she strolls down the hallway. His calloused hands twirl a closed switchblade between his fingers. The soldiers stand by the door, minding their own business. The quiet in the halls breaks as Macalov walks out of the room and slams the door behind him. His legs move quickly, with a distinct purpose and direction, as Flannery struggles to keep up with him.

The angled windows hovering over the room break up the gun-metal gray paint of the observation room. Flannery walks around the room, slowly taking in everything around him. Each enclosure, made of solid cinder blocks, is bright white. The telltale outline of the entry cut into the stone can be seen only by those who know what to look for.

The floor, made of smooth cement, holds a large metal grate in the center. The pitch of all four sides of the room lead to the center in seamless beauty. The clear glass ceiling gives a perfect view inside the rooms with a few metal air vents attached to the corners, close enough to block a small portion of one's viewing, but not enough to concern the men upstairs.

To the outside world, these spaces would rival dorm rooms, with bunk beds and desks housed in the corners, and small closets jam-packed with whatever supplies a new aspiring student would need. Instead, their occupants wander around aimlessly, their bare feet scraping the concrete, sometimes leaving droplets of blood in their wake. Their flesh is matted with dirt and sweat from the time spent in isolation.

A young child plays in the room directly in front of the observation deck. He pretends to be someone who can fly as he rushes around the room, arms wide like the wings of a plane. He cheers and laughs as he moves around the confined area. The innocent sounds radiate up to Macalov and Flannery, who show no signs of compassion or joy over the ministrations of their captives.

The final holding cell contains a woman rocking back and forth in the center of the room. Resting on her knees, her hands are clasped in front of her in prayer as her body moves back and forth. Her hair is shaved down, her body riddled with sores, and her feet are covered in scabs from previous injuries. A number branded into her neck identifies her as number seven.

A doctor enters the room with several members of an entourage, complete with tablets and holo-frames. The statistics of each individual pop up before their eyes and on the screens by the main panel display. The two men offer a slight distraction from the science at hand. The doctor salutes and waits for Macalov to acknowledge him before they go about their business.

A simple nuclear family . . . who broke the law by being Muslim. Their lighter skin allowed them to walk among society as if nothing was different about them. The arrest record scrolls up from the screen. The father was found during a raid on an underground mosque. His wife and son were pulled from their job and daycare to be brought to Riker's Island, the woman knowing the true reality of their situation, the father long since accepting his family's end.

The doctor looks over to Macalov, partially for reassurance, but also to verify his choice. The colonel general walks up to the glass facing the father. He stands stoically, arms folded behind his back, waiting.

The doctor presses one button, and then slowly spins a dial to the right. The father looks around his cell as a yellow gas fills the cabin. First, he coughs, then he claws at his skin, his nails digging deep enough to draw blood. His mouth opens and closes as he stares up through the ceiling at Macalov, his arm rising in a one-finger salute as the man falls to his knees. His body convulses as blood trickles from every orifice to the floor. His arm drops, his head wavers, and he falls face-first to the floor with a loud crack.

The doctor rattles off some statistical numbers and turns the dial all the way to the left. Massive fans kick in and suck the gas back out of the room. After a few seconds, guards enter with protective gear and pull the man's corpse out of the room. The doctor hits a few more buttons on the panel and sprinklers wash the entire room down.

"A cleaning agent, mixed with water and bleach. We found that to be the best decontaminant before the ultraviolet scans," the doctor tells the entourage behind him. They all take meticulous notes as the water stops and the ceiling changes to an opaque white, the computer blaring in the room about the disinfection process.

Macalov walks across the room to view the woman's cell. She looks up and sees the two men standing there watching. Her clasped hands rise up and her mouth moves frantically, her voice trapped within the soundproofing built in. The doctor presses the same buttons as before and turns the dial to the right. A dark red gas fills the room. The woman holds her breath and sits cross-legged in the center of the room. Her skin erupts in pustules that grow until they explode, forcing the air to erupt out of her lungs in what the men assume is a scream. Her body slowly melts as her mouth remains open, wailing for help from those who cannot hear her.

The doctor follows the same procedures in cleaning the room before turning his attention to the boy. Macalov watches the child play, bouncing off the walls like a wrestler on the ropes, his energy radiating brighter than the sun. The doctor exhales as he presses the buttons to turn on a different gas mixture.

"The other two, which gases did you use?" Macalov interrupts.

"Basic airborne Ebola and a mutated variation of it. Both in high concentrations."

"Quite effective." The boy rolls on the floor as if he's dodging bullets. "Spare the boy. Bring him to my office at once and expunge his record."

"Sir?"

"Macalov, the kid's one of them. He's got fucked up genetics, and the law is—"

"I am the law, Mr. Flannery. I will do as I please. Doctor, you will do as I say."

"Right away."

Macalov storms out of the room, leaving Flannery to stare in disbelief at the man in charge. After a few moments of being ignored by the medical staff, Flannery also storms out of the room in a huff, his anger and desire to take over Riker's Island burning just below the skin. If the man in charge could show compassion for an ignominious child, the mutiny would be easier than he thought.

Chapter Seven

Anton leans over his desk, on which several papers are scattered about. The old maps for Riker's Island with the New York Public Library mark in the lower right corner hang over the edge. A brand-new pencil rests behind his ear as he holds a piece of chalk in his dirty right hand. His work overalls with the Waste Management NYC logo over his left breast smell of garbage and chemicals.

"Anton." Osaka walks into the room and falls onto the bed. Her hands pull at her high heels before she carefully drops them to the floor, her heart heavy and her body weak from the stress of what has become a normal workday.

"Hey, baby, I'm just going over a few ideas to present to Goldman. Maybe she'll push ahead with one of them." He continues to face the wall, scribbling with the chalk onto the papers.

"Chalk is expensive. Where'd you get it?"

"Trent gave me pieces he swiped from his son's charges. There's a dark spot on the rear side of Riker's Island. The water is more dangerous there, but if we created a distraction, we might be able to swim around and begin our attack there."

"I wish you would sit down for a minute," Osaka continues softly, her eyes unfocused through the tears that silently fall down her cheeks. "I need you to stop for one second."

"We could also attack from the front. If we make a distraction at the gate, at night . . . well, depending on what's in there, maybe we could cut off the entire facility. They've got a control room on the right once you cross the bridge. If we hit that, we put them in the dark and systematically take them out," Anton continues, making more and more marks with chalk.

"And then you let the guards know you're there, which activates all of their security protocols. It's a fool's errand, Anton." Osaka's words hit Anton hard. He spins around, his face a mixture of anger, fear, and confusion.

"My sister is being held—"

"Nadja is dead," she says flatly. The guilt of knowledge rolls into the room in one fell swoop, combined with relief and pain.

"What?" He pauses. "No. You're lying."

"Her file came across my desk. They directed me to expunge her file and wipe her information from the mainframe."

"No . . . they wouldn't."

"I'm sorry, Anton, but she's gone. This battle for Riker's has to stop. We have more important—"

"More important? My sister is dead!" Anton seethes harshly with spit flying out of his mouth with each syllable. "You sound just like her! There are bigger things than what's around us . . . How many people has she sent to die? How many people need to suffer under her thumb until someone does something about it?"

"We all know what we signed up for, Anton. We all have the implant. Nadja could have broken hers and not been subjected to the torment that she experienced. She made her choice, and right now, you have to make yours. You can let the grief take you over, or you can focus on what you can control."

"Get out," he says as he turns back to the old prints of Riker's Island. She wraps her arm around him from behind. He struggles, pushing her away at first. She repeats the action, holding onto him tighter, with no space between their flesh. His chin trembles, and tears roll down both of their faces as he slowly collapses to the floor.

"She never should have gone out for supplies," he whimpers.

"Nadja was the best hunter we had. She wouldn't have allowed anyone to go in her place."

"Agent Goldman . . . she could have gone in my sister's place."

"Could she? Goldman knows the inner workings of this resistance faction. If they caught her, we would be flying blind and they could wipe us out from within."

"Like you said, she has her implant. She would have had the same decision my sister had to make."

"True, but Agent Goldman knows the risks. She's also stronger than any member of our team to date. She saved my life, and even if she committed suicide, we don't know if they can extract memories or thoughts. We don't know what the enemy is capable of."

"Maybe they're not the real villains though. Maybe we are," Anton says, pushing her off and standing to his full height. "We sit around here, controlling the minds of the weak. Telling them what they can eat or how they can speak. We ration their water for showers and force them to drink some disease-riddled concoction. We never give them hope. We never have a plan to further our existence; we just keep moving forward. That's all she fucking says: think of the bigger picture and move forward." He rambles while pacing in the small room.

"I understand you're upset . . ."

"Upset? That's my sister, Osaka! She's the only . . . she *was* the only one I had left. The only rational thing connecting me to whatever this world was supposed to be. My only connection to the hope of humanity within. What the hell am I supposed to do when I go topside now? What stops me from just going to one of their schools and shooting their fucking kids like they've done to us?"

Osaka stands up and wraps her arms around Anton again. His entire body vibrates with negative energy as she leans her forehead against his. "I've known you for four years—this pesky little eighteen-year-old who wanted everyone to take him seriously, who asked me out and grew into the man I love with all my heart. I know I'm not Nadja. I can't comprehend how you both grew up in Hamelin or fled in the cargo hold of smuggler ships from Hamburg."

Anton struggles to remove himself from her grasp. His body, calmer from Osaka's touch, begins ramping up again, the energy for action boiling in his blood like a volcano ready to incinerate thousands with a pyroclastic cloud. She holds firm, the pressure of her hands preventing the complete destruction of the man she loves.

"I do understand what it was like to come to this country on a plane and sold into slavery. I do remember my mother crying as they beat her for trying to hold onto me. I remember my father turning his back on me in shame because I accepted my place. The feel of a guard taking from me what no one had before. I know what pain felt like, because every nerve ending under my skin would scream if I moved the wrong way after a paying client came in."

Osaka places one hand against Anton's cheek, and his eyes find hers. She shows a small smile, and her lips brush against his softly, the connection a grounding force as his hand squeezes hers tighter. Breaking apart, she continues to look at him as if he were the world.

"Laskin might have saved me from future assaults until my body wore out, but you . . . God, Anton, you gave me something I never thought possible. You gave me love. You gave me hope. You helped me process all those . . ." Osaka's voice breaks as she closes her eyes to get her bearings. "You replaced all the bad touches with wonderful ones. You gave me back control over my own body. You held me through the nightmares, even when I fought against you when my brain triggered negatively."

"You're worth every bruise," Anton all but whispers through his own emotions.

"And so are you. We're a team, and that means I get to be the strong one right now. You just have to let me."

"I don't know how to live without her. Even locked up, I knew she was still around. Now, I feel so empty, angry, and someone is going to have to pay for it."

"And they will. Have faith in that."

Osaka kisses Anton again, their salty tears from past and present torment mixing into one. He releases her and walks to the door, ensuring it's locked, before walking up to his girlfriend. He pulls off his work overalls and allows them to fall to the floor before ripping off his sweaty tank top.

Osaka runs her fingers along a scar from his hip to the bottom of his rib cage, a memory of the past flashing before her eyes as his skin pebbles with slight bumps. His hands work effortlessly to remove her shirt and bra before her eyes lock back onto his. Without saying a word, she steps out of her skirt and underwear. Anton takes in her body, covered with small ridges of pink, healed skin from being in the sex trade for years.

Anton leads Osaka to the bed and begins kissing every mark on her chest, his voice uttering soft declarations of love and respect as he cherishes her body. She pulls him gently to look at her directly. His eyes are filled with love, but the storm brewing behind the dark brown orbs cause her stomach to churn in fear. He leans down to kiss her passionately, and all conscious thought rolls off her body.

Trent lies asleep on his compact cot in the corner. Everything in his small room is reminiscent of a life in the military. A photo of two men in uniform rests in an old cracked frame on the table against the wall. The walls remain empty, a small dresser holding his clothing across the room from his cot. No excess, no evidence of who lives here other than the sole image.

"You really think we can take Riker's?" Anton says from the doorway, his hair wet, and a towel over his shoulder. He's wearing a pair of sweats and black boots.

Trent rolls slightly under his thin sheet, rising and fumbling for the small switch on the wall above his head. Once the light brightens the room, he covers his eyes with his arm, blocking the unwanted light until his eyes can adjust. Anton walks farther into the room, closing the door behind him. Taking the initiative, he sits at the table, waiting.

"Why don't you come right in and sit, boy." The pointed sarcasm rolls out of Trent's mouth. "You ever hear of knocking or asking if you could come in? You damn kids and your lack of basic respect." He swings his legs from beneath the sheet, his calloused feet hitting the floor.

"I knocked, but you old people never accept that you can't hear shit. You'd rather just blame all your problems on us young people who carry your weight around like an albatross around our necks," Anton counters.

"Without us old folks, there never would have been—"

"I don't want to get into this again. I asked you a question. Do you really think we can take Riker's Island by force?"

"Truthfully?"

"No, fucking lie to me like when people said their vote mattered," Anton scoffs as he fists his towel with distaste.

"It's possible if we do it correctly, but it might be costly."

"We have the weapons in holding. I have the combinations to the armory, so that's not a problem."

"Getting men to follow the plan and turn their back on Agent Goldman is our biggest issue. We can improvise the rest." Trent reaches forward and picks up a plastic cup of water, takes a sip, and places it back down. "Why the sudden interest?"

"Maybe I'm tired of chess and would rather play checkers." Anton attempts to joke, but it falls flat. "I have ideas."

"So do I, but you're Goldman's second and maybe even her lackey. Let's just say I've kept my head on my shoulders for this long and I don't plan on changing that anytime soon."

"She's stuck in her ways, but Agent Goldman would never—"

"She's former MSC, boy. The Multinational Security Council operated outside all parameters of the law. I've seen Marines fall to their knees and cry like babies when they were around." Trent moves forward on his cot, elbows on his knees, his voice lowered more for effect than anything else. "She probably has more bodies in her jacket than Macalov. Why do you think the king wanted them exterminated before they even attempted the takeover? They would have assassinated him before he could compromise the first election. She is not innocent in this war, and she sure as hell isn't my leader."

Anton looks around the room, noting the nothingness that reflects back to him, each second giving him time to digest the additional information. The loyal side of himself wars with the anger within for the family he's lost. Agent Goldman was the one who saved him and his sister, gave them purpose after they fled their home country. She helped forge their papers for work so they could survive. If he remains steadfast by her side, it will be safe. He will never have to concern himself about anything outside of small raids and maybe preparation for the larger one in Manhattan. If he goes behind her back, she'll never forgive his betrayal. His punishment will be banishment. If Trent's words are true, death could also be on the table if the agent catches wind of his role in the mutiny.

"Did the crew for the supply run go out yet?" Anton finally says, after pondering his next move.

"No, I've held them back until I felt the timing was safe."

"It's never safe."

"Exactly."

"Smart play. No one leaves, rations run low, and people revolt. Doesn't make us much better than them, does it?"

"It's war. No one's ever in the clear, Anton. The victors write history, and I plan to be one."

"It will take time to plan, study their schedules, and figure out the best timing. Once that's accomplished, we take those individuals who volunteered for the supply run and those who stand with you on the mission. Agent Goldman will never know of the attack until it's finished." His decision lifts a figurative weight off his shoulders.

"Once we take Riker's, she and the rest of them will understand their failure to lead. They'll allow us to run the resistance in the proper direction. With one spark, the fire will ignite, and our cause will gain more traction." Trent holds his hand out to shake on their agreement.

"One condition." Trent remains steadfastly holding his hand out as he waits. "I remove the man who killed my sister."

"You can have as many of them as your heart desires."

Anton grabs Trent's hand in a firm grip. The two men break and sit back in their respective spots, staring at one another. Anton feels an unfamiliar weight slowly settle upon him. He's just agreed to send his people to a possible slaughter. The man sitting across from him, a small smile etched onto his aged skin, concerns him. It's in that moment that Anton feels he's made the wrong decision, but understands going back now is impossible. He has crossed the line drawn on the floor and has to see it through.

Osaka knocks softly on the old metal door at the end of a long hallway. A mumbled "Enter" hits her ears as she jerks the handle up. She leans her body weight into it, forcing it open one step at a time. Once inside, she pushes the door closed and latches it.

Ellie sits at her desk, frantically working on something in front of her. Osaka stands calmly, waiting for some attention from the agent.

"What's going on?" The words are soft, inviting, like a big sister talking to the younger one.

"What are you working on?" Osaka's body moves shakily across the floor, her wet hair sticking to her arms and back. Ellie lifts her jacket and hands it to her. Osaka slips it around her shoulders before leaning against the wall and taking in the map of Manitoba, Canada, with varying pencil marks scattered all over it. "That's an awful long way from Manhattan, Ellie."

"It is," Ellie replies. "But it may be the best place for us to go."

"Go? I thought you wanted to make a stand here."

"I do, yes. That doesn't mean all of you need to come with me. Our fight . . ." Ellie pauses as the air pours out of her lungs slowly. "My fight is here. You deserve a place to live away from the fear of being raped, beaten, or shot dead in the street just because."

"And Churchill? It probably snows more than here. Ellie, they'll find us no matter where we go."

"No, they won't. Churchill is off-limits by order of King Valkov and the prime minister. They had been testing biochemical agents during the early period of the war. Scientists said contamination levels rivalled that of Pripyat. They're cleaning that up for financial reasons. There's no reason to develop it."

"I've seen the plans for developing the area for prisons and low-income housing. But they're lying. Those cleaning it up will die of radiation poisoning. They'll force people to move there and never allow them to leave."

"Yes, well, that's not surprising, but this is all a lie. The Unified Canadian Resistance Front were in on it before their disappearance." Ellie pulls back a layer of pages to show a human transport system map. "They designed a small series of pathways using abandoned train tracks, tunnels, and whatever was already in existence."

"I've been privy to conversations between the prime minister and president; there is no Canadian resistance."

"Partially accurate. It's possible some sects migrated north when the walls started closing in."

"But you have no evidence they made it there alive."

"Do we have any other options? We're isolated on this island with barely enough rations to get by for another two weeks. We have innocent children who deserve a chance at some kind of life. I don't say it will be easy . . ."

"Is there a developed area? Shelter? Food?"

"It was a tourist town, so shelter is already in place. Based on old maps, most of the buildings have wood-burning fireplaces."

"And heat signatures?"

"Explained away with the chemical reactions in the soil or the animals nearby."

"Ellie, you're not a fool. They could easily use satellite imaging and see where the heat is coming from."

"I know it's a long shot, but it's all I've got. Sam can go with you, hack all the systems, and create some kind of digital camouflage. Whatever he can do . . . Osaka, this really is our only hope for a life."

"And if you're not there?" Ellie stops and leans back in her chair. Osaka takes in her expression, the look of understanding and calm in Ellie's eyes. "Anton?" Ellie nods before returning to sketch out some more notes with the nub of her pencil.

"He's fully capable of leading everyone." Ellie flips pages back and forth, marking safe travel spots or alternative routes. "I'll need you to see if the president has any information about strongholds between here and there. Once I have a plan in place, I'll let everyone know. Those that want to go, can. The rest can continue here if they wish . . . without me."

"I can do that." Osaka pushes off the wall and walks to the door. Her fingers wrap around the handle and she slides it open. "What if . . ." She pauses. Her mind swirls with questions about a future away from all of this violence, her desire to run and pull Anton into her arms and tell him the bigger picture Ellie has for them and plan. It's funny how life twists things before they rest within your grasp. "Anton's planning an attack on Riker's Island."

Ellie drops her pencil on the desk, her face stoic and firm. Osaka turns and tries to assess the situation in front of her. The negative energy buzzes from wall to wall as the muscles in Ellie's neck tense. She clenches her fists as she exhales loud enough for Osaka to hear it.

"Are you sure?" Ellie spins her chair around and takes in Osaka's nervous demeanor. "Of course you're sure. You're his partner . . . In everything, or just affairs of the heart?"

"I don't agree, but his sister . . . Her file came across my desk. She's not with us anymore."

Ellie nods her head as her fingers continue to flex and relax into fists. She stands, turns back to the desk, and folds up the papers and her notes. She lifts her mattress and places them underneath. "Thank you for your honesty." She sits on the bed and stares at the map hanging on the wall. The black X marks fill more of the country, including the cities Ellie had hoped were still functioning.

"What does this mean?"

"Depending on who's involved"—Ellie pauses and takes a moment to process the information. "—some men deem themselves holier by living their interpretation of religion. They believe they'll be accepted into the kingdom . . . This means it's time to test that theory." The words hang in the air, and Osaka isn't sure how to interpret them.

"I'll find out what I can from the office," she adds, her mind swirling with confusion. Ellie has never shown defeat in her disposition before. In fact, Osaka can't remember the last time the agent has ever looked so out of it. Always composed, even when dropping the hammer down on her subordinates, now she looks anything but.

Chapter Eight

Laskin sits in darkness on a couch in his living room, the skyline of New York City lighting up the room. He sips his brandy as the ice cubes rock into one another and clink against the glass. The papers on the coffee table remain untouched as the silence in the penthouse washes over him.

"You look all cozy up in here." Flannery walks into the room and drops himself unceremoniously onto the opposite side of the couch. "Got one for me?"

Laskin stands and walks toward the windows and the small bar. He fills his glass to the brim and pulls out another one.

"Easy on the ice." Flannery laughs to himself. "Better yet, just one cube."

Laskin places one round ball of ice into the glass before pouring the brandy over it. He turns around and hands the glass to Flannery before reclaiming his spot on the couch. "What did you find?"

"I'd say you and daddy boy have a reason to be suspicious," Flannery says, tipping his head back and taking a large gulp from his glass.

"That's a fifty-year-old brandy, Mr. Flannery. It's meant to be savored, not chugged like a commoner."

"Well, see that's the thing. I am one of those, aren't I?"

"Not really, no. You had a high-level education, tested out of most programs, and came from a very wealthy family."

Flannery stops, sits up properly, and places his glass on a coaster on the coffee table. "What the hell are you talkin' about?"

"This persona is just that. You're not a common piece of trash or ignorant killer. You're a con man." Laskin reaches for a small file folder on the table and tosses it over to Flannery. "First rule of power: maintain it."

Flannery opens up the file and sees an image of himself from grade school. He flips the pages and skims its contents before taking a sip of his drink. "So, what . . . You going to blackmail me? Your father-in-law—"

"Knows exactly the kind of man you are." Laskin sips his drink and leans back into the leather of the couch. "I need you to be exactly who you prefer to be. Consider it equality for what kind of individual you identify as."

"What's the catch?"

"Nothing. I expect you to use all the tools at your disposal to get me information as needed and some other brutish endeavors."

Flannery drops the file on the table, grabs his glass, and leans back against the couch, the leather cracking as he presses further into it. The men sit in silence, enjoying the quiet and the spectacle of the skyline. Laskin's phone lights up on the table. He leans forward, scans the information, and returns to his position.

"You said we had a right to be suspicious. Why?"

"Macalov is running all the protocols, but the doctors appear to be going behind his back to run their own experiments."

"So, his control is wavering. That's not surprising. The way to a better job is to remove the man ahead of you."

"Yeah, but his experiments have made mindless soldiers. Doc talked about them being slaves to whatever programming we give them, but Macalov . . . I know he's planning on expanding it."

"Do you have evidence to support this theory?"

"Official funding paperwork. It's the programming I'd be more concerned about."

"Which is as beneficial as a barren woman. I need documentation, actual evidence proving his disloyalty."

"What? You want me to pull it out of my ass? He's losing it. Hell, he let a kid survive. A terrorist, for fuck's sake . . ."

"Macalov saved a child? From what?"

"I don't know exactly, but the kid's parents tested out airborne Ebola of various concentrations. The effects were brutal. But then he stopped the test when the doc turned his attention to the kid's cell. He broke the law, so we can bring him in."

Laskin lets the alcohol burn down his throat and settle into the depths of his iron stomach. The last few weeks, packed with meetings and minutia from the other countries, have weighed him down some. His wife and son caught in the crossfire of his enemies, wanting his position by force if not by resignation.

"My father-in-law won't care about the minor indiscretion. He wants something more . . . volatile to the crown. Saving a boy, well, he could contort that narrative to suit his needs. 'King Valkov, I saved a sinner and converted him into a devout killing machine. He blends in with the deplorables and destroys them from within. We can now conquer the neutral zones!'" Laskin holds up his glass, toasting what he expects Macalov would say.

"Exactly! He'd listen to you."

"Right, just like I informed him Africa is a gold mine of resources. Not all of it is lost. But no, it's a wasteland with disease running unimpeded. What do I know? I'm just a Columbia University graduate with a doctorate in biochemical engineering! It's all lies. All of it."

Laskin stumbles as he refills his glass once again. He holds the bottle open to Flannery, who is quick to accept. "Macalov has been a thorn in my side since I married Maria. Every time he looks at her, it makes my stomach cringe. I won't have that piece of crap taking my place, raising my son, and taking my wife." Laskin gulps down the brandy before refilling it again.

"Then don't," Flannery pushes.

"Riker's Island has been Macalov's pet project for years, but the cost he's racked up has damaged our budget. It's a money pit. They don't say that, though. Keep up appearances with lies to get more donations. I want you to go back, play whatever con game you want. Keep your nose to the ground and find out anything you can. If we turn it into a profit machine—"

"While that's possible, there are laws in place that prevent me from doing everything I can." Flannery stands next to the window, letting his comment hang in the air, waiting for it to be digested.

"Those laws will be . . . flexible in this specific case." Laskin hands the entire bottle to Flannery. "Do as you need, but ensure it's handled."

Flannery finishes his glass, reaches in front of Laskin, and places it back on the small table. Grabbing the bottle, he smiles in acceptance as he takes in the view of the outside world. "The view's pretty sweet."

"Riker's Island has a better view of the water all year round from the warden's office."

Flannery spins, focusing his attention fully on Laskin. His neck flexes as his mouth opens to reply, but nothing comes out. The implications of the simple statement weigh heavily on his chest. The desire to take what he feels has always been his calling is a tempting offer, but the cost has always been great. Laskin casually dangling the carrot in front of him is both enticing, but also concerning. If he follows through as the president wishes, he could be in the good graces of the king and given a new position. He could also be a scapegoat for the mutiny and punished accordingly. It would all depend on the whim of a man any rational human being would regard as unfit to hold the title of president.

But desire will always win out over concern for well-being. Eventually, the king will pass and his grandson will take the mantle. A mother's son filled with compassion but easily manipulated by his parents. His advisors might not fare well against the woman who birthed him, regardless of her standing.

Flannery is well aware of the hidden lessons Laskin forces his son to attend. Images on a board showing those in power that work for his grandfather and all their negative traits. To insiders, it's an obvious message of a complete change in regime which will unsettle markets and society for a few years.

"I'll do what you ask in exchange for that view."

"Good. Then you ought to get started."

"But if you throw me under the bus—" Flannery takes a large swig from the bottle and swallows hard"—no one will ever find Maria or Maxim again." Flannery finishes the bottle quickly before placing it on the counter. He wipes his mouth with his forearm before belching as he heads for the door.

"Mr. Flannery," Laskin calls after him. "You threaten my wife and son again and you'll wake up in Africa with no papers or means of escape. Don't miscon-strue our business arrangement as weakness on my part. It would be wise to remember that."

Flannery says nothing as he walks out of the penthouse. Laskin places his glass back on the table and shoves his hands in his pockets. His eyes wander over the view, from lit buildings to the darker areas just outside of Manhattan Island.

"You threaten everyone that walks in our door?" Maria leans against the wall, pulling her silk robe around her frame.

"What are you doing up?" Laskin walks across the room to meet his wife. He pulls her into a tight embrace, breathing in her scent to calm his anxiety.

"Listening to you play war games with our son's life." She pushes her husband back a bit and looks up into the eyes she loves so dearly. "I don't want him to lead, ever. He's a good boy. Let him be."

"You know that's not up to us."

"It is. He's our boy, and I will not let my father control the future of our son!" Maria raises her voice and pushes past Laskin.

He promptly grabs her and pushes her against the wall. His arms vibrate as the muscles work overtime to hold her in place. His face is a few inches from hers, his mind racing and his body shaking out of control.

"You don't have a choice in this. You're my wife, and I treat you better than any woman in the country, but don't push me." He takes a few calming breaths before loosening his grip on her arms. "I love you, but we don't have control over the game we play. Your father's the king, and he chooses. When Maxim takes the throne, we can change the world for the better. We can push for those ideals you hold. We can help our son rule over a peaceful and just world."

"I guess that depends on your definition of the word 'just.' Until you walk in my shoes, Jerrik . . ." She lets her sentence hang in the air as she pushes away from her husband.

Laskin waits until he hears the bedroom door close. The telltale sign of the door lock engaging causes him to rub the back of his neck. The muscles, tense from the altercation, scream as he attempts to get comfortable on the couch that's mostly for show. He's well aware it will be a long night, but in the end, his wife will support his decisions and stand by his side. After all, it's her place.

Flannery walks out into the middle of Times Square, pulls out a cigarette, and lights it. The fence clicks closed behind him and an armed security guard stands by the fence, preventing him from reentering. He takes in the billboards screaming about some new product or the regime-approved Broadway musicals. He chuckles a bit to himself as he watches the masses mindlessly walking around. The major construction continues behind the gated area where the president and his family remain safely tucked away. Floors of government agencies exist between the grunts on the ground and the penthouse. The illusion of being part of something grander melts away the closer you get to the bottom.

Flannery flips open an old cell phone and sends a quick message consisting of only numbers. Closing it, he shoves it back into his pocket before taking a long drag of his cigarette. He strolls through the crowd of people milling about, exhaling smoke into the air. Several people wave their hands, pushing it away, while others cough. He laughs internally and continues on his path through the crowd to a small gate leading to an alley on a side street. Flicking his cigarette to the ground, he stomps on it and heads into the darkness. A person covered head to toe in white, face covered save for small eye holes, uses a small broom to sweep the discarded butt into a tray.

Flannery walks through the desolate, dirty walkway to the end and down a flight of stairs. He bangs on the door; the metal slat slides open, revealing nothing but a dim light. Flannery slides his hand inside and winces slightly at the pressure of his fingers being pressed on a scanning device. A green light illuminates the other side as he quickly retracts his hand before the opening slams shut. Several clicks and gears sound before the door slowly opens up. Looking behind him once more, Flannery enters, and the machine sounds echo again as it closes behind him.

The dank underground bar, full of black-market items from drugs to women, has no name. The patrons know it by word of mouth, membership to the outcast moniker, and pure addiction. Flannery's lineage prevents him from being a member by society's standards, but the man has his ear to the ground. He couldn't be a successful murdering bastard if he didn't have his informants.

The hallway, lined with a mix of white men being serviced or snorting inferior quality powder off a woman's breast, cut the walkway in half. Sliding past body after body, the stench rolls up into Flannery's nostrils before he can close them off. The main room consists of a large square housing a small stage against one wall and a bar directly across from it. Cocktail tables fill the open spaces. Flannery walks to the bar and sits in the corner seat farthest away from the lights.

"What'll ya have?" the half-naked male bartender asks.

"Whiskey, neat."

"You wanna see a menu?" The bartender grabs a barely clean glass and pours a cloudy mix of cheap alcohol into it. "Got new listings."

"He's not interested. Get me a dark beer, don't care which one," Trent says, sliding into the seat next to Flannery. "Smells like you already got a head start."

"How can you smell anything above the debauchery in here?" Flannery laughs before sipping his drink and wincing at the horrible taste. The bartender hands Trent his beer and heads to the other end of the crowded bar.

"What's the emergency?" Trent questions.

"Things are changing direction."

"You remember when you were five years old? Your daddy was a good man, outstanding pilot. He was my friend, and I promised him I'd take care of you. But if you keep talking in riddles like your old man, I'll put you in the ground."

"I went back home to see Mom."

"Why would you do that?" Trent looks over at Flannery, taking in the far-off look in his eyes. "She the one to do that to your face?"

"She didn't deserve to be lowered like that. Dad was a great man; he died fighting from the inside for the king, like you. She deserved more."

"Your father died. Everything reverted to you. That's the law. She needed to work, and that put her in a different class. This isn't news, so let's stop rehashing old history and move on."

Flannery finishes his drink and taps his glass on the counter, getting the bartender's attention. In short order, the cloudy fluid fills it again and Flannery downs it and taps again. Trent sits there, sipping his beer and letting the man slowly crumble in front of him.

"I set her free." He looks over to Trent, sincere remorse in his eyes. "People witnessed what she did, so I . . " He motions with his arms in a choke hold.

"I'm sorry you had to do that, but don't go around telling anyone you were merciful. We need your reputation to remain intact." Trent pats Flannery's shoulder in solidarity before turning back to his beer. "Now tell me what's going on."

"I got orders to get any kind of dirt on the warden. Anything, no holds barred. Once I do that, I can bring you topside."

"Kid, we've been through this. They don't like my kind."

"Keep your proclivities behind closed doors and no one will care. I'll make sure the cell cameras are off—"

"And go back into the shadows? No thanks. I did that years ago. Not doing it again. Besides, I got some people willing to plot an excursion to the island. Maybe we can help each other out."

"How do you figure?"

"You help me get in and we take the island and show the incompetence of certain people in power. If he gets caught in the crossfire, even better for your cause." Trent reasons.

"There's a militia that basically lives there to provide all kinds of security. There's a lot that could go wrong and shine one hell of a spotlight on me. You'd have to give me something that would keep the hothead focused on his presidential whims."

Trent takes a long pull from his beer as he ponders his options. "What if I gave you the resistance's location?"

Flannery sips his drink and leans toward Trent. "You'd turn in the very people who protected you all this time?"

"I threw people under the bus and traded them as commodities for less. It's war, kid. People die. We need to make a stand, and if a diversion is what I need, so be it."

"That might not be enough."

"It's run by a former MSC operative. If you want to know if there are other holdouts or hiding places, she's the one who knows. She's also hiding a pair of illegals."

"Illegals in what way? Border jumpers?"

"Of the darker pigmentation variety."

Flannery sits straight up and takes in the information. "Okay, what do you need?"

"Best access route, codes, whatever layout you can get us."

"I can do that. You get me names of those inside and the exact location. I'll take care of the rest."

"Done."

The two click their drinks together. Trent takes a celebratory sip of his while Flannery gulps his down. Feeling the full effects of everything in his system, Flannery leans heavily on Trent's shoulder. "I'm proud of you, old man, fighting for the right side—our own! Now, tonight we have fun. Tomorrow, we'll hash out the details." Flannery pats Trent's back before stumbling to the stage and the topless dancers.

"He need another one?" the bartender asks. Trent waves the option off but continues to stare at the bartender. "You wanna see the menu?"

"I already see what I want to order."

"Room Zebra, twenty minutes."

The bartender walks away and tends to the other end of the bar. Trent carries his beer and walks across the floor, not paying attention to the men and women indulging. He finds these places repulsive, but always attends them when he can nonetheless. The minute you enter, it's like signing an iron clad nondisclosure agreement prohibiting you from telling the powers that be. If someone knows you've told authorities, you're dead before the police find you to verify the information.

Chapter Nine

Tim drags Wei Ni into a small cement-lined room with a metal drain in the middle. Her face is devoid of any markings, but her arms show the beginnings of some bruising from Tim's tight grasp. Her eyes are downcast, and her body aches for rest; whether it is sleep or death, she no longer cares.

"The world is like a spider web. Its beauty shines for the world to see while hiding the true evil behind it," Wei whispers to herself as she takes in the room around her.

"All you have to do is talk. Then this all stops," Tim says, locking the door behind them. "I don't enjoy doing this . . . It's a side of me—"

"The scorpion stings the frog, killing them both because he is a scorpion. We cannot hide our true nature behind platitudes."

"Yet, that's what you're doing. Whatever I say, you have some saying or some witty comment. Maybe trying to get me to think beyond who I am, but that's the funny part—this *is* who I am. The tests proved it. I'm a protector of my own. I do what I have to do to put food on the table and take care of my mom. You could have been more to me, but you made a choice to be—what is it?—a player in the grand game of life," he finishes, the sarcasm oozing from his lips.

A simple metal table rests in the center of the room with a drainage hole lined up below it. There's a tray to the side holding a folded white gown, medical gloves, and a face spray shield. Wei Ni understands this room's use is beyond the simple talking points or normal beatings for the extraction of information. This is a room of torture, one secluded from the other inmates on her block. No matter what she says or does, she will not leave the room the same way she entered. The pristine white walls and floor hit her with their simplistic splendor. No matter how much detritus may coat them, they apparently wash clean, allowing the next person to revel in the absurd beauty of it all.

Without saying a word, Wei walks to the table and lifts herself upon it. She lies down, mumbling soft prayers to herself in her native language. Tim says nothing as he locks her wrists at her side in metal contraptions attached to the frame. He repeats the same action with her ankles. Her words hit his ears, but he ignores them.

He places the face shield on her chest, along with the gloves from the table next to her. As he opens the gown, the heavy plastic protector peels away noisily with each movement. Like a kitchen apron, Tim slides one loop around his neck and ties the heavy cords around his waist. His hands slide into the arm-length gloves, slightly restricting the dexterity of his fingers. He places the face shield back over the tools, looking down at the patient, her eyes closed and breathing steadily as she continues to pray.

"Wei Ni, suspected member of the Multinational Security Council. Born in Japan, trained in many banned forms of martial arts. Do you deny of these statements?"

Wei turns her head to face Tim. "My name and birth are well documented. My training was as well before the world ended and tyranny began."

"Are you a member of the MSC?" Tim ignores her previous comment and continues his round of questioning.

She mutters something in Japanese as a reply.

"Did you start the underground pipeline to smuggle individuals to the unin-habitable zones?"

"People fled of their own accord. I was part of the fleeing masses. The bombs dropped, decimated my country, and left me no choice."

"The government has condemned those lands. The radiation levels are well beyond acceptable levels. The government satellites retrieve updated information daily for changes. No one could survive there for very long," Tim counters, waiting for an honest answer.

"One chooses death when the only other option is slavery." She breathes deeply and exhales slowly.

"They're stupid. This isn't slavery; it's a new way of living. So, I ask again, why go to the irradiated lands?"

"The new way of living is for the white man. My people would never see the sun again. We'd live as slaves to the world above, in perpetual servitude to ones less deserving. No. I would choose the chance of survival or certain death over that." She breathes.

"You don't think like everyone else. Normal people wouldn't just go there. Wouldn't risk..." Tim stares at the wall in thought. "Unless our scans are faulty."

"That's not possible under governmental law," Wei Ni says with a smirk. "Russia is never wrong."

"So, it's possible that some or all of the land is habitable? Exiled people are living there?"

She continues her riddles. "Mother Nature takes back what man has squandered. We choose the end, to assist her in the beginning."

Tim looks over at the tray and picks up a pair of small needle-nose pliers with his right hand. Slipping on his face shield, he grips her thumbnail between the metal prongs. "Is the area habitable?"

She remains calm, breathing deeply as her body lies still. Tim pulls hard, ripping the nail from the flesh with ease. Her jaw clenches with the pain and her breathing quickens as she tries to regain her composure. Tim moves to the index finger. He waits for a few seconds before tearing it out of the nail bed. Composure lost, her scream fills the room with pure agony.

"I don't know," Wei sputters, spittle flying from her mouth. "No one has ever returned."

"So, they go to die. Radiation poisoning is painful. Why do it? Why not just shoot each other?"

"Our bodies decompose and give back to the earth. You might not understand, but it is an honorable death. One on our own terms."

"Falling on your sword . . ."

"Some did," she continues, thinking of her father. "You may not understand, but every person believes differently. The information is there, but the implementation is unique to each human."

"Your father was a general in the Final War. Did he give you any information that the crown would need? Movements of rebels?"

"When Russia turned our own people against us, my father lost." She laughs sadistically. "When you cannot protect your own back, you are doomed to fail."

Without warning, Tim pulls out another nail, causing her body to jump slightly on the table. Trained to take an enormous amount of pain, she can handle the beatings and even cutting, but this is her weakness.

"Is there a pipeline to smuggle people out of Japan?"

"No!" she screams as the pain radiates through her body. "We fled as a unit, above ground, begging for scraps of food. Many died along the way, but I assume some made it to Africa."

"Yet you survived. Why did you leave the group? Did you meet up with another MSC operative?" Tim continues, his voice cold and the pliers hovering over her ring finger. "Did you join the resistance?"

"There was nothing to join. No people left with the courage to stand against . . ." She bites her lip, causing the skin to break under the pressure as Tim attacks her last two fingernails. He drops the tool, dripping with blood, to the tray.

"They filled the lands with bodies of the unwashed. Good." He flips up the shield and looks back down at Wei Ni. "Now, are you an MSC operative?"

"The government purged them out of existence. How can I be something the ruling authority says is extinct?" She spits as blood drips down her cheek.

"If you were a coward who ran away instead of facing judgment—"

"The fly does not flee the spider due to fear, it runs for self-preservation." Her body shakes as she answers. "You were different. Yet, you are truly the spider."

"I thought I was a scorpion."

"No, he is blindly doing what nature has intended him to do. You are the spider. You capture your prey, allow it to live as you devour its essence." She runs her tongue across her lip, wincing when she reaches the split flesh. "You enjoy every aspect of this . . . task you've been given. Yet, like the beautiful web, your face hides the reality underneath. You are no better than those stopped from claiming me. You were no better when you pretended to take me as your own to shield me from harm. Your words are hollow, Tim Flynt. You are a creature of darkness who shies from the light of day. You are the coward who waits for its prey to tire, wrapped in the strings of your web, before you pounce. I am no coward, but you reek of it."

His hand connects with her face before she can take a deep breath in. His eyes darken with anger as he flips the shield down once more. His right hand grabs the first tool it comes across, a corkscrew. "How many operatives are still alive?"

"I told you . . ."

"And you lied." He places the corkscrew in her belly button, pressing down enough to make Wei aware of the pain coming her way. "How many operatives?"

Silence.

He twists as he pushes down. Wei clenches her jaw as a resounding crack fills her ears. Tim stops and leans back. "How many?"

Wei turns her head and spits out a broken tooth from the clenching of her jaw. The sweat rolling off her forehead dilutes the blood dripping on the table below her head.

"I am the last one," she says as a tear rolls down her face. "The others fell in the initial attacks. Murdered with the rebels they tried to help."

"Where is your rebel connection?"

"My connection is dead."

"Where?" Tim demands, turning the corkscrew a half a rotation.

"Toronto!" she screams as blood pours from her wound. The sound of her life's fluid drips from the table to the floor. "I tried to help Toronto . . ."

"They buried them alive. Did you know that? It was cheaper to bury them alive than try to traverse all those underground tunnels to find them."

Tim cracks his neck, lets go of the tool, and stretches his fingers.

"What do you think got them first? Oxygen deprivation or starvation? Maybe dehydration? I wonder if they turned on each other for food. Could you imagine? Attacking your best friend for flesh to eat and blood to drink . . . all in the pitch blackness. Maybe their paranoia killed them all before anything else could take hold."

"One day, you will face judgment."

"Wei Ni, I am a soldier of the law. The only judgment I will ever face is if I am doing my job well or if I need retraining."

"There is always a reckoning, whether or not you know of it. One day, you will face it, and karma will ensure it is fair and balanced to what atrocities you have committed."

Tim removes the shield and places it on the tray. He leans over Wei's face and kisses her bloody lips. His left hand grazes her cheek, but she refuses to turn away or break eye contact. "You are such a powerful woman. So bold in everything you say or do," he says softly, wiping the blood from her lip with his tongue. "You could have been more. You could have been mine."

"The body is simply a vessel for the mind and soul to live. It can be owned and controlled . . . But everything else would never be yours or anyone else's," she sputters, knowing these are probably the last words she will ever utter.

"You might be a proud people, but you are awfully dumb." He kisses her again before jamming the corkscrew in deeper. Her screams bounce off the walls of the soundproof room.

Flynt walks into a small room, his apron, splash shield, and gloves dripping with blood and parts of human flesh. He peels off one layer at a time before tossing them into a biohazard bin. He turns on the shower to his right and allows the water to warm up. He strips naked and steps inside. The red fluid rolls down his skin and circles the drain. His hair is coated with the life he just took away.

The door opens. Tim spins around, looking behind him. Macalov stands, holding a new uniform for him to wear. His boss leans on the edge of the sink and stares at the entryway. Tim swallows hard as he continues to clean himself, his entire body on display to his superior, his vulnerabilities all there for Macalov to see and exploit.

"The coroner has removed the body, and a team is cleaning the room as we speak," Macalov begins. "She was missing her right index finger, the one with the birthmark. Was there a reason for this?"

"Apologies, sir. I should have requested permission before . . ."

"I don't care that it's missing, Flynt. I want to know why you took it."

Tim brushes the antibacterial scrub across his chest, the water jets washing the orange soap away. "I sent it to the president via courier, sir. His team should be able to match the birthmark as proof the MSC still exists," he finally replies.

"Was this requested?"

"It's in the rule book, sir. All suspicious high-level individuals need to be verified upon death," Tim states, his voice almost robotic compared to the emotion he shared earlier.

"Good, following protocol," Macalov says. "The recordings . . . they were enlightening." Macalov folds his hands in front of him. "Agent Ni was a difficult subject, but you were able to get suitable information out of her."

"Sir?"

"She confirmed my suspicions. These MSC agents are alive and working with the rebels. At least one for sure."

"But sir, she stated—"

"Yes, yes, you still have a lot to learn. When someone is being tortured, they will say the minimum of what is necessary to stop the pain. If they say one, it's usually two or more. The fact is, people lie. Even when facing death, they lie."

"Toronto?"

"Oh, of that part I have no doubt what she said was true."

"But if they lie . . ."

"Flynt, how long have you been working for me?"

"Seven years, sir." Tim finishes his shower and dries himself off. Macalov hands him the crisp, clean uniform.

"Seven years." Macalov watches Tim closely as he dresses. "That's a long time to go without a promotion, don't you think?"

"I'm not sure I follow, sir." Tim buttons up the black shirt, tucks it in his pants, and tightens the belt. He turns to the mirror to brush his hair and notices a red bar with three gold stripes resting on each shoulder. Three stripes that were never there before. "Sir?"

"Put your boots on and follow me."

Tim hurriedly slips on his socks and boots before the two men leave. Macalov walks one half step ahead of the new sergeant in the hallway. Soldiers salute the two men as they pass.

"I read your file. Clean record. Not one errant action or behavior unbecoming of a soldier. Take out your genetic abnormality and you have been a superior employee."

"Thank you, sir."

Macalov unlocks his office door and waves Tim inside. The two men sit on opposite sides of the desk in silence. A single file folder rests on the warden's side. Macalov opens a drawer and pulls out a wooden box. He grabs two cigars and clips both ends. He lights one and hands the other to Tim. The new sergeant takes the cigar but is unsure what to do.

"You light it, then smoke it, Sergeant Flynt."

"Yes, sir. Just never had one before."

Macalov leans forward and holds the lighter out for him. Tim takes it and lights his cigar, coughing lightly as he inhales.

"You don't inhale like a cigarette. You just hold it in your mouth and enjoy the flavor." He watches Tim lean back and slowly get the hang of how to smoke the cigar. "Where do you see yourself in the future? What position would you like to reach before you retire?"

"Retire? Is that an option for someone of my caliber?"

"Not normally, no. However, if things work in your favor, it could be." Macalov exhales the smoke into the office air and leans back, placing his heels on the corner of the desk.

"Truthfully, I'm not sure, sir. I'd like to continue to support my family."

"Yes. If I'm correct, you take care of your brother and sick mother. But your brother should be on his own soon. He was of age to be tested, yes?"

"He took the exam, but I haven't seen him to discuss his results yet."

Macalov picks up a file closest to him and tosses it across the desk to Tim. The sergeant opens the file and sees his brother's image clipped to a page of medical jargon. He flips through it, seeing high numbers on the exam and more medical information that he doesn't understand.

"Forgive my ignorance, but what am I looking at here?"

"Nothing to forgive; you're not an intellectual or a medical doctor. I had to have them explain it to me as well." Macalov smiles and snickers softly. "Turns out your brother is jumping three ranks above you. He'll be part of the president's elite technology core."

"The ones below?"

"In the bunker; close enough to push the button, but far enough away to not cause mass destruction." Macalov's deep belly laugh fills the room. Tim chuckles a bit, trying to stay with his boss's reactions. "He will no longer concern you," the warden says flatly.

"I understand that, sir, but my mother will be. I want to provide for her properly," Tim counters truthfully.

"How has your mother been doing?" Macalov asks. His hand wraps around the cigar as he inhales. He holds it for a second before exhaling some rings in an attempt to seem friendlier than he is.

"Better. The medication keeps the fits at bay, but some days are worse than others. If she got the cure . . ."

"These fits, what happens?"

"I don't—"

"What does she do during them? What happens to her body?"

"It depends. She might have an outburst out of frustration or some other mental aspect. Other times, her entire body spasms and twitches. We have to hold her down, massage the muscles with medicated cream, and pray she can get through it. Until the next one hits."

"Like a seizure." Macalov drops his feet to the floor and faces Tim. "Would you like a drink?"

"No, sir. I'm still on the clock."

Macalov ignores the answer, walks over to the bar, and pours two glasses of whiskey. He places one glass in front of Tim and leans on the edge of the desk in front of the sergeant. Tim lifts the glass, and Macalov clinks it with his own before taking a sip. Tim sips his and chokes.

"Not used to a man's drink, son?"

"No, sir. It's not in my budget."

"What if it could be?" Macalov says. "What if you could get your mother the cure in a timely fashion, like the rest of the upper class?"

"I'd say it's impossible," Tim says. He sips the drink again, letting the alcohol wash away his nerves.

"How much time do you think she has left?"

"I don't know. The doctors say the treatments are helping but she needs them more frequently than I can provide. If Sam scored well, then he can get her the cure."

"No, he can't. You know the rules. He moves up and away like a superhero. You stay behind with the rest of us." Macalov finishes his drink and motions Tim to do the same. Once emptied, he takes both glasses and fills them again. "Now, how much time do you think your mother has?"

"I'm not good at math or calculations, sir. I'd estimate three, maybe four years without the increase in sessions. Maybe ten with them, I guess," Tim answers. He takes the offered glass and takes another sip, the warmth of the liquid making him calm down and feel more comfortable.

"But a cure could give her another thirty years, maybe even forty. Your mom is young; she could live to one hundred and ten. All you have to do is say you're interested in knowing how."

Tim leans back in his chair and sips the luscious fluid. He's always been a practical man. Do your job well and get rewarded. With his brother moving beyond him, his mother's care would fall to him alone. Even with his brother's help, the stress was a lot for him to handle most days. He also understands that nothing in this world is free. He'd have to give something up to accept the new rank and information.

"Sir, may I speak freely?" he asks.

"Of course," Macalov states. The truth of those words hang in limbo, but Tim understands he has no recourse but the one in front of him.

"What would be expected of me in exchange for these new options in my life?" Tim asks as politely as possible.

"Sergeant Flynt, do you like your new title? You would be in charge of the rebel wing of the prison"—Macalov flips the file open—"if you accept these terms and conditions." He stops on one page of Sam's medical information. "Eventually, if you decide to assist me in a specific matter, you would be next in line to be warden of this prison."

"But my ranking makes that—"

"Yes, yes, impossible. Sergeant Flynt, if I sign your name to a piece of paper, you will no longer be bound by your test or station. You will be my second-in-command, in training to keep the title of warden when I . . . move beyond this place." Macalov takes a long swig of his alcohol. "But you must accept and trust before we can continue. Understand a verbal agreement in this office is binding. The only way out of this agreement is by the end of your natural life."

Maybe it was the liquor coursing through his veins, or the promise of wealth and power, or just the promise of a boy saving his mother—but Tim felt the need to respond affirmatively. He was already a murderer; he needed to do some good to counter that dark stain on his soul. Saving his mother's life would help with that.

"I accept and understand," Tim whispers.

"Excellent." Macalov pushes the file forward. He points to one line in the file. "Your brother passed out at his testing exam today. The doctors said his sugar level was low, but they found a rare antibody in his system. One for a disease we have only seen in underlings. Do you know why your brother would be a carrier for Leptospirosis antibodies? Had he been ill before?"

"I honestly don't know, sir."

Macalov closes the file and walks around his desk to sit back down in his chair. His glass rests in front of him, the cigar in his other hand still burning. "Do you know they have found it in the rats under the city?" Macalov places the cigar on the edge of the ashtray by his phone. He leans forward and clasps his hands in front of him. "For whatever reason, your brother has been around infected rats or people infected with this disease. He might have isolated himself when he was sick or he might be immune. Personally, I don't care. Let the doctors sort that out. What I want to know is, who was he visiting and why? Would he have found himself a whore down there?"

"No, sir. My brother is still pure. I made sure he waited until his test results."

"Are you positive?"

"As much as I can be, sir. My brother . . . He's not . . ."

"Does he not like the fairer sex?"

"No, sir. He's not one of them. He is more interested in the inner workings of a computer than any physical relations, sir. He's attracted to women, but he's just fixated elsewhere."

"Then your job, sergeant, is to follow your brother and find out what he's been up to. I want to know why he's been in contact with this disease. I want to know where he enters the underground or exits. I want everything in a report by the end of the week. That gives you four days." Macalov leans back in his chair. "Can you handle that?"

Tim flips the file open and stares at his brother's picture. He was raised to do what was asked of him, fall in line, and do a good job in whatever role he was chosen for. The only thing he asked of his brother was to be better than him. He never forced him to work before his exam. He only asked that he study and help with their mother's care. Above all else, Tim always supported whatever technological endeavor Sam was interested in. Yet, the signs were there. His brother's growing attitude towards their living space. His anger at the exam and natural order of the world.

Tim's heart breaks, but his anger is stronger and bubbling over. Closing the file, he chugs the rest of his drink and takes a deep drag of the cigar. He looks over to Macalov, who waits for his answer.

"It is my honor and duty to complete this mission for you."

Macalov raises his hand for Tim to shake. "Congratulations, Sergeant Flynt. You have chosen wisely."

Chapter Ten

E llie stands alone in the main meeting room, her hair pulled into a tight ponytail, her uniform as clean as it could be with her living in the bowels of New York City. She stares at the map hung loosely on the wall, at the old boundaries of the city that never sleeps during the mid-nineties before mayhem took hold. She can remember the sound of children playing in Central Park with no care in the world, traveling through Times Square and hearing families laughing as they took photos in front of the crystal New Year's Eve ball. Sometimes she missed the crowds that she struggled to get through.

"Ellie?" Anton says, his voice soft, kind, and inviting. Yet, the knife he's placed in her back smarts as much now as when Osaka told her about it.

"Do you remember the rush of people in Times Square during New Year's Eve?" The question hangs in the air with an obvious answer. He was too young to remember the world before, but he refuses to acknowledge his ignorance.

"I've never been there, but I've seen it on the television feeds," he answers.

Ellie nods her head; her hands meet behind her back and fold around one another.

"I was in my early twenties with a rare break between missions. My friend . . ." She collects her thoughts. The best way to get them back on your side is to say enough truths that envelop the lies. "Wei Ni, the agent I always worked with, she wanted to experience it. We both grew up watching people push against the barricades and flood into the area, just for a glimpse of a crystal ball. It both amazed and fascinated the two of us. So, the year we had a break, we went."

A metal chair scratches the dirt covered concrete floor as Anton sits down, his body's weight making the old piece of furniture squeal in resistance.

"I never understood that. A waste of time really," he says.

"Not to us," Ellie says softly. "At noon, they cleared out the entire area, pushing people toward Eighth or Sixth Avenue. If you didn't have a pass to get into the area before the general opening, well . . . you were shit out of luck. Police officers on every corner checking papers . . ."

"Sounds a lot like now, but with less order," Anton cuts in.

"There was order, but also freedom. You were free to mingle about the other stores as you waited for them to set up the corrals. You could eat anywhere or talk to the stranger waiting with you. You could do whatever you wanted as long as it was legal."

"Agent Goldman," he begins. He leans on his elbows, his face softening and seeming almost cathartic. "I don't understand what this has to do with the world we live in right now. Memories are a wonderful thing, but living in the past will never allow us to free the future."

"No, maybe not." Ellie turns and leans on a chair at the other end of the table. "But we stood with one million plus people from all over the world and shared a moment with them. We had a connection for those ten seconds as the ball descended to highlight the new year. We hugged and sang with random people, enjoying the spirit of it all. Color, religions, orientations . . . none of it mattered. Every year, New York City embodied the reality of this world; we are a unit and must survive as one. It was something I will never forget."

"But it is something that will never happen again. There is no hope in bringing back ideals lost during the war and restructuring. That is a pipe dream."

"Who needs to bring back what lingers in the dark?" Ellie smiles and locks eyes with Anton.

"Riker's Island," he mutters. He leans back in the chair, his shoulders rigid, and his face firm, the sharp cheekbones of his European heritage creating shadows over his face. "Why now?"

Ellie pulls out a photo from her back pocket. She walks around the table as she unfolds it. She stops next to Anton, her eyes never leaving the image in her hand, the anger bubbling up from a place she swore was dead along with her family. Her hand releases the image, and it falls to the table. Anton peers at it quickly before pushing it away.

"Where did you get that?"

"Osaka stole it from a file on the president's desk. They're running tests to verify her identification, but I would know that birthmark anywhere."

Ellie walks back to the map on the wall and faces it.

"Wei Ni was the best agent the MSC ever had. She was quick, precise, but also humane. She defied direct orders to use a sniper rifle in an assassination. There were too many people around. She waited until he passed out from drinking and slit his throat. He died alone in his personal wine cellar. They wrote her up, but it gave her a legacy many agents aspired to. Get the job done, but in the right way." Ellie turns and faces Anton again. "It is what I live by to this day. If we are going to overtake the island, we need more than just men and weaponry. We need Sam to get the schematics and find out the easiest way in without detection."

"And all of that is being handled." Trent walks into the room, looking angrily at Anton and Ellie. "You are no longer needed in this mission, Agent Goldman."

"Major Trent, what makes you think I would allow such an act of mutiny to go unpunished?" Ellie says. Her steps quick, she stops directly in front of the major and presses a small blade to his femoral artery. "You are an old man with nothing but pipe dreams of power, while the rest of us do the heavy lifting. Tell me again why I shouldn't make you bleed out on the floor for treason?"

"Because we need each other," Anton says. He continues to look straight ahead, away from the rest of them. His tone is filled with rage as his teeth grind against one another. "As much as it sucks, we all need to do this together. Otherwise, we'll die for nothing."

Ellie pulls her blade away and safely stores it in a small sleeve. She taps the chair Anton is sitting on, and he reluctantly stands. He pulls out a chair on the side and sits. He points to the one across from him for Trent to take. The old man grumbles and curses under his breath as he sits. This was the last thing on his mind when he walked into the room this morning. He fully planned on taking control of the entire operation and running it as he felt it should be run. Instead, he continues to work with what are the weaker links in his mind—an inexperienced boy and a woman. In his day, neither one would have the positions they held.

"What's this?" Trent pushes the image of Wei Ni's cut off finger toward Ellie.

"That is all that remains of my colleague, Agent Wei Ni. I assume Macalov's doing," Ellie says. "If we are going to attack, we need to have a proper plan."

"We'll look over the old schematics of the buildings and figure out which is the best area to enter. Then we take one building at a time. They don't have as many guards during the night shifts according to our intel," Trent answers.

"The same intel that's over two years old?" Ellie asks. "What about getting on the island? Over the bridge—what about cameras? By water—what are the currents? What about the spotlights?"

"This is still in the early stages of planning, Ellie," Anton says. He shifts, trying to keep the tension in the room from exploding. "We obviously need to get more current information."

"We need to talk to Sam. Has anyone heard from him?"

"He was taking his placement exam today. I'm sure he's home. I can try to get word to him through the underground network," Anton answers.

"Then we'll adjourn until he arrives," Ellie says firmly. She stands, but Major Trent grabs her arm. "Is there something you need, Major?"

"A minute of your time, in private."

Anton takes the hint and quickly leaves the room. The hinges of the old rusty door scream at being bulldozed. Major Trent and Ellie remain in the same position, his hand squeezing her arm in and her attention remaining on the door.

"You're losing control, Agent Goldman," Trent says. He violently yanks her arm, forcing her attention back to him. "You never should have been running this group, but they voted you in for some obscure reason. Be aware, I aim to remove you. If it comes to it, I will turn you in to the authorities to save any and all of my men."

Trent finishes his diatribe, his spit dripping from the corner of his mouth onto the worn-out insignia of a rank long ago. Ellie stares at him and takes in every wrinkle, every line on every inch of his face, her eyes and expression blank and unreadable.

"Do you have something to say for yourself?"

Ellie steps into Trent's grip and pulls him flush against her body. She continues her silent stare as Trent's heart rate rises. His cheeks flush and his grip loosens.

"You are nothing to me," Ellie whispers. "You walk high and mighty around here with a rank you probably stole from a more deserving soldier. You push others in front of you for the genuine tests of courage, yet you spew words as if you embody their meaning. You are simply a man well beyond his prime trying desperately to hold on to what he remembers as a better age of living."

Trent tries to push away from her, but Ellie pulls him by the shoulder harder than before. Her boots firmly planted on the ground, she lifts the major slightly in the air, his toes holding him upright and level.

"What you don't understand is you are a means to an end. You feed the detritus and watch it grow like a massive blob of violence. You encourage it like a newborn child, but you don't control it. They simply tolerate you because you give them access to what they need. I am the one who gives barriers. I am the one they listen to, not because of my words or the tone of my voice, but because my actions have always proved my worth to them. I would lay my life down to protect every living soul here, including you." Ellie raises her knee quickly to smash it into Trent's groin. He crumbles like a lump to the floor. She pulls her pants up slightly as she kneels over his writhing form. "But don't think I won't remove you from this plane of existence to protect the greater good. Men like you brought on the Final War, and women like me will correct it."

Sam slams some notebooks into his backpack and zips it up. His skin is pale, his eyes shining, devoid of their normal rich hazel tones. He dumps an authorized military hat his brother gave him on his head, covering up the mess of hair after his traumatic day. Sliding on his jacket, he struggles to lift the backpack and carry it.

Sam turns to his computer, a small eagle blinking in the bottom right corner in Morse Code. He opens up the command prompt and types in a long string of letters, symbols, and numbers. Hitting enter, the eagle disappears from the screen. He shuts his computer down and waits for it to come to a full stop before heading down the stairs.

Tim sits at the dinner table, feeding his mother while Nurse Anna checks her vitals. His mother's mouth barely opens as he pours the broth from a child's spoon into her mouth. Some drips out and he catches it with the utensil, like a mother with her baby. Tim hums as he continues his motions. One spoonful, clean up, repeat. It's all very normal, but he understands this won't last.

Sam trudges down the stairs and passes the table, his feet dragging along the floor with a squeak every other step. Tim glances over to him but keeps his focus on his mother.

"Where are you going at this hour?"

"Meeting up with some friends. I need someone to talk to about today. You wouldn't understand," he answers.

"Try me," Tim tosses out. He's praying Macalov is wrong about his brother's true intentions, but he trusts the law. "You never talk to me about what's going on. Maybe it's time we start."

"Tim, I love you. You're my brother . . . but you wouldn't be able to get this kind of stuff. I'm meeting people in my test range." Sam reaches for the door. "You were right. I'm moving up." He turns the handle and opens the door, his feet frozen to the floor. "I'm sorry." Sam exits quickly, slamming the door behind him.

Tim stays calm as he feeds his mother one last bite. He places the spoon in the half-filled bowl and wipes his hands off on a napkin. Standing, he grabs the jacket off the back of the chair.

"Nurse Capellini, would you mind staying later than normal? I need to make sure Sam isn't getting into any trouble. I'm sure you understand." He grabs his cell phone and a military grade baton. The new stripes on his shoulders give him enough pride to hold his head higher than he has before. "I will pay you double for your time this evening."

Without waiting for her response, Tim walks out the door and into the cover of darkness. Finding a glimpse of Sam's backpack, he follows his brother at a safe distance. They traverse through the masses of people heading home after work or those working in the darkness because of their deformities. Tim hangs just out of his brother's sight. Sam moves toward the subway tunnel, headphones in his ears, and oblivious to his tail. Sadly, Tim realizes his brother might be intelligent enough to work with the elites, but he is still dumb. If the world needed men to stand up and help, Sam wouldn't know the difference between a rifle and a pistol. Tim was smarter and more powerful.

The bile rolls around in his stomach then. He knows more about the inner workings of the city than his brother, yet he is in a lower grade position. Even with the red flag on their DNA, thanks to their mother's illness, they expected Sam to jump several levels to one of the highest positions in the country. Now, here Tim stood, on the front lines of the continuing war, and no one met his gaze. Well, not before his stripes.

People seem to take notice, nodding their heads in appreciation of his status. Respect for the hard work he had put in all these years. He'd earned this position doing everything the right way. If Sam couldn't understand this, then he was simply one of the masses that needed to be purged. His mother would forgive him in time. She would be healthy enough to remarry, have more children, or adopt a child of the king. That would be a tremendous honor for a once lower-class family like themselves.

Sam darts down the stairs to a lower subway line, the only mode of transportation their identification passes will allow. Tim follows suit, tapping his card on the turnstile, and entering the platform. People move out of his way, some afraid of his rank, while others don't wish to hit such a solid mass. Tim's eyes remain focused on his brother as he steps onto the 2 train headed to the city. The rattling old metal tube shows signs of age with rust spots and ads from decades ago promoting dermatologists. The sign hanging directly above Tim makes him stifle a laugh. *If you see something, say something.* According to history books, they saw something and told the world about it . . . but no one listened.

Sam sits at the far end of the car, his head down with the bulky backpack on his lap. Tim stands by the doors, trying to make himself seem smaller as he monitors his brother. Stop after stop, people move on or off the car, but Sam remains stoic. The numbers keep rising, but soon Sam stands upright, slings his backpack over his shoulders again, and waits by the door. The Ninety-Sixth Street station comes into view and the doors open promptly. Pushing against the rush, Sam and Tim exit onto the platform. Sam hurriedly walks down to the end of the platform, mixing into the crowd of those unable to travel by train.

They all walk through a small pathway, down steps, and onto the side of the tracks, the expansion created by removing the inner train tracks when congestion decreased significantly. Walking with the crowd now would make him look suspicious. While Sam fits in with his look and demeanor, Tim stands out in his crisp military uniform. Cursing himself for following protocol and always wearing his colors, Tim slips his jacket off and turns it inside out.

Hanging it over his arm, the dark black uniform passes with the lack of light, but anyone up close would notice how clean and new it looks. No holes or patches to be found. He hopes the mass of stench-ridden humans will be too lost in their own misery to notice him.

People deviate from the trail and head down the walkways under the signs showing Ninety-Fourth Street, Ninety-Third, and more. Sam keeps moving forward, head down and focused. As the thinning crowd dwindles to just one, Tim is wondering where he's heading when his brother spins around, looking behind him. Tim presses up against the indentation in the wall, his face against whatever grime has formed on the cement over the centuries. He gags as his brain contemplates all of the bacteria he's exposing himself to.

Sam's footsteps crunch garbage as he continues walking alone. Tim pushes off the wall and continues following his brother. After a few minutes, Sam stops at an indentation in the wall. Tim hides in the shadows and watches.

Sam knocks one time, then smacks the door, then taps again. He pauses before banging once more, another pause followed by three quick raps, then another two, and another three. He then slaps the door with his open palm. Tim instantly knows its code, but is unsure of the cipher. The door opens, and the muzzle of a gun presses up against Sam's forehead. Tim takes one step toward his brother before Sam hands over his identification card. A hand grabs it, and the unmistakable sound of it being scanned hits Tim's ears. The weapon retreats and Sam walks inside, leaving his brother in the dark.

Tim looks up and sees the sign for Ninety-First street above his head. Maybe Sam isn't fully involved with the resistance, but his activity is too suspicious. Opening up his coat and placing it back on, the sergeant understands what the implications mean. There would be no trial, no excuse that could hinder the punishment. Tim knows he would watch over Sam for the rest of his life . . . as an inmate of Riker's Island.

Chapter Eleven

The conference room is a flurry of activity. Ellie sits at the head of the table, silent. Major Trent sits to her left, half out of his chair, waving his right arm around as his mouth moves quickly. Anton, standing to her right, points down to some papers on the table as he voices his opinion rather loudly. Sam sits next to Anton, his head in his hands. Jason and Milo sit at the opposite end of the table, quiet, their concern evident on their faces.

"Stop," Ellie says in a calm tone as the two men on either side of her continue to rant. Sam raises his head and meets her eyes. She holds up her hand and stops him from getting involved. Ellie counts to ten loud enough that the men on the other side of the table can hear, but those in front of her ignore her. "I said STOP!" Ellie screams with a force that shocks everyone in the room. "We either discuss this properly or not at all."

"We need to—" Trent begins.

"I didn't tell you to speak. Sit down and shut the hell up for five seconds, will you!" Ellie commands.

Trent sits back down in his chair with a huff. Anton seats himself next to her as quietly as possible. When everyone is calm, Ellie lowers herself back into her seat and pulls it closer to the table. She grabs a notebook with a myriad of notes written within it.

"Sam, what am I looking at?"

"I decoded by brother's card and got access to his rule books. They have a ton of codes that the guards use to communicate with one another. I wrote down the most important ones, what the colors on their uniforms mean, and some basic rules that we need to follow if we want to try to fit in."

"We don't have the time to get uniforms to fit in, Sam," Anton says. Ellie raises her hand to quiet her second-in-command.

"Anton's right. Time is of the essence."

"But you will know who has more power than the other on the island. That would help us find the prisoners we're planning to rescue."

The table quiets down, and Anton looks over to Ellie. Even Major Trent remains silent. All of them are willing to run into the bloodthirsty battle, but none of them are willing to discuss that this will be an attack on the island. Saving anyone from the cells is a secondary operation, and then only if it's feasible. Otherwise, this is a straightforward all-out assault.

"Sam, things have changed," Ellie begins, her tone soft, as if talking to a younger sibling. "The two main individuals we planned on rescuing are no longer with us."

"But there are other people there, innocent people. We can help them, bring them into the fold," Sam argues.

"Yes, we could. But we don't know what they're doing to those people while behind closed doors. The torture . . . it changes you. They might not want to be saved," Ellie answers calmly.

"So, what? You're all just going to run and gun over there? This isn't some old ass video game; this is real life with real human beings!" Sam replies harshly.

"We can talk more about this later, but we have no plans to send our people into this mission blindly. That's why Anton asked you to bring everything you've dug up since your brother took the position."

"Just please consider the human cost in all of this," Sam begs. Ellie nods in response as Sam stands up. He pulls out several pieces of paper and aligns them on the table. Once connected, the image of Riker's Island comes into view. Sam has drawn a map of every building and access points.

"Going over the main bridge is suicide. The main security checkpoint would radio ahead, and all the defenses would activate. In the time it would take to cross the bridge, they would have assembled at least twenty men with high-powered weapons to greet us." Sam points to the skull and crossbones he's drawn over the bridge.

"Okay, we get it. Bridge of death," Anton says.

"This isn't Chernobyl," Trent mutters. Ellie nods in agreement with the reference, but the rest of the table stares at him in confusion. "The nuclear meltdown? The rumored bridge of death when the radiation wafted over the people who were watching the fire? Don't any of you know our damn history?"

"One can't study what the regime has deemed inaccurate or a threat to the hierarchy," Ellie says. "They wiped the accident from the history books because it showed the USSR was inept at handling things of that magnitude. They lied and kept things hidden. Russia was stronger at corruption and control. Find dirt on someone, make them do your bidding, and focus blame elsewhere."

"Thanks for the trip into something that isn't important at the moment," Sam says softly. "If we could get back to the map, I'll get home before I miss curfew and my brother sends out a search party."

Ellie holds up her hands in understanding as Trent shuffles in his seat to get more comfortable. Sam wipes a small amount of sweat off his forehead with the back of his sleeve.

"Are you okay, Sam? This can—"

"No, I'm good." He points to the side closest to the airport. "If we want to take a risk, we head to LaGuardia Airport. We'd have to break through the barricades, but if we could make it to the end of the runway, the distance to Riker's Island isn't that far. We'd need to fashion rafts—"

"We don't have the time or materials to do that," Ellie answers, her eyes searching the map. "Did you add currents?" Her fingers hover over the lines around the island itself.

"Using what I could find, yeah. The East River is strong."

"There's no telling the condition of the runway. It's been in various stages of renovation since the war destroyed it. We'd have to assume parts of it no longer exist, and that would put undue strain on the men trying to travel across the terrain carrying equipment," Ellie says.

"I think our only option is the bridge," Trent says, his voice calm and his hands folded in front of him. "I know the objections, but it seems like the only safe way to get the men on the island. What happens from there . . . well, we can't control it."

"The mission would fail before it began." Anton interjects. "We need our men alive to search buildings, kill soldiers, and release as many civilians as possible. This helps us grow in strength and in reputation. Your idea is to walk right into their hands, allowing them to slaughter us all!"

Trent and Anton go back and forth with varying levels of ego as Sam sits back in his chair, defeated. He continues to rub his forehead and looks more tired with each passing second. Ellie looks from Sam to the map on the table, her mind racing with possibilities, but the toll of losses also add up in her thoughts. Knowing the two men arguing have lost sight of all rationality, Ellie faces a tough decision to support this mission.

She had always struggled with the idea of sending human beings to their deaths. When she was deciding what branch of military to enter, the recruiters had always picked up on her inability to put someone else in harm's way. She would sacrifice herself to fulfill any and all aspects of a mission; however, she could never delegate. When pressed, her answer was always the same: "They have a family at home. I have none." That attitude did not fit in a normal chain of command.

Eventually she was recruited into the MSC and found her niche within their ranks. Her ability to morph into another human being like an award-winning actor was simply a bonus. She always knew anytime she walked out the door, it might be the last time. If she was killed or captured, the organization would disavow any knowledge of her existence.

The MSC was a well-known secret that NATO pushed forward as a last resort. When dictators dropped white phosphorus on innocent children with total disregard for laws, the MSC was dispatched overnight. Those involved with the sale, distribution, and usage of the illegal substance were all removed within a week, each death attributed to a documented medical issue or a car accident. The conspiracy theorists tried and failed to find anything connected to the underground organization. They were ghosts from Satan's worst nightmare.

"Trent is right." Ellie's voice silences everyone else in the room. She continues to stare at Sam, who has a nauseous look on his face. Anton opens his mouth to argue, but Ellie's hand snaps up faster than the words exit his mouth. He lowers himself into his chair, dumbfounded by her statement.

"Agent Goldman, you . . . agree with me?" Major Trent says. Ellie's eyes rise to his level and she nods. He sits back down and slides the map in front of him. "Right, well then, we should begin with—"

"No," Ellie spits out.

"You said you agreed with my tactics," Trent fires back.

"I agree with your point of entry. Your tactics would never suffice on a mission of this scale." Ellie stands up and moves the map so she can read it. After a few moments of silence, she folds it back up and hands it to Sam. "This is going to take diligent planning and precise execution. No room for error, not one bullet wasted."

"That's almost impossible. How do you plan to save ammo when you're actively being fired upon?" Trent argues.

"Cut off their sight." Ellie looks up at Jason. "Can you scrape together parts for shivs and other weapons for close quarters fighting?"

"Yeah, but I don't see how that would help when they've got armed soldiers."

"It would help because without power, they won't know what they're shooting at."

"You want to knock out the power," Milo says.

"They might have taken over our land, but they've never upgraded the aging grid. The backup generators would take five to ten minutes to come online. If they're like any other jail, I'm sure keeping inmates locked inside is more of a concern than the exteriors. Darkness would be on our side."

"That wouldn't help with their larger numbers," Milo pipes up from the back of the room.

"Sam, how trustworthy is your brother?" Ellie asks bluntly.

"I . . . I don't know. I think he's reliable, but I don't talk to him about this stuff," Sam answers.

"I want you to test him. I don't care how you phrase it, but we need to know more information about the inner workings of the jail. Primarily, how the food is prepared."

"I'll see what I can do."

"Good. Milo, I need you to come up with a poison. If we can't kill them outright, we can at least thin the line."

"Agent Goldman, I don't know if I can . . ." Milo blanches. "That would condemn people to die."

"If you can't handle it, I can," Anton interjects.

Milo nods frantically as he stands up and heads for the door.

"This meeting is not to be discussed with anyone, Milo. You understand?" Ellie asks, her tone hard and cold as the smaller man nods again before rushing out of the room. "Okay, Anton will work on the poison. Sam, work on knocking out the grid of the jail—you knock out all of New York City if you have to. Jason will handle the close quarter weapons. Trent, you get the men ready and in battle form."

"What is your job, Agent Goldman?" Trent asks suspiciously. "You are a trained agent after all. Would you sit on the sidelines while your people fight your battles?"

"You know I work best alone, Trent." Ellie takes her small notepad out of her torn cargo pocket. She flips open to a page with mission notes. Reluctantly, she hands them over to Trent. "The president will notice the attack within minutes of the grid going down for obvious reasons. While you are all on the island, diverting the attention and resources of the city, Osaka and I will head toward Times Square. We will infiltrate the penthouse and assassinate the president and his family."

The entire table remains silent as Ellie takes her notepad back from Trent. He stares at her, astounded at the information she has just shared. None of them dare speak. "We all know this might be the last offensive effort our chapter ever partakes in. If we are all going down, then we will make damn sure the rest of the world knows who we are," Ellie touts.

Anton nods in agreement before leaving the room. The connection to his girlfriend makes the two-pronged mission hit home. Trent stands, smiling foolishly, pats Ellie on the shoulder, and walks tall out of the room. Sam remains, staring at his hands.

"Are you okay?" Ellie asks.

"Yes." Sam shuffles his weight from foot to foot. "No, I'm not. I took my test today."

"I know. What were your results?"

"I passed out before they told me everything. I didn't expect there to be so much pain."

"It's a drug concoction to lower your inhibitions and allow your mind to be free of restraints. People usually disassociate at that point and remember being asked questions of varying skills. It's not meant to be pleasant." She tries to remain calm as she watches the younger man struggle with his words. "What's really bothering you?"

"What if they did something to me? During the test. Like what if they injected me with something to make me become like them?"

"They're bound to the laws they uphold. None of those individuals would have the courage to go against those words on a page. If they did, they'd lose everything for their families and serve a lifetime sentence in jail. People are too afraid of losing the things they love. It's been the same since mankind first walked the earth. I doubt it will change in the immediate future."

Sam stands and packs up his bag. "Thanks, Agent Goldman."

"Just take it easy for a day or two. This will take that long to plan at least, so rest up."

"Yes, ma'am."

Sam walks out of the room, leaving Ellie alone. Leaning back in her chair, she pulls out the small tattered photo of her niece and nephew. Her thumb runs across the well-worn path along their faces. Her smile deepens as her eyes fall closed.

"Soon . . ."

Sam closes the door behind him as quietly as possible. Everyone in the house should be sleeping by now, especially Tim, who rises before the sun.

"Where have you been?" Tim says from the darkness of the living room.

Sam stops dead in his tracks and flips on the living room light. His brother, in full work uniform, sits in a chair with his patrol baton on his lap.

"Do you know the time? I was worried sick. I almost called my friends to start a search party," Tim hisses. His tone is mixed with anger and fear for his brother being alone, but also for what he knows about Sam's resistance dealings. "What were you doing?"

"I . . ." Sam stops. He needs to choose his words wisely, but also follow orders. He needs to test his brother's loyalty. "I was at a meeting with some friends. Then I walked home. I needed to think."

"Meeting about what? What's so important it can't be during daylight hours? If anyone caught you out after curfew, I wouldn't be able to help you."

"I know. We were discussing our tests, what we all got, and what it means for all of us. Like one of us tested lower than his current ranking. Can we still be friends with him? What does that mean for his family? Is it really fair? He's smart and sort of athletic, but just not as good as the rest of us."

"Sam, that's the way the world works. Survival during these times means making tough decisions and putting the weaker ones into positions no one cares about. We all have a role, and it's easier to just play it," Tim says. He looks down at his baton, the words of the warden filling his mind. His mother would have her cure if he made the tougher decision. A life for a life. That was what his rules told him constantly. You sacrifice one inmate to ensure a disease never reaches the general populace. You remove another for information that could stop an attack. It was basic math. "I understand how hard it is," Tim says, the words feeling foreign on his lips as the lie flows easily out of his mouth.

"Tim," Sam says, taking three steps into the living room. "What if something happens to Mom and I'm not allowed to go to her funeral? Would you come get me? You'd be breaking all kinds of rules, right?"

"We're not there yet," Tim answers quickly. "And I really don't want to think about it."

Tim stands and pulls his brother into a tight hug. Sam remains stoic for a moment before his arms find purchase along his brother's back. "I'd get to you," Tim mumbles.

"I know you would." Sam allows the warmth of his brother's embrace to envelop him. Signs of affection between the two of them have always been scarce, but maybe his brother isn't as bad as he seems.

Tim pulls away from the hug and holds his brother at arm's length. "Next time, let me know where you're going. Maybe I can get you a pass until you've got your working ID."

"I will." Sam looks at the new red bars with a gold stripe on his brother's jacket. "These are new." He notices a smell coming off Tim that he had ignored before. "And you smell like a dumpster. What happened at work today?"

"It was a rough one." Tim laughs, playing along. "New inmate who smells like he slept in raw sewage tried to escape. Had to chase him down and tackle him. The warden calls me into his office a little while later and tells me that my yearly review came in; I was exemplary in everything I did. So, they promoted me to sergeant. I'm in charge of an entire section of the prison, and I can change things now. To top it all off, it comes with a raise and a bump in class. Not like yours, little brother, but still."

"That's so cool. Can you really put a stop to all the things they do there? Are the rumors true?" Sam asks.

"All I know is my ward, but I can make sure inmates aren't treated poorly. Maybe I can get certain guards transferred from my team. I don't know the full extent, but we'll see." Tim ruffles Sam's hair. The two look at each other uncomfortably after the display of affection. "Yeah, well . . . you better get to bed. You've got an early morning tomorrow."

Sam backs away and scurries up the stairs. Tim falls back into the chair and picks up the telephone on the small table next to him.

"Sergeant?" Macalov's voice wafts through the phone.

"Hey, Arnold, it's Tim. Can we meet in your office before the first bell tomorrow morning?" Tim says, his tone off as he tries to act like the conversation is normal.

"I abhor code, Sergeant Flynt," Macalov seethes. "Tomorrow morning, before the bell of your shift. Good evening."

Tim hangs up the phone, his eyes never leaving the staircase Sam climbed earlier. His heart pounds in his chest as he repeats his mantra over and over in his head. A life for a life. His brother for his mother.

Chapter Twelve

Anton bursts into his room and slams the door behind him, knocking off pieces of chipped paint and dust with the violent motion. Osaka jumps up, her hand on her chest in fright at the intrusion. Seeing the look of utter dread on her boyfriend's face, she knows he is fully aware of her part in the upcoming missions. He paces, saying nothing, but the tension rolls off his body like water.

She pulls herself to a sitting position, her back against the cement wall, waiting. The idea of launching a secondary operation was mostly Ellie's, but she couldn't deny her part in its development. Osaka would provide entry into the construction zone and the penthouse. They were both fully aware of what that meant for her career as well. Her job—and the safety that came with her title—would be gone. She'd be fair game for the sex trades or any of the global prisons that enjoyed torturing traitorous women. It was a risk deemed necessary, even if fear gripped her inner core.

Anton was wired differently. Having already lost his sister, Osaka was aware he wouldn't find her part in the task acceptable. Even though he was young and a fighter for the greater good, he couldn't see past the same protectiveness men walking topside felt. It was their duty to protect women at all costs, even if it meant hindering their ability to live a normal life. A good woman, that is. No one protected the unwanted. They were merely toys to be played with, broken and tossed away.

Not Osaka, though. She was a respected woman in the president's office. Even with her lack of suitable skin tone or facial features, staff within the office treated her well at work. Any other behavior would offend the president's choice of assistants. Laskin would take that as a personal attack.

An oligarch once tried something during a meeting with the president. He left with three fingers missing and the promise to never disrespect her again. Laskin could show compassion to her, but it never fully covered up his propensity for violence. He'd get what he wanted, and she knew that. As long as she stayed on his good side, she was safe.

She was independent and continually got information out to the resistance. She was in danger daily, and seeing Anton move about their room made her angry. His innate need to stand up and protect her now, when she had needed it all along, felt cheap and unwarranted. The hypocrisy radiating into the air was enough to suffocate her.

"Will you stop moving like a sugared-up child!" Osaka screams.

Anton pauses. He turns to his girlfriend with an unreadable look on his face. His hands wave about, but no words pass between his lips. He motions to the door, shakes his head, and tries to find his words.

Osaka begins the conversation for him. "I assume you heard." She pulls his pillow toward her as her knees press into her chest. Her arms wrap around her legs for security, but also to give her the confidence to keep talking.

Anton remains silent. Stoic and almost indignant, he pulls the chair out from the desk and sits down, his back ramrod straight as his jaw flexes as he fights to keep it closed. He'd learned from an early age to speak after you could collect your thoughts.

Time was a precious commodity that most people didn't have. They were always on a tight schedule, so spending precious minutes on a child unable to speak was a waste. His sister helped him process faster And organize his thoughts so he could speak to the elders without a stutter or wild story.

He hadn't been able to stop Nadja from running into danger when they were older. He couldn't protect her or their mother. Even when men around him were demanding he grow up, take the test, and fall in line, his sister deferred. She fought against the laws, but the rules always won. As he sits, staring at the woman he sees forever with, Anton is truly torn.

"Did..." he sputters. Anton closes his mouth, swallowing the emotion to calm his voice. "Do you truly understand what you've signed up for?" he says with pregnant pauses between each word. His fists grip his knees as he continues clenching his jaw.

"I do," she whispers. "Do you?"

"No, I don't," he answers. "You don't need to do this. You should stay as far from this as possible. Maybe Ellie's lost her mind, but you're not going. There's no way in hell I would let you risk your life—"

"Like you are," she says, cutting him off.

He stops. His shoulders sag and his fists loosen. That is the elephant in the room. Anton was demanding Osaka follow his words but not his actions. Like he owned her. His head falls into his hands as he weighs what to say next. The discussion gets heavier with each passing moment.

"I'm a soldier. It's what we do," he finally says.

Osaka lets the words sink in. She shakes her head as she tosses the pillow to the side of the bed. She slides down the mattress, which squeaks with every motion.

"A soldier?" she scoffs. "You?"

His head darts up quickly. "Yes, me. I'm the second-in-command. I'm the fighter in this family."

"Anton, I love you, but you're no soldier. The only way you would take another life is if my life was at stake. You don't know how to kill." She sighs and catches her breath. "You don't have the stomach for it."

"They killed Nadja. I am more than capable of killing every one of them."

"Who did? Specifically. Which one killed Nadja?"

"I don't know, but they're going to—"

"No. Think a minute. You want to go there and kill people who are simply doing their jobs?"

Anton stands upright, his anger returning full force as he hovers over Osaka. "Doing their jobs? You've heard the rumors about torture and medical experiments. No one's ever come out of that place alive. They're all a part of it!"

"And no one has told the truth about it, either."

"You're defending them?" Anton stops. "Knowing what they've done to people?"

"Anton, please. Just listen to me." Osaka stands and grabs his shoulders. After several moments, she gets him to sit back down as she rests back on the bed. "I don't know the details of what's done on that island. They encrypt the emails for the president and the president alone. I get to read the notifications of recent deaths, not the how, why, or what have you."

"But you—"

She raises her hand, cutting him off. "I understand there are men in that place who would rape me the second they saw me, just to see if it differed from all the other women. There are soldiers who would carve my eyes out to see if my eyeball was the same shape as its socket. I know the horrors they inflict on people."

"Then why do you feel some are innocent?"

"Because some are just guards walking patrol with no understanding of the horrors behind the doors. Some are paper pushers or drivers. They do their jobs to bring enough home to survive—like we all do." Osaka tries to show the other side of things.

"They're complicit."

"They can't fight against what they don't know. They're not high enough in the ranks to understand. Do we take away someone's son, husband, or father just because they work at an institution we regard as evil?"

"It's not up to me to teach them the right way. Besides, they'll shoot us without a second thought," he yells.

"We live by example and maybe teach along the way. If that fails, then we rise above and be better than the rest of them."

"And we will die if we don't fight back."

"I never said don't fight back. I am saying there might be people on the other side worth saving . . . recruiting to our cause."

"I doubt a man with a rifle in my face cares about my reasons for being there. Plus, they're just mindless followers, right? So, what makes you think they'd listen to us when they're brainwashed into believing we're terrorists?"

Osaka leans back on the bed, her head hitting the mattress with a thud. Her words and emotions all jumble into a mess of thoughts swirling in her mind. "I just . . ."

"You wish we didn't have to hurt anyone," Anton finishes for her. "You want to save everyone, and it's part of why I love you."

"This never would have happened if people stopped worrying about someone else's house and cleaned their own," she spits out. "People are inherently different. We're supposed to be." She props herself up on her elbows. "The president has this thing for the history of the old world and what it was like. Courts sided with the rights of people to live free and love who they love. Women could vote and hold a job the same as a man before . . ."

"Before the Final War."

"No, the war was the inevitable culmination of our hatred and fear. I read about men and women putting money and corporations over people. Where one religion deemed their word to be greater than the freedom of another to choose. It started long before we were both born and just festered like a cancer. Then Russia started interfering in elections and slowly taking land back to form the original border of the USSR. No one stopped them. Everyone claimed it was—they had a term for it—alternative facts."

"How can a fact be alternative?" Anton scoffs.

"It can't. Yet, it was. People followed the masses and hate spread across the globe as Russia kept working in the background unimpeded. By the time the world woke up, it was too late."

"And once they had full control, the purges began," Anton adds somberly.

"The newer books said they organized those raids to remove those who fought against change and were a strain to the system. The ones who took more out than they gave back."

"I know the rest," Anton finishes. He lies next to Osaka and takes her hand in his. "Why are you telling me all this?"

"Because we have to be better to change the world for the future," she whispers.

Anton rolls on his side and kisses her nose. She turns to meet his gaze and pulls their firmly clasped hands up to her chest.

"My love, that's where you've got it wrong." He kisses her lips softly and presses his forehead to hers. "We can't fix what people don't view as broken. We can't make it better if people don't want to change. We're fighting a war we've already lost to history."

Osaka pushes Anton onto his back before resting her head in the crook of his neck, her silent tears flowing as the realization of death lingers over the two of them. They'll never get married. They'll never have the family they fancifully dreamed about. The world has no place for people like them.

Tim stands by the warden's door, waiting for him to arrive. He managed only a few hours of sleep last night after their phone conversation, his concern evident as he tossed and turned, unable to calm his mind. It wasn't the action itself that was weighing on him heavily, but the outcome and the subsequent effect it may have on his mother. If she ever found out about his choices, she'd never forgive him for betraying his brother. There was one thing Tim could not handle, and that was losing the only woman who ever showed him love. He couldn't.

"Sergeant. You're early," Macalov says. He holds a briefcase in one hand and a travel mug filled with coffee in the other. The warden masterfully opens the door while juggling his items, refusing the help Tim offers. "I'm capable of opening the door, Sergeant Flynt."

The two enter the office, and Tim clicks the door shut behind them. He stands at attention while the warden walks through the office, preparing for the morning. The briefcase is placed in the center of his desk and the coffee perfectly perpendicular to it. Macalov opens the blinds, letting the morning sun peer in through the window, illuminating the room and forcing Tim to shield his eyes.

"I normally have the morning hours to go over the briefings and new files from the previous evening," Macalov states. He opens up the briefcase and removes several files of various thicknesses. "But I see that today shall be out of order. While I will accept this once, let's not make a habit out of it, understood?"

"Yes, sir," Tim answers, squinting at the light hitting his eyes at the perfect angle.

Macalov stands, watching the young sergeant hover by the door. "Shit, are you waiting for an invitation? Sit down already."

Tim swiftly moves to the chair, removes his hat, and sits down. His right knee bounces as his hands fumble with his cap. Macalov sits, sips some of the liquid from his mug, and waits. A soft knock on the door breaks the silence.

"Enter," the warden grumbles.

A younger soldier, shorter than Tim but stockier in build, walks in and salutes. He hands the warden an envelope before saluting again and leaving the office. Macalov opens the letter and scans through it. Folding it back up, he leans back in his chair and takes another drink from his mug.

"This job . . . it is more difficult than most people think. I control the safety and livelihood of around two thousand men. They come to work, do what's required, and go home. They make one mistake and I have to decide if they lose a day's pay, their jobs, or their lives." He takes another long swig of his drink. "Alcohol helps, of course."

He holds his mug up in the air with a side smirk.

"So does being calculating when it comes to personal things."

Macalov places the mug back on his desk and grabs the letter again. He opens it and looks it over. "I saved a boy yesterday. The experiments were a success on his parents, so the need for his death was . . . unnecessary. But to the outside world, I gave an infidel a free pass. Do you understand?"

"No, sir," Tim answers quickly.

Macalov drops his feet to the floor with a loud thump. "It means that the outside world will never truly understand your motives because they aren't you. They will view your actions through their experiences and decide based on those alone. Soldiers took the boy to the medical wing so we could learn everything about his people. Study their differences over his entire life for a better picture of who they are."

"Sir, why are you telling me this?"

"I assume we are here to discuss your brother and his connection to a resistance cell within the city limits."

"Yes, sir."

"Then understand your peers will view your decision as a difficult but necessary one. Those below you will consider you a traitor. Your mother might not forgive you."

"But she'll get the cure?"

"I will make that call once I know the information you have given me is accurate," Macalov says, his tone deeper and filled with venom. The calm, lighthearted man from earlier has slipped away like the liquor down his throat.

"I followed my brother last night into the tunnels. He took the subway to the Ninety-Sixth Street stop and walked down the path for the others. When we got to Ninety-First street, he was alone and stopped by a blocked passageway.

The nozzle of a gun became visible, and someone asked for his ID. They scanned it and let him in. I couldn't follow beyond that," Tim finishes.

Macalov sits and studies the man before him, his psyche easily swayed by promises of aid for the one person who makes him feel valuable in the outside world. The rank Macalov tossed his way was a mere means to an end. A slight bump in pay and prestige in the social hierarchy was enough to convince this man that he was in with the warden. Macalov has always been well aware of what humanity will sell to save their own skin or get more coming their way. The idea of enough or too much falling to the wayside with thoughts and prayers.

"That's all?" the warden presses.

"No, sir," Tim stalls. "My brother is a good kid, but he can be naive in the ways of the world."

"Are the inmates in here naive when they broke the law?"

"No, sir."

"So, why would your brother and his associates be any different?"

Tim's hands continue to fumble with his hat to deal with the nerves coursing through his body. He's fully aware of what his brother has done, and the test scores alone back up his intelligence. He knew a defense of ignorance or manipulation would fail. He whispers the mantra in his head: a life for a life. He needs to focus on that now.

"It shouldn't, sir." Tim swallows. "He came home awfully late, discussing his meeting with friends and asking me about laws, and breaking them, and if I felt it was fair. He wanted to know if I'd come get him if Mom passed away. I told him what he wanted to hear and told him to go to bed."

"Interesting." Macalov stands and turns to look out the window. The activity outside was getting busier with each passing minute. "I want you to continue to tell him what he wants to know. I mean everything."

"Sir?" Tim looks up from his hat. "He might ask for some intelligence I shouldn't share."

"But you will. I want you to share everything you know. If you don't have an answer for him, be honest. We need to have him trust you, Sergeant Flynt. Do you understand that?"

"Yes, sir."

"I expect you to report back to me when anything new arises. You're excused."

Tim stands, salutes, and spins on his heels to leave. Macalov turns back to his desk and uses a key to open the top right drawer. He pulls out an old-looking cell phone and dials a number.

"How is he?"

"Are you on a secure line?" the voice on the other line asks.

"Of course I am. Do you take me for a fool?"

"Maybe. You did take in a stray that should have been executed with the rest of the filth," he replies.

"Need I remind you I can reinstate your conviction and bring you back here. Next time I might consider you for our research wing."

"I get it, old man. I'll protect the kid with my life."

"I need you two to remain in the secure bunker under my house. Under no circumstances do you come out. I will ensure you have everything you require."

"Fine by me. It's like a castle down here."

"Just be careful and make sure he continues taking the medicinal protocols I put out for you."

"I get it," the voice replies. "Why you really saving this kid? It's not like society's going to accept him."

"Just do as you're told."

Macalov hangs up the phone. Sharing his plans for a presidential coup was not on his agenda for the day. Truthfully, he didn't care what anyone thought. This child was his son's doppelganger. Once the chemicals in those pills lightened his skin, there might be no need for exoneration. The child will pass as his own. Slightly tan in complexion because of the location of their birth, but nothing more.

The warden understood he was playing with fire, but he needed to fill this hole in his heart. If the boy never saw sunlight again, he could accept that. He would live within the walls of the secure room and venture out when his father was home. When company came over, he would hide once more. In the end, it would satisfy the warden to replace part of the past he lost.

Outside the warden's office, Flannery hides in the shadows with a smirk on his face. The warden was hiding several secrets, all of which he would report back to Laskin by lunchtime.

Chapter Thirteen

Iris stands along the wall of a common room as Toby plays with old battered toys with other children. His smile is bright and his laughter rich, as if the world outside of the walls doesn't exist.

"He's doing well," Ellie says.

Iris turns and notices the agent standing in the doorway. In seconds, the older woman has Ellie wrapped in a hug so tight the woman can barely breathe. Unsure of what to do, the agent's hands falter as they hang at her sides.. Iris continues to hold her, like a grandmother would, and Ellie eventually succumbs to the warmth. Her arms wrap around the woman and her head falls into the crook of her neck.

Memories flood the vision behind her eyelids. Her niece and nephew running along in the park, their curls bouncing freely as they ran away from Auntie Monster. The way their smiles could remove any negative emotions from the day. Visions of themed birthday parties, movie nights, and impossible puzzles make her heart ache with a pain she had long since locked in a trunk.

The first tears trickle out of their own accord, the emotions welling up inside Ellie, pushing against the boundaries of her skin and finding a way to freedom. Iris just stands there, holding her body close, allowing it to crumble in her arms. The older woman never moves an inch as the strong military agent fights a losing battle. She whispers soothing words into Ellie's ears, telling her to let it all out, encouraging the agent's arms to tighten their grip.

Toby drops his toy and stumbles over to the two women. His little arms wrap around their bodies as far as he can reach. Ellie pulls back from Iris's embrace when she feels the little boy on her leg. Without thinking, she picks him up into her arms and squeezes tightly. The tears continue to roll down her face as she walks over to a rickety table along the back wall.

"Why you cry?" Toby whispers. Ellie leans back, surprise filling her face.

"He's been talking more over the last two weeks." Iris turns back to the children playing on the floor. "He's made friends, and they're helping him open up. I never thought it was possible."

"Why you cry?" Toby asks again. He squirms in Ellies arms, seeking her attention.

"Because . . . " Ellie ponders if she should be truthful or let the child live in his innocence. "They're happy tears. Seeing you laughing and running around here is so wonderful. It makes me super happy, and sometimes that makes adults cry."

"Why?" Toby inquires.

"Because it means a lot to me. I want you to be happy and safe." Ellie tickles his stomach, and the boy squirms with laughter.

"Down," he says through his giggle fit.

Ellie lowers him to the floor. His feet barely touch the ground before he launches himself out of her arms. Toby makes it to his new friends and hits the floor in a fit of giggles, their innocence filling the room with pure joy as a reminder of what the world could be.

"Most adults would have told him the truth," Iris says, watching her grandson play. "Why didn't you?"

"What difference would it have made? He's too young to understand and he shouldn't have to. Let him be a child as long as he can."

"You can tell me, if you'd like to," Iris says. Her voice reminds Ellie of the soothing tones of her grandmother when she was growing up. "You don't have to, of course. We can just sit here and let those kids' joy just infect us both."

Silence falls over the two of them as the world around Ellie seems to close in on her. Those she trusted have forced her hand, making her execute her plan before she is comfortable. Those she thought would understand the greater issue at hand fell back into the mindless emotional knee-jerk responses. It was much easier in the field when she only had herself to depend on. On the rare occasions she needed a partner in crime, Agent Ni was always her first choice. Now, the only actual relationship that tethered her to the world was gone.

"I think about my family," Ellie says softly. "What happened to them, if they suffered . . . things like that."

Iris leans back against the metal table. Her hands rest neatly on her lap as her gaze bounces from child to child in front of her. "You know thoughts like that won't help you get through the day, but we all do it, don't we? Wonder what happened, if we could have done more for them . . . saved them all."

"I know I couldn't save them, but the thought of them . . . that they survived long enough to be imprisoned. I know what happens across the water."

"Stop doing that. In the beginning, they didn't round people up like you're talking about. They just walked through the towns, shooting any person deemed abnormal to the crown. Anyone who helped them met the same fate."

"I know soldiers brutalized women during the purges. Sometimes for days at a time. It was the worst kept secret," Ellie counters.

"I know. But if you think about what might have happened, you'll go crazy," Iris says. Toby runs over and hands her a broken matchbox car, the paint long since gone, along with the driver's side door. "Thank you, sweetie. This is a really cool car." Toby smiles, takes it back and rushes to the kids again.

"If I don't think about it, I'll forget the reason for all of this," Ellie huffs. She leans back on the table, her elbows denting the aging metal. "I don't want to forget those who suffered. I don't want to think about the future and erase the past so we repeat it."

"Oh, I'm sure you won't repeat it. No one who has seen what you have could do that."

"Yet, we do it. Over and over again, we do the same damn thing and it never changes."

"You can point out all the problems, but what are the solutions?" Iris asks.

"I don't know," Ellie answers solemnly. "How can you fix something that's so broken you can't figure out where to begin?"

"I'm going to share with you a bit of wisdom my momma gave me. If you gotta do something, just start. It don't matter where." She laughs at Toby dancing around with another young boy to music only they can hear. "If you don't start, you never will."

"For the next week, I'd appreciate it if you and Toby stay away from all our entry points," Ellie says seriously.

"Should we be concerned?"

"Not yet. If we need to evacuate, listen to the guards. They'll make sure you get out. I give you my word."

"That isn't very comforting, Ellie."

"Iris, I promise you and Toby will be safe. I will do everything in my power to ensure it," Ellie answers. "There are some things going on that will put this community on edge. I need to know you are deep inside our nest. If necessary, stay in my room and lock the door. It's the least deteriorated. Should hold for a very long time."

"You're telling me this and saying I shouldn't worry? I don't understand, Ellie. I've been on the run with my grandchild for a long time. If we need to go, I'm more than capable of handling it. You've helped us have a life with your people here. You seem different from everyone else here. Please don't break my trust."

"I give you my word," Ellie says again, more firmly.

Toby runs back over and grabs Iris's hand. He pulls gently, but her focus remains on Ellie. He tugs a little harder, and she finally relents. The two walk to the other children. One of them hands her a book to read. She smiles and sits on the floor so she's eye level with the children. Holding the pages open for the children to see the illustrations, Iris reads.

Ellie watches as Iris acts out different animals with accents and hand motions. In another time, this would be in a library with brand-new books and families enjoying it together. Maybe there would be refreshments after where everyone gets to know one another and the children play. A fantasy that only lives in her mind now, but even there, the memory is dim. Ellie is fully aware of her main option for humanity. It is time for a clean slate, but she will keep her word to Iris. She'll protect them from all the torture and torment outside their doors. She'll make sure it's peaceful.

They will not suffer.

Laskin sits at his desk, rifling through the latest news on the yearly budget for the United States. Congress seems hell-bent on cutting back on funds that he has always deemed necessary. Yet, to get the money for it, the wealthy need to pony up more than they want. He's quite aware of the fight he has in front of him, but the outcome will end in his favor.

A soft knock on the door pulls him from the piles of pork and useless things thrown on the page.

"Enter."

Osaka enters, with Michael Flannery behind her. "Mr. Flannery is here to see you. He's here without an appointment."

"It's okay. Please cancel anything that can be and push back the rest," Laskin answers.

Osaka hesitantly closes the door, leaving the slimy-looking Flannery with her boss. The oil on his hair is so thick, his hair is slicked back without products. His clothing is rife with fresh dirt and the smell to match it, and his shoes leave black marks on the rug marked with the presidential seal with each step he takes.

"Is there a reason you're here smelling like an outhouse and looking like you've rummaged through dumpsters for your last meal?" Laskin asks, disgusted.

"Had a tussle last night with a woman." Flannery plops himself down on a chair with light upholstery. Laskin makes a mental note to burn the furniture when he leaves. "Apparently she was married. Husband didn't take too kindly to me poaching his whore."

"You want to be warden of the most prestigious institution in the United States of the Russian Federation and yet you still fornicate with lower-class humans. What is wrong with you?"

"Nothing. I've got needs. Besides, she was a two-bit piece of trash with a farmer for a husband. She should thank me for allowing her to take my—"

"I don't care." Laskin raises his voice. "You represent me and, indirectly, the crown. You cannot continue to make such a fool of yourself. You can do what you want in the privacy of a brothel or bedroom, but my god, man, shower before coming to work!"

"Nah, makes me fit in with them better. Then they don't know what hit 'em." Flannery smiles, the right corner of his mouth rising higher than the left. His eyes darken with the memories of the previous evening's events, the pride over the lives he destroyed rolling off him in waves. He's drunk with power, like they all are.

"Let me put it to you nicely: if you show up here again reeking of feces and walking around like you own my office, I will put a bullet between your eyes before you finish saying hello," Laskin says. The venom in his voice brings the temperature of the room down several degrees.

"Maybe you could. Maybe you couldn't. Remember, Jerrick Laskin, all it takes is one wrong move and your son learns to fly," Flannery counters. "Now, considering I like the kid, I'll meet you halfway. I'll shower before I meet with you high percentage freaks, but I will do what I want, when I want, how I want. Or you don't get the information I have on Macalov."

Flannery lifts his dirty boots and drops them on Laskin's desk with a loud bang. Dirt pops out of the treads and lands on papers and the telephone. The president shivers at the number of bacteria spreading like wildfire in his office. Flannery was a loose end. One he'd eliminate once the information stopped rolling in. You sell your soul first, then question how to get it back.

"Agreed."

Flannery launches his body forward, hand outstretched for confirmation. Laskin looks at it and leans back in his chair. The dirty man laughs as he falls back to his previous position. The sound of his clothing sticking to the fabric as he shifts makes Laskin gag.

"Tell me what you know," the president continues.

"Our friendly warden has one of his men following around a member of the resistance. Seems he wants this Flynt guy to give the traitors whatever they need. Don't know why, but from what little I heard, they were in the subway tunnels around Ninety-First street." Flannery says. He immediately thinks of Major Trent. If this was the cell he was a part of, there would be no way to extract him before the attack. His hands were tied.

Laskin frantically writes notes on a small piece of paper near him. "Anything else?"

"Yeah. The kid he saved, the infidel? He's alive and living in his house. Something about a safe room and someone with a criminal record with him."

Laskin jots down more things before dropping the pen to his desktop. He pushes further back into his chair and ponders all the new information.

"Does he trust you?"

"Does anyone?" Flannery retorts.

"No, I guess not." Laskin taps his fingers together in front of his chin while he thinks. "I want you to lead a raid on Macalov's house. I want everything you can find in his office that would show the improper use of . . ." Flannery looks lost. "Secure files, computers, anything and everything we can use to prove he's a threat to the crown. Then find this boy and bring him to me."

"Sure, but doesn't this require a higher authority to launch it?"

"Leave that to me. Just be ready."

"When?"

"I'll need two days to get things in order. Some of my men will assist you while the rest take care of the resistance cell. We'll broadcast the executions of any survivors."

"Great. We good?" Flannery asks. Laskin nods and the man retreats from the room. Osaka opens the door carefully and stands waiting for the president to give her orders.

"Have this chair removed and someone clean my office immediately. That . . . man is disgusting."

"Yes, sir." She closes the door behind herself.

Laskin picks up the phone and shakes the dirt out of it. He hits a few keys before ringing sounds on the other end. There are several security prompts where he types in various combinations of numbers, each longer than the one before it.

"Please hold," a computerized voice says every few seconds into his ear.

Laskin holds the phone while scanning the piece of paper. If things were to go in the right direction, he could remove two thorns from his side with little to no loss of his men. That would always be a preferential outcome.

Once he proved himself with these military operations, Congress would have no choice but to respect his position. He would be a man of action instead of the poster boy of nepotism. The grumblings of old white men wanting him out of power would stop. His son would begin his studies for a future in the presidential office. The name Laskin would be revered and remembered for a millennium to come.

"Jerrick, my son. How are you? How's my daughter and Maxim?" King Valkov's voice breaks Laskin from his fantasies.

"Maria and I are well. Max is succeeding in all his studies and athletic endeavors. He'd love to see you, if you can maneuver it into the schedule sometime," Laskin says. The phone call is a simple cat and mouse game of pleasantries neither one truly feels. If not for Maria or Max, the two men would be at each other's throats, intent on murder.

"I'd love to see my grandson. If a trip to your country isn't possible, maybe a summer here to learn our ways. He's going to be president someday; he should see how it's done in the motherland."

"I'm sure he'd enjoy that." Laskin takes a deep breath before continuing. "I apologize for the intrusion on your time, sir. New information has crossed my desk, and I was hoping to proceed with military retaliation. I need your permission to move forward."

A heavy sigh comes through on the other end of the line. Another muffled, angry voice adds to the conversation. A door slams, and Laskin hears a glass hitting the table and fluids pouring. Something in Laskin's words must have upset the king enough to warrant a drink and privacy.

"Go ahead."

"One of my men uncovered a resistance cell living in the old subway tunnels."

"You have proof of this?"

"That's where it gets a bit . . . difficult, sir. It appears Gregor Macalov knows of its existence and kept this information from the hierarchy. My informant has given me the location and in one strike, we could remove the threat."

"Gregor is a good man. I'm sure he has his reasons," Volkov counters.

"Yes, sir, but he's putting New York City's people at risk. Our water and food stores have seen an uptick in violence. We've done the best we can to secure them, but it must be these people."

"Yes, yes, but the people who matter are happy. We do not worry about the ants, my boy."

"True, but I will protect your daughter and my son. These people are dangerous. If they plan an attack to harm either of them, or our people. I could not live with myself. If we were anywhere else in the world, I would ask for patience to let it play out. But this is our home, and I'm concerned for my family's safety from retaliation."

Ice cubes rattling in a glass are the only sounds Laskin hears through the phone. The silence is deafening as he waits patiently.

"What do you need?" Volkov finally concedes.

"I would need to reallocate the majority of the guards from Riker's Island and deploy them to the subway lines."

"Would that put undue stress on the remaining soldiers at the jail?"

"The island is a fortress. If anything comes across the bridge, the remaining forces can handle it with minimal fuss."

"Agreed. If that's all?"

"No, sir. It's about Gregor Macalov himself. My informant tells me he is hiding a child of dubious upbringing in his home. I'm unsure of his reasoning, but he spared this child a proper death in the jail itself. His behavior has been erratic as of late, and concerns are high about his ability to handle the stress of his position. This child might be the most visible in a long line of criminal activity on his part. I would like to send a team into his house to search for evidence and the boy himself."

"You're asking permission to prove a high-ranking and trusted official is a traitor?"

"No, sir. I'm asking for the opportunity to prove the allegations—"

"Just do it." The glass shatters on the other end. "But you better pray you're not wrong, son. If you are, Gregor will have your position and the rights to do with you as he pleases. Your son will return to me with his mother and learn to become king one day. Do you understand?"

"Yes, sir." Laskin gulps.

"I'll give you two days to report back to me. If you do not . . . Let's not allow it to get to that point."

The phone call disconnects. Taking a few deep breaths to compose himself, he dials Flannery.

"Miss me already?"

"You've got clearance. If this goes south, it's both our heads."

"I expect nothing less. I'll bring everything to the geeks in the basement," Flannery states.

"No. Take the most experienced ones only. They'll be meticulous. I don't need the added stress of you trampling the crime scene. Just get me evidence and that damn boy."

Laskin hangs up the phone and throws it wildly against the wall. Osaka rushes into the room and looks at the new hole in the sheetrock.

"Sir?"

Laskin walks across the room and picks up the pieces of the phone. "I need you to get me the general on the line. We need to process several new military positions before nightfall. Tell him it's urgent and we only have two days to move forward. And cancel all my appointments for the rest of the weekend. I'll be in the bunker assisting our team."

"Yes, sir." Osaka turns but stops at the door. "Should I pick up Maxim, sir?"

Laskin stares at the clock and rubs his eyes. "Yes, get me the general and then head out. Take extra security with you. Please."

She nods and leaves Laskin to his thoughts. He wrings his hands, nerves taking over his body with the decisions rolling off his tongue. The confidence of his earlier thoughts has long since melted into the dirt Flannery left behind. In forty-eight hours, his name will elicit cheers or warrants for his death. The lack of gray area makes the acid in his stomach bubble up his throat with a belch that burns his innards.

He has to be right. Otherwise . . . Laskin can't focus on that now. Death came for everyone, regardless of time or place. But Macalov wouldn't just kill him. No, the psychotic fool would never give him the satisfaction of a quick end. That fact worried him most of all.

Chapter Fourteen

After another confusing day at school, planning his life around a job he has no intention of working, Sam walks into the empty house. His brother not being home was one thing, but his mother missing caused a chill to ram his body hard. The backpack hits the floor as he rushes from room to room, screaming her name, praying she would moan or knock something over to give her location away.

But the house is empty.

Sam rushes out the back door to the empty and overgrown backyard, the weeds cloning themselves over and over, filling the lawn with sharp leaves that never die. The fear buries deeper into his chest as his hands grip the old railing.

"Be careful of splinters," Tim says.

Sam spins around as a small piece of wood juts into his skin with a prick. He pulls his hand back as he hisses. Tim waves him over, a cigarette hanging out of his mouth. The younger brother moves cautiously, picking at the offending foreign object.

"How was school?" Tim asks.

"Usual. Talked about our positions today. No one is being placed with me," Sam says.

Tim pulls out a pocket multi-tool and flips it around to a small blade. The collected ash falls from the end of his cigarette and onto his work pants. The sergeant makes no move to wipe them away as he grabs his brother's hand. Sam struggles a bit, but his bigger brother moves quickly, placing the offending limb in an arm bar. Sam squeaks in surprise.

"Stop moving and I'll get it out. Crap, how much of a baby are you?" The smell of alcohol wafts over Sam.

The negative feeling settles into his stomach. The likelihood of his mother's death rattles around in his brain. The image of her in a box, ready to be burned, forces his eyes shut and his mind to rage against the machine. He mumbles numbers to himself as the anxiety takes hold. Goosebumps form on his flesh like a parasite gnawing away at dead skin. The pressure mixed with pain in the palm of his hand instantly sobers him up.

Tim finally lets his brother go and holds the tip of the blade up to inspect. A small piece of wood rests at the very top, and Sam looks at his hand to check the wound. Nothing. Just a small line. No blood or hole where a chunk of skin should be.

"You think I'd cut you, Sam?" Tim asks.

"No, just . . . it's a knife."

"It's for work." Tim laughs. He leans back into the yellowed wicker bench and inhales deeply on his cigarette. He coughs a bit.

"I didn't know you smoked."

"I don't do it here. Don't want you to do it. It's not very professional for an intellectual like yourself," Tim says, trying to sound like the higher classes.

"You shouldn't do it," Sam replies, concerned. "Those things can kill you."

"Yeah, but they have a pill to treat any kind of cancer now. Just one pill and BAM!" Tim pops up toward Sam, hands outstretched. The sudden movement makes the younger brother jump back in fright. "It's gone and you never worry about it again. Miracles happen, little brother."

"But we can't afford that," Sam adds.

"No. No, I can't," Tim says, flopping back into his chair. "I'm so tired, Sam. I just . . . I need more . . . more than this."

"Where's Mom?"

"Nurse Anna took her for her treatment. She'll be in the facility for a few days."

"But I usually read her favorite story before she goes in. And I get to say goodbye in case she doesn't come home . . ." Sam rambles on.

"Sam, it's okay. Doc says she needed to go in. I promise you, if something happens, we will both say goodbye together." Tim inhales again before releasing it with another short cough. "I have a good feeling about this treatment, though. My promotion gave me access to better medicine. She could be okay. No more maintenance, just living life."

"Like we used to?" Sam asks. The innocence in his question hits Tim hard. They used to play like two normal kids, beating each other up and running toward a future with no knowledge of the past.

"No, Sam. You get to move forward. Mom and I will always be here. You just need to get a pass to come visit. Anytime, anyplace . . . I promise we'll be there," Tim says.

Sam merely nods as tears run down his face. The emotional toll of the resistance plans, his mother being missing, and the idea of living without his brother was too much. Tim embraces him and the tears fall.

"It's okay. I know that's not what you want to hear, but it's our reality. Unless we can change the way the laws work, we just have to follow along."

"What if we could?" Sam whispers.

Tim pulls back and holds his brother at arm's length. "What are you talking about?"

"What if we fight back?" Sam says again.

Tim jumps up and looks around the yard. He stands on his tippy toes and looks over the neighboring fences. Thankfully, every area is empty. He puts the cigarette out on his boot and runs his hands through his hair.

"Watch your mouth. Talking about things like that . . . in the open? It's not safe, Sam. What if someone heard you and called it in?"

"It wouldn't happen, Tim. Our neighbors are too dumb."

"That's not the point!" Tim yells. He waves his arms wildly about as he lowers his voice. "That's not the point. If you get comfortable doing it here, you'd open your trap in the middle of Times Square. You need to be more careful."

Sam pauses and watches his brother. Tim's cell phone rests on the side table with a glass of cheap moonshine and an ashtray. The younger brother considers the entire situation. His older brother could easily call him in right now and grab a large reward. Yet, he stands still, arms holding the railing as his back presses against it with an expression of concern.

"Why haven't you called it in?" Sam asks.

"What?" Tim asks, surprised. "Why would I do that? Why would I turn my brother in?"

"People do it all the time for money. I mean, it's also your job, right? Take in the people that break the law. Put them in the cells as convicted traitors without a trial," Sam continues at a normal decibel.

"Lower your volume," Tim says. His hand hovers in the air, begging his brother to stop talking so loud. Tim might be playing along, but he didn't need an overzealous neighbor to destroy everything he's worked for. "I'm not a cop, Sam. I'm a soldier. I protect and patrol the federal penitentiary on Riker's Island, not Manhattan Island or anywhere on Long Island. Riker's."

"Would you turn me in?" Sam questions. The serious nature of the question hangs in the air. Tim knows full well the ramifications of his brother's actions and the agreements he has already made. If he came clean now, he could get his brother out of the country and somewhere safe. If that existed, that is. That choice would leave his mother alone to die. Tim was fully aware that life was a series of choices, and he had already made his.

"No," he lies. "You're my brother. Blood is thicker than all this crap swimming around us. Just like you'd protect me if you had to from your big office and paycheck."

"So, would you?"

"Would I what?"

"Want to change it?"

Tim grabs his glass and allows the cheap liquor to burn down his throat. The satisfaction of being able to handle the flavor and getting his brother to trust him sits on his tongue with a slight bitterness.

"Yes, I would," Tim answers.

"Then you'll need to trust me and meet my friends."

"I don't think that's smart. I don't want to spook any of them. Besides, with my size and look, I'd never blend in enough. I'd draw too much attention. Just tell them, I'm in. If it means we can still be a family . . . I'm in."

Sam hugs his brother again. Tim's phone vibrates incessantly on the end table. His brother pulls away and rushes back into the house, the fear and concern from earlier long gone. Tim catches his breath and counts to ten. He looks at the caller identification before answering.

"I'm in."

Macalov stands looking out the window with his cell phone pressed tightly to his ear. Tim's voice comes through the receiver as lights from the courtyard highlight tiny droplets of rain.

"Good. Give them whatever information they need. If they need you on their side, join them. I don't care. I need to know what they've got planned so we can end this." Macalov ends the call before Tim can comment further. "Before that little piece of crap does no work and takes all the credit."

Macalov finishes his brandy, the ice rattling around in the glass as he clenches it tightly. He spins and throws the glass against the wall, shattering it, his breathing increasing in pace as his anger rages through his veins. His left hand grabs a letter off his desk. The embossed presidential seal stares back at him mockingly. Macalov lights the edge of the paper on fire and watches it burn.

The flame curls over the edges as the words singe away, the new rules and regulations dictated by the king himself being forgotten and cleaned. Macalov drops the page into his empty wastebasket and turns to a note on his desk. Several names listed one after another, most of them crossed out, and some circled. One name stands out among the rest: Flannery.

The middle man always concerned the warden. He demanded access to everything, including the special operations that had yet to be cleared by the government. There were studies pending with evidence to support their substantial price tags that the traitor had witnessed. There was no other man with the means and connections to pull a maneuver like this. Flannery and Laskin were up to something to undermine his credibility with the boss. A knock on the door lifts the warden's head from the name on the desk.

"Enter."

Arnold George, Tim's friend on the ward, enters the office. He stands by the door, hands shaking, one boot untied and his shirt askew. The soldier tries to tuck his shirt in as Macalov looks him over.

"What is this?" The warden waves his hands up and down. "Can you not dress yourself?"

"No, sir. I was told to get here right away, but I was in the middle of something and . . ."

"And you couldn't take five minutes to correct yourself? To make yourself presentable to your superior?"

"I'm really sorry, sir. It won't happen. . ."

Arnold drops to the floor and ties his boots correctly. Macalov stands with his arms crossed, watching the feeble private continue his machinations while his mind runs through all the scenarios.

"What was her cell block?" Macalov asks.

"Block A, number one-nine-four-zero," he answers as he buckles his pants properly.

"I have an off-the-books project for you. Complete it, and you can keep her as your personal pet."

Arnold smirks, but remembering where he is, drops all emotion and stands at ease. "That would be an honor, sir."

"Excellent. It's a simple order. If you see this man anywhere on the premises, you are to kill him." Macalov hands the private a picture of Michael Flannery. "I suggest you use your pistol, unless you want him to stab you in the throat."

"But he's a fellow officer, sir. A higher-ranking one . . ."

"Yes, he is." Macalov moves behind his desk. "Is that an issue? Let me sweeten the deal. You get your whore and a promotion to corporal." The warden moves papers around his desk, already getting impatient with the private in his office. "This is a limited time offer, Mr. George."

"But isn't the punishment for killing a superior officer . . . death?"

Macalov stops and raises his head. "Indeed, it is. So, I suggest you don't get caught." The warden turns his attention back to the mess of information and the smoldering wastebasket. He grabs his vodka bottle and pours it into the trash before grabbing an expensive brandy. He pops the top, takes a rather large gulp, and places the bottle next to his lighter. "I won't need proof other than his dead body on my campus. Until then, you can see yourself out."

Arnold wastes no time in leaving the office of the increasingly drunk warden. The office phone rings, and Macalov answers it without thinking.

"Macalov."

"Tell me, how many men have you set loose on me?" Flannery's voice wavers through the line.

The warden drops into his chair and the springs squeal with displeasure. "What do you want, Mr. Flannery?"

"I'm curious. How many?"

"I don't know what your question pertains to?"

"Don't play stupid with me, Macalov. We both know we're on opposite sides of the same coin here. We both want a different job. I want yours. You want Laskin's."

"What do you want, Mr. Flannery? I have a facility to run." Macalov chugs from the bottle now. A small amount of liquor leaks out of his mouth, rolling down his chin and neck before finding a home in his white shirt.

"How many men?"

"One." The warden leans back, much to the chagrin of the chair. "But on an island of hundreds, you won't know which."

"Hundreds? Didn't you get the notice? You're losing more than half your men. I'll figure out your man and kill him before he blinks twice." Flannery laughs into the receiver. "But in the guise of military sharing, a man in a glass house shouldn't throw stones . . . or something like that."

The line disconnects. Macalov's aware of the letter the president sent him. In the morning, his defenses for every shift are half what he's used to. The rest transferred without a thought or approval from him.

The warden knew he could run the facility with less due to half the current population being under sedation. He chose not to. Riker's Island stands as an imposing and inescapable place. To have one of the major deterrents removed from his repertoire made his nerves stand on edge.

Flipping through Sam's file on his desk, Macalov continues to drink heavily. The brown fluid runs freely down his chin, the excess dripping onto the file below. His man on the inside would uncover what the boy and his ilk were up to. Hopefully, before Laskin undermined his plans.

The president might have more information, but the warden knew he had the better avenue for attack. Any major battle in history that pushed humanity headlong into gunfire always ended up with the most casualties. He could be the rotten fruit at the bottom of the basket. Rotting the core, one person at a time.

The random words from Flannery roll through his mind. "A man in a glass house shouldn't throw stones." He remembered that saying from years ago. The alcohol blurs his mind from connecting the dots to the past, but concern rises up his spine, and he can't shake it. He stands, swaying as if a breeze wafted in from his window, and waddles to the couch. He pulls out his burner phone and types out a message he thinks is coherent. His body hits the soft material, and within seconds, Macalov passes out. The bottle hits the floor as his hand relaxes, the liquid spreading over the floor one drop at a time.

His phone blinks with a reply from the criminal in his house. It reads: *Locking everything down.*

Chapter Fifteen

Trent and Anton sit in the center of the table, mulling over the homemade map of Riker's Island. Small rocks lay in different sections, with a small designation underneath them. Various notes litter the rest of the table. Mentions of tides, shift changes, and more tedious information is written in chicken scratches on a notepad by Anton's side.

Trent grabs some small army soldiers from the kid's toys. He places them strategically around the buildings, each figure moving through the island with a job and a path to decipher. If they can know the full machinations of the men around the penitentiary, then they stand a good chance of survival. Though Sam has gotten them somewhat updated information, there's nothing to prove its accuracy. The men lean on their old books, underground legends, and prayers that what they have will suffice. The reality of the battle hangs heavily in the air.

"Do you think it's too soon?" Anton asks. "We've got barely enough information to launch a small-scale attack, let alone one for the ages. Are we doing the right thing?"

"History says we have to stop talking and start doing. September 1901, the United States had a vice president by the name of Teddy Roosevelt. He stood up and gave a rousing speech. Most of it doesn't matter, but he said we have to 'speak softly, and carry a big stick.'"

"History has also shown us that resistance is a joke. People die for arguing about their bread rations," Anton counters.

"Yes, yes, but in the good years, the country's formative years, we would always talk softly when negotiating. But the thing is, if that failed, our military could crush you."

"Sounds like Russia and the bullies they've become."

"Oh no, the United States was never like that. We fought for peace and justice throughout the world. People just hated us for it. We only did what we thought was right."

"There's a difference between thinking you're right and actually being right," Ellie interjects. "Was it right to pardon former soldiers who raped innocent women overseas? How about those in positions of authority who murdered people of color? Cheating to get elected and then jamming the court system with unfit justices that support your cause, effectively ensuring the rights of citizens would be in jeopardy for decades to come? None of that was right, but they thought what they were doing was."

"You fight apples with oranges."

"I fight reality with psychology. Again, a difference."

Trent huffs and looks back to the map in front of him. "None of it matters if we're all dead."

"If they handled it properly the first time, we wouldn't be here at all," Ellie counters, her tone harsh and colder than she intended. The years of tormented sleep are into her skin as permanent dark circles and worry lines. The stress of moving the small ragtag group of people across the country before making home the underbelly of New York City has aged her greatly.

"None of that matters now," Anton shouts angrily. "Sam, what've you got?"

Sam comes fully into the room, his baby face looking even younger around the rapidly aging adults. He tosses a pad of scribbles on the table for the two men to see. "My brother gave me all the information he had. He can get me onto the grounds and to the electrical area. I can shut off the power long enough for you to get over the bridge and into some kind of safety. Then it's up to you from there."

"What about the food? We need to cut their numbers down," Trent comments.

"Unnecessary. My brother told me the president pulled almost fifty percent of the soldiers from there. Something about funding and not needing the resources as before. He thinks they might plan on taking Long Island. There's a rumored resistance nest in Nassau County."

"I don't remember seeing anything like that in the area," Ellie says. "Can you verify they exist?"

"They don't," Sam says with pride. "I searched everywhere, but there's nothing doing. Maybe it's that old program I ran when I first joined. The one that would bounce our activity all over the world like a virtual private network ..."

"We need to focus on the mission. What are we doing?" Anton asks.

"We don't have transportation above ground in the city. We take the subways out of the main boundary to a bus, and the last stop is Riker's," Trent says.

"You want armed men to just casually climb on board a subway and then fill a bus with no one noticing?" Ellie asks. The idea sounded more irrational when she repeated it.

The attack itself was a rational idea. The getting there seemed almost impossible. Moving a militia across the water to an island with weaponry was posing more of a problem than originally planned. The men stare at the map, their faces empty, almost defeated as they try to think of another way. Ellie sits in her chair quietly, her mind running several options through. There has to be a simpler way they have failed to see.

They can't deviate from the point of entry, but they could change the dates upon which people went out there. "Have the men break down their weapons and carry them in waste management bags. Milo should have a ton of them in storage. Then we stagger into smaller groups traveling to the site." Ellie leans forward and points to a small outcropping near the bridge on the Queens side. "It might be dangerous footing, but they can hide here in the demolished areas. That way all of our men will be in position by nightfall tomorrow."

"That's putting undue stress on our men," Trent counters.

"She's right though. I don't see any other way to get our men there without raising suspicion, let alone explain why everyone wants to ride a bus to a defunct stop," Anton cuts in.

Sam looks over the map and the toys placed haphazardly on it. He removes several of the green army men and tosses them on the table. The young man opens up the notes his brother gave him and continues to move them around to new locations. He jots down the name of the previously unmarked buildings and other small markers. On the one building in the back, the most protected, he writes *warden's office.*

"Are you sure this is accurate?" Anton whispers.

Sam nods.

"Can we truly trust your brother?" Anton presses.

"My mother is dying of Alzheimer's. If we break this hold the president has . . . the warden has. . . . we could get her cure from the medical wing," Sam says.

The other two men immediately understand. Ellie remains stoic and calm. People's sob stories stopped breaking her heart when she was overseas. She remembered a man with a family and an ill mother-in-law. They were truly beyond poor for the country's standards. He worked for the allied fighters and was being paid a fair wage. This man was putting his life on the line every day as he traveled with the military forces through the unknown lands. He was an asset—until he wasn't. Money will always trump righteousness, and this man led his team into an ambush. No allied soldier survived. The man walked away with a large sum of cash in his bank account and blood dripping between his fingers.

When Ellie found him through her rifle, she didn't think of the poor man's family. She never once worried about the mother-in-law's health. She visualized the men and women slaughtered for a dollar or two more. As the man walked through the market, her finger squeezed the trigger as she thought of the children's missing parents back home. When his head exploded all over the stall and locals near him, she worried about the person screaming with flesh on her hands. Those were lives she never wanted to harm. This man . . . his sob story was pointless. His death inconsequential. He was simply a puppet that created forty-seven caskets.

All kills were like that during her entire tenure. She would see the facts, know the reality of the situation, and head into the lion's den. The victims would go about their day as if life was simply a beautiful thing to enjoy. It never mattered what they did for a living or who they killed or tortured. At home, they were with family.

Here now, she had to remember that Laskin and Macalov were simply criminals. They might have family and people they cared a great deal about, but in the end, their blood would spill.

"Ellie?" Anton asks.

"Yes?"

"We're set then? The men will break down their weapons, travel to the location, and bring some rations with them. Tomorrow night, we attack."

Ellie nods. Trent stands and salutes her. Finally, after traveling together for so long, he gives her the respect she deserves. Of course, it only comes after he has got his way. Ellie salutes from her seated position, her mind too far off on her own mission to pay attention to the unimportant details going on around her. Trent marches out of the room with Sam hot on his heels. Anton turns, but Ellie grabs his forearm.

"I'm trusting you to lead them, Anton."

"I understand."

"Bring as many of them home as you can, and never let Trent run it. If you do . . ."

"No one comes home," he finishes.

Her grasp loosens, and her hand falls to the armrest of her chair. "Send Osaka in please." Anton hears her, but just barely, her voice just above a whisper as the reality sinks in.

Her desire from the moment a Russian asset became president of her country was to eliminate him. The need to remove an enemy on domestic soil burrowed under her skin like a parasite. It burned through her soul with its constant desire to be fed. One by one, the members of Congress fell, replaced by those who towed the line. Each time, her list became shorter in one breath and longer in another.

Right now, the beast roars in her mind, the idea of killing the president so beautifully clear without the need of a vivid imagination. The agent was in full control of her destiny at this point. Ellie was the one who held the cards that no one else knew were missing. In the end, she would do what no one else had the courage to do. She would pull the trigger and remove the threat, regardless of the outcome. This time, there would be no respawn.

"Agent Goldman?"

Ellie returns to the present and Osaka sitting next to her. The woman points to a steaming cup of tea in front of her. Ellie places her hand on the glued handle and brings it to her nostrils. Authentic green tea. Her eyes dart to the woman beside her.

"I took some from my boss's office with filtered water I could take home with me," she says proudly.

"The last time I had this, I was in Tokyo with Wei Ni. We were on a rare break in ops and we stopped by Tokyo Disney."

"I can't imagine you running around in a child's paradise," Osaka says, taking a sip of her tea.

"I went shopping for my niece and nephew for Christmas. I got some themed shirts with Stitch on them; had to prove he was the best character that company ever created. Wei insisted I get some toys and craft things too. Plus, all the snacks I planned on smuggling into the country. It was . . . peaceful."

"What else do you remember?"

"I don't think it really matters now."

"Anton talks about the world like it's best to look forward and fight on. My father taught me we learn a little from victory, but a lot from defeat. We've lost so many times over the course of my life; I'd like to know what you've learned when humanity has won."

That's a more troublesome question to answer than Ellie has ever pondered before. People lost the idea of winning or a victory with every small backdoor deal made in secret. The high of thinking of equality and choice as established law fled the moment another's religious freedoms became more important than the actual teachings within it. The sad answer to Osaka's question is nothing. There has never been a genuine victory.

"I wish I could tell you what it felt like. But I can't. Each victory kept our attention away from the bigger issues—the larger, more important battles. These small tokens were rungs on a ladder to ensure those with the most to gain continued to gain. Then the rules tipped in their favor, and all the small wins dripped off the walls like wet paint into a puddle of nothing."

"I don't understand," Osaka says.

"Wei Ni . . . she was gay, and in our country, same-sex marriage was legal. It had been made the law of the land. People screamed from the rooftops that love had truly won. Yet not three years later, these extreme religious groups kept denying things to members of that community. Kept saying it went against their religious beliefs. They elected politicians that began legalizing the discrimination. Once that set hold, states refused to allow its members to officiate those kinds of marriages for the same reason. That swelled into denying interracial marriages. Eventually, only the extreme evangelical institutions had the legal right to hold any ceremony, mass, or whatever. Before any of us knew it, there was no First Amendment. There was no freedom of or from religion. These people were front and center, taking away the rights of the rest of us when *they* were the statistical minority. They lived by a Bible they never read or understood."

Ellie sips her tea and lets the warmth fill her soul.

"Now they're all dead because the king didn't like 'em. They were so busy fighting everything they deemed wrong that they never knew their judgment was coming. So, victory teaches us nothing. The loss . . . that is everything," she finishes.

Osaka sits and stares blankly at Ellie, who continues sipping the flavorful tea, both women in their heads about the rules and regulations of a time long gone and the unknown future of tomorrow.

"They're attacking tomorrow night," Ellie continues.

"Anton told me."

"I need to get into the building."

"I know." Osaka slides a small, plain, white piece of plastic across the table. "I had someone make me up a visitor's pass for Anton. They owed me a favor, so there's no image on it."

"How'd you manage that one?"

"I gave them access to a torture porn website," she spits out in disgust. "I'm not proud of it, but everyone has their price."

"You did what you had to do."

"Doesn't make it any better. It makes me nauseous." Osaka shakes the visuals out of her mind. "By allowing him access, I contributed to it. I . . . the views will perpetuate the cycle, and I did that."

"We all do things we may regret in the future, but it's necessary to accomplish the greater goal." Ellie drains her tea and exhales slowly. "We go in together?"

"Before we do, I have your word you won't harm Max? Laskin's son. He's an innocent in all of this . . . madness."

"He's next in line."

"He's a child." Osaka stands firm. "Do I have your word?"

"I disagree with you, but yes, you have my word," Ellie agrees.

Osaka pulls out a small file full of printed pages. "I don't know why you needed these documents, but this is everything about the bunker. All the changes, security codes, everything."

"If we shut down the entire country's electrical grid, then fighters all over stand a chance to take the US back," Ellie lies, her training enabling her to cover up the genuine reasons behind her decisions. "Maybe I can get a signal out to other cells and give them some information to assist in future raids. I don't know, but this is the beginning of a new tomorrow."

Osaka stands, reaches into her pockets, and drops two small packages onto the table. "I don't know why you needed that, but be careful. One bite. The medical team uses it when interviewing traitors. They beg for the treat . . . then . . . well, you know."

"I understand and thank you for this."

"Meet me at the fence tomorrow at dusk. I'll help you get in, and then we'll take care of the rest. Just promise me this will work."

"There are no guarantees here, Osaka. I can only promise that after tomorrow, the sun will shine freely and warm the earth below, healing the soil one grain at a time."

Osaka nods her head in understanding and leaves the room. Ellie picks up the small, silver-wrapped squares and plays with them in her hands. Just like in poker, you always ponder the best way to win: a straight, a flush, three or four of a kind. You have to make a decision early on and let the hand play out, for better or for worse. Ellie was about to play her first card and allow the others to fall where they will. Unlike the others, though, she would play this round alone.

Ellie walks through the tunnels to her bedroom. People mill about the open spaces, some children saluting her as she passes by. Families move about their day with no concern for the battles being planned behind closed doors. They feel safe here, at home. Who was she to remove that peaceful feeling? The people deserved to enjoy what brief moments they had, and if the battles went well, there could be peace for everyone on the horizon.

Her door creaks open and Toby rushes to smush his face in her legs. The young boy wraps his arms around her as Ellie shuffles her feet to enter the room. The laughter bubbling up from her chest sounds foreign to her ears, but she relishes it just the same. Reaching down, she grabs Toby by the waist and flips him upside down. His legs kick wildly as Ellie holds him with outstretched arms. Iris takes her cue and tickles his belly before sitting back down, a cough ripping through her body like an explosion. Ellie turns Toby right side up and places him on the floor. He rushes over to his grandmother and rubs her back. Ellie grabs the cup of water on her desk and hands it to the older woman.

"You okay?"

"Nothing I can't handle." Iris sips the water and turns her attention to Toby. "Why don't you go back to drawing that picture for Ms. Ellie."

Toby jumps off the bed and struggles to climb onto Ellie's office chair. He grabs the small pencil on the desk and begins moving it around frantically, the swirls, lines, and shading making nothing but a mess of lighter and darker gray coloring. Perfection for a child of his age.

Iris coughs harder this time, her fist covering her mouth as her body shakes with each violent motion. Toby continues drawing, knowing his grandmother wants him to finish it. Iris pulls her hand back, revealing a small amount of blood.

"You said you were more than capable of taking care of him. Yet you're sick."

"Because the will to protect a child is stronger than any damn disease, Ellie," Iris says through her coughs.

"When?" Ellie asks.

"Long time now. It's why Wei Ni helped us. She knew I needed to get him here. To safety. To you." Iris tries to clear her throat.

"Contagious?" Ellie tries to calm the swell of emotion surging through her system.

"I reckon it was too many years of living underground, eating diseased animals, and drinking infested water."

"I'm sure we can make you more comfortable."

"I'm fine with how this is playing out, Ellie. Leave the rest for the children. You promised to take care of Toby. I'm holding you to that in the future."

"I gave you my word."

Iris nods her head and leans forward a bit as exhaustion overtakes her body. Ellie helps her lie down on the bed, the springs squeaking with every slight movement. The older woman presses into the pillow as Ellie pulls the blankets up to her shoulders.

"I need a favor from you as well."

"What is it?" Iris yawns.

Ellie pulls out the two small, silver squares and places them on the table by the bed. "I have to go out of the area tomorrow evening. I need to know you two are safe in here."

"We'll be fine, Ellie. Don't worry." Iris coughs lightly.

"I got you both a bit of chocolate. I want you to enjoy it as dessert with dinner. Okay?"

"How did you manage that?" Iris's eyes widen as her mouth waters. "I haven't had chocolate in, gosh, I don't remember when."

"Remember our earlier conversation. Tomorrow, men from here will fight topside against the hierarchy. The chocolate might help keep him calm. So please, promise me you'll have it tomorrow. I will ask nothing further from you."

"If it's that important, yes. We'll wait on the guard's orders to evacuate if necessary. Until then, we'll stay here. Quiet as church mice. You be safe out there. We need you down here."

"I will try." Ellie ignores the raging bull in the back of her mind screaming at how wrong this is, her innards rolling over and twisting around themselves, forcing acid to burn every section of her esophagus. She has to go through with this. She has to finish what she started all those long years ago. She's tired, and her queen needs to rest. It is time for checkmate and knowing they might suffer . . . she couldn't handle that.

Chapter Sixteen

Darkness falls across the East Coast as it always has, with a sunset raging in reds, oranges, and a hint of yellow. The fiery colors turn the metropolitan area of New York into a burning concrete jungle, where the light dances around the shadows of people. Mostly empty at night except for those who have a pass and soldiers and police officers roaming the streets, Manhattan is beautiful. The simple streetlamps highlight the roads paved with high-tech solar tiles, the massive billboards in Times Square long since manipulated in favor of turning it into the propaganda of Presidential Square, though few called it that. The construction had begun over ten years ago, but the ego of man and the desire to be bigger and better kept pushing the finishing point further away.

Riker's Island had been an exception to this rule. Money freely flowed into the penitentiary for medicinal and governmental purposes. The development of new technologies, seemingly out of thin air, always came out of their facilities. The aura of impenetrability flows over the compound like the morning fog in fall. Soldiers walking around the perimeter would discuss the swirling waters around the rocky shore, talking of the one-way bridge and the security of it all.

The same had been said for Alcatraz. The island known for housing the worst offenders, tainted by the escape of three men. As the resistance clicks their weapons together, the soldiers on patrol are far too complacent. Future generations might talk of ignorance being the reason for their fall, but that's only if it's approved writing by the state. Either way, everyone hiding in the rubble alongside the entry point knows today will live in infamy, one way or another.

Sam looks out the window of the bus and tries to see the men in the shadows. Only seeing a small reflection of what could be a gun sight, mirror, or piece of broken glass, he sits back, trying to calm the nervousness spreading through his veins. His brother Tim shares the bench seat, eating a sandwich they'd made at home. Sam couldn't handle eating anything before leaving, but his brother has always had a stomach of steel. He could laugh about that now. Maybe it was the absurdity of it all, his brother eating peanut butter and jelly before walking into a gunfight, or just nervous laughter. Sam couldn't be sure, but it gave him some peace knowing that some things stayed the same, even when the energy around them changed.

The bus screeched to a halt and the doors flipped open. Systematically, one row at a time, the occupants stood and exited in an orderly fashion. Tim swallowed the last of his food and shoved the used napkins into his backpack. When it was time, he pulled Sam with him as they filed out onto the compound grounds. The two men walked with a few others, following solid white-line barriers like lanes for pedestrians. A flatbed truck whizzes by the two of them, black elongated bags stacked in the back of it. Sam can only speculate as to what they are, his imagination filling in the gruesome details.

"This way. Stay in the lines," Tim whispers as he pulls Sam back into the painted barriers. "Don't need you to get run over, little man." Headlights illuminate the path as they speed by once again.

They enter a small building, and Tim dumps his bags on a conveyor belt. Walking to a massive, upside-down, U-shaped device, he removes all the metal from his pockets and places them with his baton in a small square bin. A soldier moves the bin to the other side and waves Tim into the contraption. A red laser pops out of both sides of the machine and descends over his body to his military grade boots. It switches to a bright green and scans back up to his head before turning off. The soldier on the other side waves him through, scans Tim's identification, and waits for the handheld device to beep. Once clear, Tim rounds up all his personal items and waits for Sam.

The younger boy empties his pockets of a few pennies, chewing gum, and a small, smooth stone. The soldiers move him into the machine and continue the monotonous process of checking every individual in and out of the penitentiary. Sam twitches as the lasers scan over his eyes, the desire to blink almost winning over the need to stay still and alert. The process is faster for the younger brother than the older.

Once they're finished, Tim grabs Sam by the elbow and funnels him through another room to a locker. He types a complex code into a keypad before leaning forward and scanning his eyeball. The lock disengages, and Tim quickly stashes all of his personal items within it. He slams it shut and walks the two of them out of the room and into a darkened alley behind the building.

"Okay, you're here. Now what do you need?" Tim breathes.

"I need access to electrical control," his brother answers.

"The computers usually run everything, but passwords change in regular intervals."

"That's why we planned on accessing the box itself within the power building."

"Yeah, okay. So, I get you in there . . . Then what?" Tim asks.

"I access the mainframe with my computer chip, knock the island out for about twenty minutes, and you get me out of there before they turn the power back on," Sam answers.

"Got it. Okay . . ." Tim looks around nervously.

"We got this, bro. Stronger together, right?" Sam says.

"Yeah. Just got a lot of people around here with guns . . . Not my kind of party," Tim answers, the lies so easily flowing out of his mouth he's unsure what the truth is anymore. The adrenaline funneling through him causes anxiety, but the reasons for it at this point are so muddled. Sam looks up at him, waiting for confirmation. "We're good. What time?"

Sam looks at his watch. The small countdown on the bottom of the screen has fifteen minutes and forty seconds remaining. That's how much time he has to get his portion of the mission completed. "We need to move now."

Tim walks, with Sam at his side, through the white lines and around the compound in under five minutes. The lack of soldiers patrolling gives Tim pause. He feels understaffed and vulnerable for the first time in his tenure. They always outnumber inmates by three or four to one. Now it is almost even. The worst offenders would require several of them at once; they would leave the unconscious ones to rot should the island fall. Tim shakes his head to clear the cobwebs and focus on the task at hand. He has to get Sam into the building, to the box, and then he has to show his true colors. He prays he can last that long.

Sliding his identification card into the power building, the light flashes green and allows access. Tim looks around the darkness as he pushes Sam inside. The two men head down the flights of stairs until they enter a large server-like room.

"Where's the card thing you have?"

Sam smiles, grabs a small loop off his molar, and dry heaves as he pulls up the small computer component. Once the balloon is free of his esophagus, he vomits on the floor, all the acid from nerves and lack of food spilling onto the metal grate and dripping to the level below.

"Jesus, Sam!"

"Sorry, couldn't help it."

"How the hell did you hide that?"

"Remember that odd pocket the doc said I had in my throat, the one where all the food got stuck? Apparently, I can slip a small USB-sized chip in there. Cool, right?"

"You're insane, little brother."

"You learn your strengths when forced into a corner; I learned that from you." Sam smiles.

The techie scans the numbers of all the boxes in front of him until he comes across one labeled *MAIN*. He pulls at the door, but it doesn't budge. With Tim's help, the two pull the cover off of the electrical control panel, which shuts off the computer system that controls everything from machines in the medical ward to the power in the open spaces.

"People might die when you do that. You think you can handle that?"

Sam pauses. The small device filled with a virus hangs above its entry point. Unsure, his hand wavers a little. "I never thought of that . . ."

"Neither did I," Tim murmurs. "There's no going back from this. I need to know you're sure."

"I don't see what other choice I have." Sam takes a deep breath and shoves the drive into the port. "We all have to face our judgment, eventually. I can only do what I think is right. You taught me that too."

"I taught you a lot of stupid stuff, little brother."

The lights go out. Immediately, sounds of chaos erupt outside.

———

Flannery sits in the back of a cube truck the NYPD once used for local raids, the logos and distinctive markings all scraped away to make it look more unassuming. His knee bounces in anticipation as he whirls the two 9mm handguns on his fingers. The soldier across from him flinches every time the barrel spins to face the opposite direction. Flannery says nothing but keeps playing with them, the thrill of the other man's fear causing his lower half to liven up. The safety is securely in place, but no one needs to know that.

The back doors pop open, revealing two NYPD officers with full riot gear on. Flannery laughs at their attire as he shuffles out of the truck. Hopping down, the two officers salute him and point to the back of a police cruiser.

"What was the point of us being squeezed into that crap box if you're gonna park that thing right in front of the house?"

"We used a drone to scan the house; no traces of a warm body in there. You've got the wrong house," the officer says with a smug look on his face.

"I don't care what your tech says, we're going in."

"I've got my orders. We only enter the building if there's a warm body. You're on your own."

Flannery steps back from the man wearing a white shirt and crisp blue pants. He spins around and sees the rest of the patrolmen standing around, waiting for their orders. He walks back and forth in front of the higher-ranking official. The dark gray house behind a white picket fence calls to him like prey to a spider. This man, this holier-than-thou individual, stands between a presidential order and a lack of initiative. Flannery has never been one to follow the rules unless it suits his needs. He's also tolerated no kind of cowardice. Technology has been helpful in providing information during the course of their careers, but it never decided for them. Each individual on the street standing around him could fully make up their own mind.

Without a second thought, Flannery raises his pistol and fires. The higher-ranking officer's head erupts in a spray of red as his body slumps to the floor. Flannery walks over to the small gate in the now red fence and flicks some brain matter off the latch. Using the nozzle of the smoking pistol, he flips it open and takes two steps inside.

"You can all sit out here and screw around, or you can come inside and do your damn jobs. Remember, nerds in the back and only enter when someone comes and gets you. Got it?"

Four unarmed men in the back nod frantically in understanding. Some officers fall in line behind Flannery; others remain firmly in place. Flannery leans over and whispers in the closest soldier's ear. The soldier raises his hand, signals to his men, and they open fire on the others remaining in the street. Their bodies fall quickly, the sounds echoing through the quiet neighborhood.

The neighbor across the street flips on the front lights and opens the door. He takes two steps outside before rushing back into his house. The lights go out.

"Make sure he saw nothing," Flannery says to two officers. "If he did, make sure he forgets by any means necessary."

They jog across the street and bang on the front door. The man refuses to answer. They bang again. One soldier uses the butt of his machine gun to smash the door handle off. The two men enter the house as a woman screams.

"Now, like I said, we have a job to do. Search every room in this house for a young kid. If you find him, bring him to me. If you don't find him, tear the place apart for intel. If you find a neighbor sticking their nose where it doesn't belong . . . they are expendable. The only person we don't kill is the kid. Got it?"

The men's heads all bob up and down like buoys in an ocean storm. They all funnel into the house, guns raised with laser sights activated. Room by room, they search, looking for any signs of life. Finding none, the techs from the bunker enter the house and begin scouring Macalov's office for more information about his crimes.

Flannery walks around the living room, marveling at its high ceilings and hardwood floors. The furniture is perfectly aligned for viewing the full wall-sized television, every piece in place but the small wooden table next to a leather chair. It fits the colors, settings, and the overall motif of the living room, but something about it feels off. It is farther away from the couch than the chair next to it, and there is nothing on it at all, while the others hold lamps, a remote, and a telephone.

Flannery walks over to the piece of furniture and kneels down. The floor beneath it looks normal. The table looks cheap, but again, functional. Maybe Macalov has crappy taste. Flannery moves to stand, loses his balance, and grabs onto the table for stability. The hairs on the back of his neck stand on end. The table didn't move under his weight.

Standing upright, Flannery places both his weapons in their leg holsters before cracking his neck. He grabs the table and lifts. The offending item doesn't move. The soldier pushes the nearby couch farther away and then the reclining chair. He kneels against the floor, rapping each area with his knuckles until he hears a hollow sound. He pulls out his bowie knife and digs into the groove of the wooden floor. After several passes, the board breaks, revealing a hinge. There is some kind of trap door under the floor.

Without thinking, Flannery chips away at the floor, breaking more pieces off. The tip of his knife breaks and remains embedded in the wood, but he keeps going. The entire hinge exposed, Flannery stands to his full height and admires his work. There has to be a trigger somewhere in this house. The bookcases on the far wall draw his gaze. The rest of the men watch in disbelief as Flannery pulls down all the books on a shelf with one swipe of his arm. He moves the bookshelves individually, but nothing happens.

He tosses statues, furniture, and anything else not nailed down. The trap door doesn't budge.

"Get me the acid from the truck. We'll melt the damn thing," he says, rage dripping from his lips.

Flannery reaches over the fireplace and lifts Macalov's family portrait: His wife, her blue eyes and blonde hair highlighting her full smile. Their son, youthful, happy and alive with every stroke of the brush. The soldier shoves his knee through the canvas. In anger, he shreds the entire painting.

"Sir," an officer says behind him.

"What?" Flannery tosses the frame into the fireplace.

"The wall, sir."

There, resting on the bricks, is a dirty handprint. Flannery reaches up and presses the stone into the wall. There's a small click, and the door rises from the floor. Flannery waves the officer to the opening. The man stands at the top and aims his weapon down to see if it's clear. His body flies backwards as a bullet blows his chest apart.

"See? Living, breathing human beings." Flannery points to another officer. "Go ahead."

The officer hesitates, wavering in his commitment.

"Don't worry." Flannery laughs. "He'll run out of bullets, eventually."

One by one, the NYPD officers walk over to the entryway. They move the body of the previous victim and then try to plan a different way down. A few make it several steps down by using suppressing fire, but eventually they all die.

"Sir?"

"What now?" Flannery turns to see the four techs standing there with boxes.

"We've found several files that need to be verified, two laptops, three external hard drives, and a burner phone. We need to bring it back to the office to begin our analysis."

"Fine, go wait outside." Flannery turns to his soldiers. "Take them to the truck."

Once they're out of sight, Flannery grabs several books and throws them into the underground hatch. He keeps flinging them around like basketballs. Most of his shots hit their mark, some miss by a wide margin. He keeps laughing and hands a few books to soldiers to do the same. Ten minutes into the odd behavior, Flannery stops on a dime.

"You lock down the perimeter of the house. No one in or out but me."

No one questions his authority or the sudden change in direction.

Flannery kneels close to the opening, but where he can't be visually targeted.

"You can come out, ya know. We won't hurt the kid."

"Go to hell," the male voice echoes up the ladder.

Flannery tries again. "Let the kid go."

"I got my orders, and they ain't from you. I ain't goin' back there, ya hear! I ain't doin' it," the man screams.

Flannery stands, reaches into his pocket, and grabs his lighter. Flicking the metal top open with a click, he lights it and watches the fire dance in front of his eyes.

"Their work will be shown for what it is, because the day will bring it to light. It will be revealed with fire, and the fire will test the quality of each person's work. First Corinthians three thirteen." Flannery tosses the lighter into the hole. "May God have mercy on your soul."

The books burn, and smoke rises from the trapdoor. He can hear the man trying to put it out, but the amount of inked kindling is overwhelming and blocks their exit. It would be so easy to lean over the area and shoot the criminal dead where he stands. But there would be no fun in that, Flannery muses. The two people downstairs cough and the young boy cries in fear.

The soldier moves around the living room, music playing in his head. He grabs several more books and heads into the kitchen. He systematically lights one at a time on the stove, carries it to a room, and drops it in an area sure to increase the flames.

The men outside watch in horror as the house is engulfed in the loud roar of flames that seem in tune with the whistling of a madman. Screams from the two trapped inside reach the outer perimeter, but no lights go on at neighboring houses. All of them are too afraid of retribution.

Flannery walks outside, swinging around to music only he can hear. He lifts himself up on the trunk of the cruiser as his tune stops. With the house bathed in fire, he leans back on his hands, feet kicking out like a kid on Christmas. The child's death might upset Laskin, but he can find one downtown in the poorer districts. He'll hand a family a few hundred bucks and commandeer their child. No one will be the wiser and none of his men would turn him in.

"Shall we head back, sir?"

"No," Flannery answers. "I want to watch it feed. We need to make sure they're dead."

"That could be awhile," the soldier answers.

"You have any place to be?"

"No, sir. Not at all."

Flannery waves him off as he turns his attention to the burning building. The screams have silenced, but the crackling of wood, shattering of glass, and minor explosions of technology are the orchestra of his heart.

Milo and Jason walk through the subway tunnel to the primary entry point to the underground resistance safe house. The normal sounds of people heading home after a long day seem more distant than usual. Jason stops the moment he sees the outline of men in black uniforms with gas masks on their faces. He reaches out for Milo, two steps ahead, but the man keeps going, talking as if Jason is still behind him.

In a matter of seconds, a soldier opens fire, riddling Milo's body with more bullets than his flesh can handle. Jason watches as the young man falls to his knees and sits on his heels. Blood trickles out of the puncture wounds, but Milo seems almost confused as he struggles to breathe. The soldier walks up to the dying man and squats in front of him. The two men stare eye to eye. In another life, they might have been colleagues, but here, one is the hunter and the other prey. The soldier stabs a blade into Milo's throat, forcing blood to bubble up and out of his mouth, spilling onto the man in front of him. His hands flail about, trying to grasp anything, but they only smudge the Velcro nametag: Private Miller.

Miller pulls the knife out of his victim's throat and watches the body fall to the floor. He wipes the blood off on Milo's dirty shirt before standing and turning his attention to the group of men behind him.

"Listen up." All the men turn to face Miller. "We're all the same rank here, but the boss told me to run things. So, here are the rules: we go into the terrorist nest and we eradicate every living thing in there. If it moves, it dies. Clear?"

"Yes, sir," they mechanically answer.

"Then let's go hunting."

Jason pushes into a small hatch and heads down the side tunnel, scraping his leg along the way. The group of men still have a few blocks to reach the main entrance and break in. The guards will return fire, so he'll have an extra few minutes because of that exchange. If he hurries, he might be able to warn the women and children hiding there. Maybe, just maybe, he can save a few people.

The makeshift flashlight dims in the darkness. Jason grabs the handle and rocks it, causing the light to brighten up a bit. He continues his journey through tunnels with sewer water up to his knees, the bacteria surely making its way into his bloodstream through the broken skin on his leg. He'll worry about that later if he survives long enough to be concerned about it.

Coming to a small section in the walkway, Jason pushes hard against the door, and it creaks open slightly. Gunfire erupts from the front doorway, and the sound bounces off the walls like ping-pong balls. The screams of pandemonium hitting his ears cause an urgency that fills his muscles with the energy to push the door fully open.

What greets him makes the hairs on his arms stand on end. Children cry as they run with no guide through the winding tunnels. He grabs one of the older children.

"Get all the kids and go out this way." Jason points behind him. "It leads back to the main entry tunnel. Then run and keep running. Don't look back; don't come back. Just keep moving forward. Understand?"

The young boy nods his head and the two maneuver all the children near them into the tunnel. Taking a deep breath, Jason closes the door and moves a piece of furniture in front of it. His mind is made up. The children will survive and live to fight another day. His life ends here.

Jason takes two steps into the hallway before muzzle flashes force him back into the smaller room. He presses his back up against the metal as a body hits the floor right outside. The woman lies in the mud, twitching as blood flows onto the floor. Her eyes blink a few times as she gasps for air. A soldier steps over her and puts a bullet in her head before moving on.

Jason moves behind the soldier in the hallway. Once he's close enough, he wraps the private in a choke hold. The private fights, punching Jason in the side and the leg. The pain of the last punch radiates throughout his body, but Jason tightens his hold until he hears a soft snapping sound. The soldier's arms go limp and Jason drags his body into the smaller room.

He removes the belt with added clips and drapes it around himself. He grabs the gas mask and wraps it around his head to ensure he isn't easily subdued before grabbing the assault rifle on the floor. The plan at this point is simple; death is inevitable, so take as many of them with you as possible.

Stepping over the soldier and the older woman in the hallway, Jason heads toward the mess hall. Smoke hovers around his ankles and rises as he gets closer to the kitchen. Bullets fire past him, forcing his body to hit the floor. A soldier takes a few steps closer and into full view. Jason rolls to his side and opens fire. The soldier falls to the ground in a heap.

Crawling, Jason hovers over the fallen man. He grabs the clip belt and slings it across his chest with the other one. He picks up the second assault rifle and lifts himself to a standing position. The white smoke getting thick and difficult to see through, he kicks the bodies of his fellow resisters as he marches through the mess hall.

A flash of movement to his right pulls his attention, and his trigger finger fires rapidly in its direction. The body vibrates in the air before hitting the ground. Jason moves with caution as he steps over the body of a young man in his teenage years. Walking through the door, he kneels and sees a young man on the floor choking on his own blood. No uniform. No gear. No gun.

Jason falls to the floor and slides the boy's head into his lap, the tears and screams of anger muffled by the mask on his face. The boy shakes before his body goes limp. Jason slumps to the floor. His wounded leg, drenched with redness, aches with significant pain. Reaching up, he pulls the mask off his face and coughs as the chemicals fill his lungs.

"I'm so sorry," he scratches out. "I'm sorry." His tears fall now, his body wracked with sobs as he pulls the body to his chest.

The gunfire slows around him. Either the military has moved farther into the tunnels or there are fewer targets to kill. The latter is more likely. Jason slides the body to the floor and stands to his full height. Wiping away his tears, he smears blood all over his face and mouth. The simple repairman walks toward the bedrooms. If nothing else, he'll see if there are people hiding under their beds. In his mind, it's a fool's errand, but at this point, he has nothing to lose.

Slinking around corners and sliding along the walls, Jason avoids any further confrontation. The smoke thins as he gets closer to the door leading to Ellie's bedroom. Pushing open the door, he sees Iris sleeping soundly on the bed with Toby in her arms, two silver wrappers with half-eaten chocolate candy near her hands. They look more peaceful than anyone could in their current world.

Jason reaches down and grazes his hand across Iris's face. Her cold skin shakes his soul to the core. He checks Toby and finds the boy colder than his grandmother. They've been dead for hours and left alone. He struggles, but stands. Painful pricks hit his back, one after another, in quick succession.

Private Miller pulls his knife out of Jason's back and stabs him ten additional times. The resister stumbles, but the soldier holds him on his feet. Blood drips out of Jason's mouth as he tries to remove the man from behind him with his arms, the piercing pain of each new puncture forcing his eyes shut in agony.

Miller laughs behind the middle-aged man, holding his weak body in the air as he presses the knife to the other side of his jaw. The tip of the blade enters his skin easily as the soldier presses it deeper. Jason struggles with what little energy he has left as the soldier slices it excruciatingly slow across his throat.

The private cleans his blade on Jason's shirt, just like he did when he killed Milo. He continues to hold Jason as his body convulses and oozes all over the floor. The arterial spray coats the walls, sheets, bodies, and anything else that gets in the way. Finally, Miller drops the body to the floor. Another soldier comes up behind him.

"Are we clear?"

"Found two of our men. Looks like people fought back," the other soldier comments. "Our guys outside found a group of kids trying to escape."

"The president's orders were clear."

"They've been purged."

"I'll meet you outside."

The other soldier leaves the bedroom as Miller kicks Jason's corpse. He notices the shiny silver wrappers on the bed and picks them up. He smiles; one has half a piece of chocolate inside it. Laughing, he chews and swallows the treat. Looking around the room, Miller grabs the stuffed bunny from Toby's arms. He shoves it into his pocket as far as possible as he turns to leave. Before he gets to the door, he stumbles and hits the wall. His eyes droop, and he struggles to stay upright.

Miller grabs at his eyes, trying to keep them open as he slides down the wall into a heap on the floor. He blinks several times before his lids fall shut. His breathing slows as his hand falls to the ground, holding the silver wrapper.

Chapter Seventeen

T he ragtag militia rushes over the bridge under the cover of darkness. A few flashlights shine across the concrete from soldiers on patrol. Once they reach the main compound area, the resisters fight in silence. Anton slides behind a patrolman and snaps his neck before he can make a sound. The light flashes oddly as the body hits the floor. Anton twists it off before anyone comes to the fallen man's aid.

Anton pulls out a small sketch of the island and tries to decipher the buildings based on his location. He has one goal in mind, and that involves the medical building. The rest of his men can handle the grunts walking around the premises. He wants to prove the rumors to be true before slaughtering every single doctor and soldier responsible for the torture of their patients.

Trent slides up next to another guard and stabs him in the neck. The soldier fights, but the old man pulls the shiv out before slamming it back into the boy's flesh. He hits the ground hard as the major continues his silent assault. The unbridled violence shocks Anton, who views him from nearby.

The major ignores the look of disgust and forces his aching body to follow another man on patrol. Following the same procedure, he kills the soldier before anything can be done. He whistles loudly, drawing the attention of soldiers and his militia as well. Anton follows the lines and markers for his destination as Trent waits in the shadows for the next unsuspecting patrolman to cross his path.

Stepping outside of the power building, Tim drags Sam behind him as they dodge soldiers moving toward the madness.

"Tim?" Arnold says from behind him. "What were you doing in there?"

"Nothing. I need to get my brother to lock down. He's not safe out in the open," Tim says, trying to defer the attention away from him.

Arnold moves in front of his friend. "You were in the power box. Why were you in there?"

"I was trying to find a place to hide my bro. I just told you that," Tim says impatiently.

"No, you didn't. I might not be a genius, but I can see you're lying, man. You had something to do with this . . . whatever it is."

"It's a power failure, you idiot," Tim says, trying to move past his friend.

Arnold raises his weapon and aims it directly at the two men. Tim watches as the other man's finger dances over the trigger. It's in that moment Tim switches gears. His hand flexes around his brother's bicep as he pulls Sam behind him.

"You don't know what you're doing, Arnold. Just walk away."

"You're a traitor to the crown. My duty prevents me from walking away."

Tim grabs the barrel of the assault rifle and raises it to the sky as Arnold pulls the trigger. He elbows the lower ranking soldier in the chest, spins to get the weapon out of his hands, and elbows him again in the face. Arnold stumbles, but recovers quickly to knock the weapon out of Tim's hands.

"I can't believe you're doing this," Arnold says, cracking his knuckles. "Makes sense though, doesn't it? Crying over your mama, too compassionate to be a real soldier. You're a freaking bleeding-heart traitor."

Tim attacks with several swings of his fists. Arnold dodges a few, but one connects with his face, breaking his nose. Blood and saliva spray to the side as Arnold spins away from the force of the hit.

"You broke my nose!" the soldier screams.

"That'll be it if you just walk away."

"We've been friends since we were kids, took the test, and got placed together. I thought it was perfect, us working together, but you always think you're smarter than me. Time for the sidekick to step into the light and be a hero." Arnold fakes a punch to the left and jabs with his right.

Tim's head snaps back as Arnold follows it up with a left hook and a right uppercut. The boxing lessons he hated in basic training come back with a fury as Tim fights to defend himself. Arnold pulls a knife out of his holster and holds it in the palm of his hand. Tim's eyes, blurred by blood and lack of light, can't see the metal as it slices into his forearm.

Sam tackles Arnold to the ground and kneels on his biceps, digging deeply into the muscles. He leans forward, preventing the soldier's legs from grabbing him from behind. Sam grabs a palm-sized rock and hits the soldier in the head. Arnold's screams echo in the darkness.

"Sam, stop." Tim tries to reach his brother.

But Sam can't hear him. His arm swings wildly as the stone hits the bone of Arnold's skull, cracking it open. Arnold's voice fades away into nothing, but the sickening suction sound of the weapon hitting brain matter repeatedly, and his own head trauma, causes Tim to throw up next to the body. Seeing his brother bent over, Sam's arm slows to a stop. He sits back on the victim's chest and stares into space. His hand, still holding the rock and coated in blood, hangs in the air ready to strike once more.

His fingers spring open, dropping the rock onto the chest below his legs and then the concrete. Sam's eyes focus on his hand, the blood-soaked one that took another person's life. Tim knows the situation has escalated worse than he ever thought imaginable. "A life for a life," he keeps mumbling in his head. He has to stay focused, but watching his little brother fall apart is giving him second thoughts. They could grab a truck and be off the island in minutes. He calculates how far they could get before Macalov would have every person looking for them, a handsome reward flashing next to their images for everyone to see. Only the topsiders would get it, of course, but you let everyone think they're eligible. It's more effective that way.

"We need to go." Tim says, trying to lift Sam off of Arnold. "Now!"

Sam doesn't budge.

"Dammit, Sam. We need to get you out of here!" Tim yanks his younger brother hard, and the movement forces both their bodies to hit the ground with a thud.

"I killed him."

"Yeah, well, he wasn't a saint either. Raped and murdered half the women in my block. Now, can we get moving?!" Tim stands up and grabs Arnold's weapon.

Sam wipes off as much blood as he can before following his brother through the maze of people and buildings. Gunfire by the bridge makes Sam jump and move a little closer to his brother. With the main power out, flashlights are all the soldiers have, and hiding from them will prove difficult the closer he gets to his destination.

Sam sees Anton run past them and up to the medical building. He kills the one guard in front of the doors before going in. Sam instantly regrets ever getting involved in things like this. He was a peaceful guy and believed in helping the little man, giving them a hand to get back on their feet.

"I just wanted people to be free." Sam stops walking.

Tim turns around and grabs his brother's arms. "We can talk about this later, but right now I need to get you—"

"I killed a man," Sam mutters. "I just wanted people to pay their fair share. I wanted love to be equal and the world to give people the choice of religion, doctors, whatever. I wanted what Mom talked about when we were kids."

"I know you did, but that was then. The world's changed, Sam, and right now . . ."

"How did I go from that to planning an attack and killing people? Where did I go wrong?"

"You didn't go wrong, little brother." Tim pulls Sam to the side of a truck, the metal providing some cover from the bullets soaring through the sky, looking for a home. "People did what they thought was right, and most times it's wrong for everyone else. But we do the best we can. We're just flawed and messed up and loud and . . . and broken. The world's broken, and you can't fix it with ideas and hopes. You can't overpower corruption, Sam. You can only survive. That's it."

"I don't want to survive. I want to live!"

"Then you should have taken your job in the bunker and left this all behind you." The bright light of a patrolman bounces closer than before. "We need to go. Come on!" Tim and Sam rush in the opposite direction.

Tim pulls open a door and slams it behind him. Walking by pure memory, he leads Sam down the hallway. He pushes Sam into a room and closes the door behind them.

"Tim, where are we?"

The fire of a lighter illuminates Gregor Macalov's face as he puffs on a cigar. Sam stumbles backwards, but Tim blocks his exit.

"What's the rush, Mr. Flynt?" Macalov asks. He grabs a walkie-talkie on his desk and presses down on the side. "Turn on the power."

In a few moments, every single light on the island comes on. Macalov sits at his desk, boots resting on the corner as he puffs his cigar and places the walkie-talkie down.

"Thank you, Sergeant. Go, do your job, and rid the island of these men." The warden waves him off.

"Sir, I was hoping . . ."

"Mother or brother?"

Tim looks at Sam. The betrayal etched on the younger boy's skin feels like ants crawling all over his body. The sergeant says nothing as he exits.

"Turned you and your gaggle of friends in for a cure for little old mommy. He really is a mama's boy, isn't he?"

Sam says nothing. He remains standing in the center of the room, his hands shoved in his pockets to hide the evidence of his rage.

"Your brother's an outstanding soldier. Loyal . . . fiercely loyal. But you, you're smart. When I'm president, I could use someone like you in my inner circle. No rules, no restrictions. Hack who you like, steal from the wealthy to give to the poor . . . feed that compassionate heart of yours. I wouldn't care. All you'd have to do is ensure I am always aware of who is conspiring behind me, and if I tell you to destroy someone—you do it."

Macalov slithers around his desk, his feet barely leaving the floor. He leans back, puffs cigar smoke into Sam's face, and takes in the full appearance of the young man in front of him. He stops when he sees the red stains on his skin. A smirk crawls across his face.

"What'd you do?"

Sam looks down at his hand and tries to shove it deeper into his pocket.

"I don't need to know, not really. It doesn't matter if you decide to work with me. You say no . . . well, you'll work for me from behind a set of bars. Either way, I win."

"What about Tim?"

"He'll be sergeant here for the rest of his life."

"And my mother?" he questions.

"She'll be living with you in Manhattan, high enough that she'd have a view of the Hudson River."

"But she's not that . . ." Sam stutters.

"You think too much. Stop worrying about the what-if's. I'm offering you a life, a future . . . What's there to think about?"

"Integrity," Sam whispers. The warden locks eyes with the boy. "I'm not better than anyone else here, but I can decide to set myself apart from them."

"Excellent choice." Macalov walks back around his desk and grabs a glass. He opens a bottle of brandy and fills it. "Once this brief distraction is over with, we'll get you all set up."

"No, thank you," Sam says firmly.

"You're saying no?" Macalov drags out each word in disbelief.

"I choose integrity over money, power, health . . . all of it. I choose me."

Macalov grabs the small caliber pistol resting next to the liquor. "You chose"— he turns and fires one shot directly between Sam's eyes—"poorly." The body falls to the floor. Macalov sits back down in his chair and sips his drink. He grabs the walkie-talkie and presses the button. "Release Zero and One. Let's see how our experiments work in a real-world scenario."

Anton lowers the body of a doctor to the ground, his neck twisted awkwardly, the bones protruding from the skin. He's been making his way through each room methodically. Any person coming across his path, he takes down silently. Whether they are women or men doesn't matter. They were all complicit in the damage done to these people. In his mind, they are all to be punished, and they've elected him to do it.

He lifts a keycard off the doctor's body and heads to the next room. As he slides it through the reader, the light turns green, and the lock disengages. Anton opens the door, peeking through the crack to see if there's any movement before walking fully inside. Unconscious pregnant women greet him, the beeping of the breeder's machinery the only form of communication. He grabs a chart from the first bed he passes. The medical jargon is like another language, but he picks out bits and pieces that enrage him.

The woman in front of him has birthed eight children since her admission. She stays pregnant for nine months, then after the baby is born, they rest her body for two months before impregnating her again. How could a human being be treated so callously?

"What are you doing in here?" a doctor asks him.

"Who is she?"

The doctor walks closer to Anton, closer to the panic button by the door.

"She's a breeder."

"She has a name, a family."

"Her designation is breeder, and she has no one."

The doctor moves behind Anton and the soldier finally pulls himself back to reality. He grabs the doctor before his hand can reach the alarm and body-slams him to the floor. The older white man struggles against the pressure of Anton's forearm pressing into his throat.

"Just let go . . ." Anton whispers in the man's ear. The man keeps squirming around as Anton loses his patience. He lifts the man's head up and violently snaps it to the right. The doctor falls limply to the floor.

Anton stands and walks to the first woman's machines. He looks over the cabling, following IV lines and power plugs until he finds the right cords. "I'm sorry," he says to her before pulling all the plugs out of their sockets. The machines go off, leaving the woman to die. One bed at a time, he disconnects all the victims from the depravity keeping them alive. He looks back at them all, regret on his face.

"I'm so sorry," he murmurs before he leaves the room.

The door clicks closed as a body-slams into him, knocking him to the floor. A man with wild eyes and a massive scar on his head rests above him, his thin frame showing the outline of lean muscle, bone, and fresh bruising. Anton elbows him in the face and scurries back up. The other man has no gun, no weapon of any kind in his hand. Anton's confidence soars, unaware of the experiments done on the man in front of him.

"One hungry," the soldier says.

A door smashes open against the wall behind Anton. Another man, more muscular than the man in front of him and less scary but with wilder eyes, cracks his neck and knuckles. "Zero . . . angry" he stutters.

Anton moves as fast as his sore limbs allow and reenters the breeders' room. The two men bang on the door as Anton resets the locks. Looking around for any kind of weapon, Anton considers everything in the room. Beds can be taken apart, but it would take too long. He'd only get one hit in with the poles holding up the IV bags and they're too clunky to use consistently. They'd also leave him open to attack as he prepared to swing. The small shiv was all he really had, but would that penetrate the skin of whatever those things were? It's at that moment that he wishes he had picked up a weapon from a patrolman outside.

The pounding on the door stops, and Anton turns back to the main doorway. A thought hits him suddenly. How did the doctor get in here? He turns around and comes face to face with Zero. The experiment punches him hard in the rib cage, cracking several. Anton's back hits the wall, then the floor, hard. Struggling to breathe, he fumbles with his shiv and tries to wave it at the creature. Pain shoots through his body with every motion.

Zero leans down and picks Anton up off the floor. With every ounce of energy he has, Anton stabs Zero in the throat. The soldier stumbles, but doesn't fall. He tilts his head curiously, not understanding the blood trickling out of the wound. His hands grip Anton's throat and presses him against the door. Inch by inch, Zero lifts him up as he squeezes harder.

Anton's fists hit Zero, but the soldier shows no response. Anton pushes the shiv further into the other man's neck but again, it's as if he feels no pain. Gasping for air, Anton's tongue hangs out of his mouth like a dog's. His arms go limp, and Zero drops the dead fighter to the floor. His hand goes to his neck and the wetness he feels. Grabbing the shiv, he removes it, and blood spurts out like a river. His body hits the floor right next to Anton's. Zero blinks and tries to move as the pool of blood expands around him. In seconds, he stops breathing.

One walks into the room, slower than his counterpart. He drops to his knees in front of the two dead men and pushes their bodies. "One . . . wins?" he says, his voice weak with confusion. He sits down, crosses his legs, and lifts Zero's arm to his mouth. He bites down hard and tears the flesh from the bone. The experiment smiles and rocks in place as it finally sates his hunger.

As promised, Osaka is waiting for Ellie at the gate and assists in her entry. The guards, fewer of them due to the outside missions, pay no attention to either of them beyond the proper identification scans. The front desk is more of the same, the minds of men fallen to their blind faith in technology giving them truthful information. Osaka had planned on the late shift being ill-equipped to handle new people or just visitors. Even though the president lives on the premises, they always considered the evening the easier shift. Less traffic, fewer people wandering around, and less actual work to do.

Walking through the majestic entryway, Ellie keeps her eyes firmly forward.

"Most people visiting look around at all the money spent to make it look beautiful. You might want to fit in," Osaka says softly. She hands a small duffle bag to the other woman.

"Everything inside?" Ellie asks flatly.

"Yes, including a guard's piece," Osaka answers.

She tilts her head back, looking at the high ceiling and the mural painted to look like the outside world, with fluffy clouds and a blue sky. "I've seen better, but it's an interesting choice of design."

"It helps those who come in through the tunnel to feel like they're experiencing the outside world. The medical personnel thought it would be a pleasant touch."

"How many of those people are allowed in the main lobby?" Ellie asks.

"None," Osaka says with a soft laugh. "I guess it really was a pointless waste."

The two women walk down a long hallway to a dead end. Osaka looks behind her to ensure they haven't been followed. She presses on a tile in the wall, and it pops open, revealing a keypad. After sliding her identification card and inputting a corresponding code, the light turns green. The wall in front of them clicks and rolls on a track back into itself before sliding to the right. The two women enter, and Osaka presses a few buttons on the inside wall. The door closes.

"Down the spiral staircase." She points to the hole in the floor.

"Down the rabbit hole . . ." Ellie mutters as she follows the other woman descending into the depths.

She half expects the old hallways to be filled with chipping lead paint and hints back to when the bunker was originally built in the 1940s. Instead, she is met with bright LED lights and pristinely painted white walls more similar to a hospital than the war shelters of old. Osaka enters her card and code once again at the only door at the end of the walkway.

"Ms. Yen, thank heavens you are here. Have you heard anything from Flannery or the team in the tunnels? There was a power outage at Riker's . . ." Laskin turns around and sees Osaka with an unknown woman behind her with a gun raised. "What's this?"

The lone tech left behind stands up to run away. Ellie fires one shot in his direction and the man falls to his knees quickly. "No one moves."

"What do you want?"

"You will sit down in that chair, and Ms. Yen is going to duct-tape you to it." Ellie hands the small bag she's been carrying to Osaka, and the woman plays her part. She stumbles down the stairs and shakes with alleged fear as the man looks her over.

"What's going on?" he whispers as she runs the roll of tape around his shoulders.

"She caught me in the square; I'm so sorry." Her voice trembles. "She had a gun, and security didn't catch it." She continues to play the damsel in distress, regardless of what happens after. With the president dead, her future will be in limbo, but if the other tech in here vouches for her, she might get a decent job. At least she wouldn't be a whore on those torture porn websites.

"It's okay. Max is upstairs. She can't get there."

"She won't. I locked the door at the top of the stairs. No way out."

"Stop talking!" Ellie screams as she heads over to the tech. "I want you to bring up every grid in the country."

The tech remains on the floor, so Ellie kicks him hard.

"Get up!" She continues playing her part. "I said get on the system and bring up the country's electrical grid."

"Do it," Laskin calls from the front of the room.

"Tape his mouth shut." Ellie points the handgun in their direction.

Osaka mouths "I'm sorry" as she places a torn piece of tape across the president's mouth. The tech uses the desk to pull himself up to the chair. Without looking, he taps away on the keyboard and pulls up the entire electrical grid of the United States.

"Can you pick what you shut off?" Ellie asks, pressing the weapon into his back.

He nods, unable to trust his voice.

"Good, shut off everything but these locations." Ellie pulls out a small piece of paper and drops it in front of the tech.

"I . . . I n-n-need auth-authorization," the man stutters.

Ellie walks down the stairs to Laskin. She rips the tape off his mouth and leans down to his eye level. "Give him your codes."

"And if I don't?"

"I'll shoot you both and hack it."

"If you could, you would have already," Laskin answers defiantly.

Ellie stands up and turns her attention to the techie. "You said there was a raid in the tunnels. Where?" she asks him.

He doesn't answer. She turns to Laskin. "Where?" she asks, pressing the weapon against his groin.

"You can kill me, but you'll have no backup, no more resistance fighters, and nowhere to run." He smirks.

Ellie nods her head as the thoughts of her people suffering runs through her mind like wildfire. She walks up the steps to the male tech and drops in a seat next to him.

"Show me Riker's Island," she mumbles. The tech brings up current satellite video of the island. "Zoom in as close as you can get."

He does as she asks, and Ellie can see bright lights, dark shapes on the ground, and numerous men on one side with a dwindling group on the other. Her men were losing, just as she expected them to.

"Shut off everything but those locations, now."

"Don't do it," Laskin yells. "You have nothing. Kill us all, fine, but you can't do anything."

"I was trying to be polite, but we can play it your way." Ellie lifts her weapon and fires. The force of the bullet knocks the tech's body off the chair and a short distance from them. Osaka jumps at the sound of the bullet and rushes to meet Ellie.

"You didn't have to do that," she says.

"Your fiancé is dead, your friends are dead, your home destroyed. Yet, you still have this idealistic view of the world, Osaka. Why? Why protect him and the future villain?"

"Because I believe in people," she spits out.

"What's going on, Ms. Yen?"

"See, Laskin, your compassion was your weakness. Your lovely assistant has been our man on the inside for years. Right there under your nose, spilling your secrets and blueprints to the rest of us. Raising your son, teaching him about peace and hope . . . about equality, while your father-in-law wanted him to be a ruthless murderer."

"Ms. Yen?" he asks, dumbfounded. "Is this true?"

"I . . ." She ponders her options. "Yes."

"I should have listened to the rest of my team when I hired you. You turned out to be a stereotypical whore. Not to be trusted, just to be used in the bedroom, and thrown away with the trash," he seethes.

Ellie pulls out the notebook containing various codes and begins typing them in one at a time. The first five fail, but Osaka places her hands over Ellie's, stopping her from trying another one.

"He always uses the same numeric code. Maxim's birthday," she says through silent tears. She types the numbers in and the board lights up, giving her total access to everything.

"Your son's birthday? Seriously, have you learned nothing from history?"

"What do you know of it? They slaughtered women like you for fun. Dumped you in menial camps, and made you carry children for our medical facilities. You're nothing."

"I'm Ellie Goldman, number 120306, the last surviving member of the Multi-national Security Council. At least I think I am." She pauses. Ellie pulls out an old USB Flash drive and shoves it into the machine. The screen comes to life with lines of code scrolling past. Ellie enters various coordinates each time a prompt comes up. Osaka stops her boss from entering another one.

"What are you doing?"

"MSC operatives were given backup protocols should the countries fall."

"What does that mean?"

"It means Valkov never should have networked the world as one unit. His confidence will be his undoing." Ellie frees her hands and continues entering longitudinal and latitudinal numbers at the various prompts.

"You think you're walking out of here alive. You're fucking dead. When they find my body, you'll both be tortured, and trust me, Macalov will have fun with you, Ms. Yen. Just to see if your eyes pop out of your head as he lets every guard rip you apart one at a time. Maybe he'll let Max take part and get justice against the ingrate who killed his father."

Osaka rushes down the steps and slaps Laskin across the face. She replaces the tape to shut him up as Ellie scans the screens in front of her. She enters a few codes and finally her MSC operative number. Alarms sound overhead, getting the attention of the two women. The large screen at the front of the room flashes the word *armed*.

"What the hell is going on, Ellie?"

"Washing the slate clean," she says simply. "Protocol."

"This was not what we agreed upon. Stop it." Osaka takes two steps toward her, but Ellie points her weapon at Osaka.

"Please, I don't want to waste time." She uses her left hand to activate more weapons and lock their destinations. "It'll all be over soon."

Osaka looks at the main screen—the nuclear warhead locations and their approximate parabolic curve destinations. The global map, littered with these lines, causes fear to rise up her spine. She moves up the stairs in a flash and almost makes it to the top before Ellie fires blindly. The bullet grazes her ribs; she rolls on the floor in pain and crawls toward the operative.

"You can't do this."

Ellie finishes her work, stands up, and fires several shots into the computer. "I'm sorry, but there was no other way."

Osaka pulls herself up to a sitting position against the computer desk. "Who made you the judge, jury, and executioner? Who allowed you to put billions of people to death?"

"They did. The minute they ruled according to their extreme ways with no thought to others. They forced my hand."

"And you're no better." Osaka laughs as she spits up blood.

"I never said I was. I only said there was no other way. A rat can be cornered for only so long before it hits you back with the force of a thousand animals. Just like the Final War, men rose up to keep their weapons and shot children who simply stood in their way. The hackers who destroyed hospitals all around the world, killing thousands to protest healthcare costs and keep profits in the hands of already wealthy men . . . we're all the same in the end. Society just forgets that part."

"You're going to live, though, while everyone else dies. You become king of your domain. King of the destroyed world."

Ellie struggles to catch her breath as Laskin passes out. She stumbles and falls to the floor as the two women gasp for oxygen.

"Nothing can remain. No connection to anything . . ." She coughs. "Nothing."

"You cut off . . . the oxygen."

"You can't have a clean slate if the roach remains," Ellie whispers.

Osaka coughs violently and rolls on her back as her breathing slows. Ellie looks up at the screen and sees the countdown hit zero. The ground shakes as her eyes close for the last time.

Trent rests alongside a truck, bodies littering the floor. His leg, wrapped tight with a tourniquet, continues to bleed onto the concrete. A sound similar to a fighter jet pierces through the battle, pulling his and the rest of the men's attention. He stands, follows the sounds, and sees several streaks of fire in the sky. A bullet pierces his chest, and his hand touches the wound. Blood drips over his fingers as he falls to his knees. He watches as an enemy soldier, a young boy who looks barely eighteen, picks off his men one by one.

The ground rattles beneath them as New York City erupts into a cornucopia of color. A wave of fire rolls toward them as Trent falls to the floor, blinking one last time before the cloud incinerates them all.

Flannery watches the small embers continue to burn in front of him. The smirk remains on his face as the sky lights up with a reddish-orange streak. In the distance, the weapon strikes the ground in silence. A mushroom cloud the size of Texas erupts from the ground with a violent shake and roar as the concussive force rushes at them like a stampede.

"Oh, fu—" The explosive force hits all the men, incinerating them on contact, leaving nothing but an outline of the humans they used to be.

Epilogue

Those who cannot remember the past are condemned to repeat it. ~ George Santayana

The craters around the world remain. The last vestiges of the old world fade with each passing change of season. The power plants still pump radiation into the air as the compounds remain untouched.

Mother Nature, true to herself, took back the land and survives. The waters swallowed coastlines and life mutated to adapt to its new environment. Life evolved.

The trees of the Congo Basin still rise to the sky, but the fresh growth still struggles to come close to the height of its ancestors. The okapi's stripes are a rich reddish brown from the toxic water it has ingested. Its new eye, resting directly behind its head, giving it an edge against the other animals within the bush.

These animals include a newly developed form of Homo sapiens, these quadrupeds who mutated to survive in the heavily radiated lands of Africa. These new hairless humans with blood like acid and skin like snakes still live and thrive among the beasts, unaware of the past misdeeds or victories of those who came before.

These new individuals, with their wooden poles with sharpened points, hide within the overgrowth as they hunt the okapi. The weapon flies with precision, hitting the animal in the chest with a sickening sound. The humans crawl out from the brush to grab their meal, each face and naked body only distinguishable by the degree of their molted skin. Some pink with newer flesh while others seem scaly and peeling.

Two men work as one to drag the okapi to their village, the others standing guard against the other hungry creatures within the trees. The sounds of agony rip through the edge of the forest and hit their ears. The hunt forgotten, the men rush through the remaining trees and into their village.

Biped Homo sapiens with dark black scaly skin, white eyes, and manes of dark hair ravage the village, their arrows slicing through the flesh of the men crawling on all fours. One by one, the fighting villagers are murdered. Like fearful rats searching for a way out, the rest of the people rest on their knees, waiting for their fate.

The crunch of leaves forces the villagers to raise their heads and see an elephant approaching. A man slides down the side of the massive beast and walks up to the kneeling people. He steps over the fallen victims and speaks to his fellow men in a foreign tongue as he enters a small hut in the center of town.

The smell of fresh flowers and rotten flesh fill his nostrils as he stands in the doorway. The stench does nothing to stop him as his feet carry his body all the way to the other side of the room toward a circle of dim lights around a metal cylindrical shape. The unexploded nuclear warhead rests on a bed comprised of leaves, brush, and undergrowth tied together like the ones the villagers slept on.

The glow from the mutated blossoms highlights the markings of a dead country. A dead people. A dead time. But here, in this time, the warhead is alive. The leader pulls out a blade and presses the rusty jagged end into his hand. The thick black sludge drips out of his flesh. He presses his hand against the bomb as his body convulses and he screams in tongues.

A warrior rushes in and holds a similar dagger up, ready to strike. His leader continues to tremble and chant while his head tilts back to the heavens. Everything stops in seconds. The leader's hand slides down the metal bomb, leaving a streak of black. His breathing shallow, he reaches down and grabs a few flowers and leaves the hut with a confused soldier on his heels.

The rest of his men stand outside at attention, as if waiting for the high ruler to issue a command. He turns to the villagers as his blood drips to the dirt below.

The bipeds have hogtied all the male villagers; they'll make for decent slaves and for sport. The leader's gaze turns toward the women, inspecting each one from a distance. All but one look away. His swift steps bring him to stand in front of her in moments, his muscles flexing, the odor of his dominance pumping out for all to inhale. She holds his gaze, refusing to avert her brown eyes. The leader raises his hand and places it gently on her bald scalp. He mutters to his men as he coats her head in his oily black blood. The woman wails as he lifts her up effortlessly and carries her off to the largest hut.

Once he has chosen, the rest of the men scramble to pick one of the remaining few. The village will eat well and increase in size. Those who follow the new leader shall stay alive. Those who do not shall pay the metal god with their lives, their flesh and bone used to further the needs of the camp.

Homo sapiens might not have walked the earth for hundreds of years, but nature always finds a way to return. That includes the evolution of man. So once again they can devolve into greed, political gains, and murder. But as long as there is breath, there is hope for a better future. And that keeps us going.

About Author

Kimberly Amato is the author of the Jasmine Steele Mystery Series and Enemy. Having won awards for a TV Pilot she co-wrote & produced, she dove headfirst into writing novels. Always creating, jotting down new ideas & unafraid to try new genres, Kimberly writes mysteries, crime, romance, sci-fi & more. Beyond that, she's a podcaster with her wife, Sheila, for the show Forever Fangirls reviewing TV and film on streaming services and in theaters. Kimberly enjoys keeping in touch with her readers. You can find her by using the links below or going to her website KimberlyAmato.com.

amazon.com/stores/Kimberly-Amato/author/B00RKJDIXA

bookbub.com/authors/kimberly-amato

facebook.com/thekimberlyamato

instagram.com/kimberlyamato

Go to the link below to stay up to date on new releases and more!
https://www.kimberlyamato.com/newsletter

Also By Kimberly Amato

THE STEELE SERIES

Steele Intent (Book 1)

Melting Steele (Book 2)

Breaking Steele (Book 3)

Cold Steele (Book 4)

Steele Shield (Book 5)

Steele Influence (Book 6)

STANDALONES

Enemy

www.ingramcontent.com/pod-product-compliance
Lightning Source LLC
Chambersburg PA
CBHW072126170626
46813CB00004B/1717